TAKEN: A MOTHER'S SECRET

Dan Lawton

Also by Dan Lawton

Deception
Stolen Mercy
Plum Springs
The Green House
That Was Before (That Was Before #1)
Now Was After (That Was Before #2)
Here It Ends (That Was Before #3)

For more information, contact:
info@danlawtonfiction.com
or visit:
www.danlawtonfiction.com

Cover designed by Juan Jose Padron
jcovers.com

ISBN: 978-0-9964076-8-7

Originally Published as: AMBER ALERT
Originally Published By: Solstice Publishing,
solsticeempire.com
Originally Published First Edition: November 2016
Second Edition: May 2024

This book is for Carol, who was vocal about her passion and encouragement for the project from the first draft—she'd said it was a "home run" from day one.

CHAPTER ONE

From a good distance away inside his mother's station wagon, Scott Baker's dark, jealous eyes study the driveway. Seeing her brings back the memories, the good times and the bad, and all those feelings: the hurt, the abandonment, the love. The love, even after all this time, has never wavered, despite everything.

In the driveway, Abby Janis approaches the mailbox with grace. She glides like a cloud, her toes barely touching the blacktop, almost hovering above it, as if floating. The sun gleams off her teeth as she smiles, and her skin sparkles with an undeniable happiness. It's been just over a decade since he's seen her last, and her beauty is just as he'd remembered.

Except now, she's actually happy.

Her unblemished skin shines like it never has before, her radiance warming Scott's insides, even from a distance. A gentle Pennsylvania breeze whirls Abby's silky blonde hair into a funnel at her back, her perfume hitting Scott's nose as if she were standing right next to him. Scott lets his eyes roll back in his head and enjoys it. It's been so long.

Scott opens his eyes and feels lighter, less tense. A tingle rushes through his body as if it were a thousand spiders, each of the tiny legs tickling him until his muscles convulse. A looming eruption develops underneath his skin. He digs the fingers on his free hand into his thigh to brace himself, his fingernails as sharp as needles. The physical pain is only temporary. It passes.

From where Scott sits, Abby appears to be living the dream. With the way she used to live, the woman she used to be, Scott can't help but be surprised by that. She's come a long way since then, and, admittedly, he didn't think she'd make it this far. Part of him regrets she did. At her back is a two story colonial with an attached two car garage and golf-course-like green grass surrounding it. The dark shingles on the roof are free of peeling and cracking, and the shutters around the windows are a crisp red. A black sedan idling in the driveway is luxurious. There's everything except the white picket fence.

It pains Scott to see it all. The pain digs deep, so deep that he can't look. He shifts his eyes and allows himself to give in to the sadness for a moment.

Ten years ago Abby would have never wanted this life. Fifteen years ago she wouldn't have even dreamt about it. Scott remembers the real Abby—where she came from and who she used to be. Before her last name was Janis. Before the lies even began.

Scott turns back as the mailbox swallows Abby's arm, only to spit it back out with a stack of envelopes in her hand. The one from Scott is somewhere in the middle of stack, he knows, and it's only a matter of moments before Abby finds it. Scott pushes the sadness aside.

***

For Abby Janis, life is good. She and her husband, Kurt, are as affectionate and passionate toward each other as they were when they first met. The best part of her day is still when he comes home and kisses her, and the saddest part is when he leaves for the office in the morning. She misses him when he's gone, loves him more every day, and agonizes when he's not well. Abby has felt like a newlywed every single day of her marriage.

Their daughter, Chloe, has just finished the third grade at Mifflinburg Elementary School and she's already excited about starting fourth grade. She routinely receives high marks and has lots of friends, and for that, Abby couldn't be happier. Everything Abby's ever wanted in life is resting in the palm of her hand, and her life, in many respects, is perfect.

At the end of the driveway with the sun at her back, Abby sorts through the stack of mail. The wind gusts almost sends one of the envelopes from the stack sailing. The waft of fresh cut grass flies with it, tickling Abby's nose, threatening to make her sneeze.

The mail is mostly garbage—bills, junk, and local advertisements—but right in the middle of the stack, one of the envelopes catches Abby's attention. It's not like the others. It's solid white, unsecured, and missing a stamp from the upper right corner. There's no return address and Abby's name is handwritten in the center. It's out of place.

Abby opens that one first.

She moves it to the top of the stack and flips it over, then slices the back with the white tip of her nail. The seal breaks quickly, a sticky dampness transferring to Abby's fingertip. Inside the envelope is a single sheet of lined paper, torn and folded in half like that of a note one might pass around in junior high. Curiously, Abby unfolds the note and reads it.

FOUND YOU.

Abby nearly drops to the blacktop.

Oh, God.

The two words are written in uppercase letters and scribbled in pencil, much like Abby's name is on the front of the envelope. The handwriting is amateurish, childlike, like whomever wrote it hasn't written anything in a while.

Abby recognizes it. She's seen that handwriting before, and after a moment, she remembers from where. From whom.

A lump forms in her throat. Something heavy pounds inside her chest. She chokes as the wind is knocked out of her.

Abby looks up and frantically scans the neighborhood for an out of place jogger or a car that doesn't belong, but she sees nothing. Lawn mowers sound, dogs bark, and neighborhood children play, but nothing is out of the ordinary.

Where is he?

Abby looks back down and reads the note again. As she does, someone places a gentle hand on her lower back and wraps their fingers around her waist, making her muscles tense. She crinkles the note into a ball and gasps aloud, ready to attack, and drops the stack of envelopes to the pavement.

"Didn't mean to scare you." It's her husband. Kurt pulls his hand away from Abby's back and holds it up to show his surrender.

Abby puts a hand to her chest and breathes hard. Air pinches her lungs and a sharp pain stabs her side, making her wince. Quickly, Abby slides a hand down the side of her blouse and slips the note into her hip pocket, pushing it inside with her thumb, before Kurt sees it. Kurt crouches and scoops up the dropped mail from the driveway, then hands the stack back to her. He doesn't seem to notice the empty envelope on top, so Abby grabs it and hides it underneath the others.

"You okay?" Kurt asks.

"Yeah, I'm okay," Abby says, her breath slowing. "You just scared me."

"Sorry, babe." Kurt rests his hand on Abby's hip and pecks her cheek. "Are you ready to go? Chloe's waiting."

"Where is she?"

"In the car."

Abby nods and allows Kurt to lead her back up the driveway. He looks at her and smiles, and mouths his affection for her. Abby returns the smile the best she can, and Kurt buys it. As they walk toward his Mercedes, Abby slides her pinky into her jeans and pushes the note further into her pocket. She wishes it would go away.

Thinking of the note, she knew this day would come eventually, and it finally has. She's been dreading it for years. Even with all the time that's passed, she still isn't ready to face it yet—the truth. But here it is, hidden away deep in the pocket of her jeans, just waiting for the opportunity to tear her life apart.

***

Scott clenches his teeth and seethes as Abby's husband puts his hands all over her. Even though it's been so long, the pain of seeing it firsthand doesn't hurt any less. If anything, time makes it worse. Kurt caresses Abby's shoulder blade, moving his hand slowly downward until it rests on the small of her back. They walk arm in arm further away from Scott. Scott squeezes his fingers into a fist.

White exhaust from the idling sedan spits into the wind near the garage. Kurt disappears into the driver's side while Abby walks around to the passenger's. Before climbing in, she stops and glances over her shoulder as if looking for something or someone, and Scott gets a good look at her. The color has left her face, a white sheet now covering her features, and her eyes have sunken. Scott knows that look—it's the look of forfeiture, the loss of hope, the look of remembrance. It's the look of desperation.

Scott can tell by the blankness in Abby's eyes that she knows what's happening. She knows he's out and that he's come to find her. She knows her husband is finally going to learn the truth after all these years, and that the truth might devastate him. The truth might be unforgivable. The truth might remove her veil of years of deceit and reveal the woman underneath, the woman she's tried to conceal for so many years.

It's all on the verge of coming to an end.

Once Abby climbs into the sedan with a halo of dishonesty surrounding her, Scott lowers his binoculars and tosses them on the seat beside him. He huffs as he relaxes his fingers. With the flick of a wrist, he starts up the wagon and winces when the drive belt squeals, the screech ricocheting off the bay windows and enclosed grand foyers that surround him. The colonials in the neighborhood are enormous, and Scott is using them to his advantage. Abby couldn't find his location even if she tried.

Scott hasn't formulated a specific plan yet and will wait to see where the Janis's are headed before doing so. Part of him wasn't expecting to actually find her so soon. Plan or not, its flawless execution is imperative. Anything less will send him back to where he came from, and Abby will vanish from his life once again.

Then it'll remain a mystery forever.

The Benz cruises around the corner, noiseless, and makes a right at the stop sign at the end of the street. Scott lowers his head, just in case, but keeps his eyes locked firmly on the Mercedes. It eventually fades away beyond the hill without incident, merely becoming a speck of black, until it disappears out of sight. Scott holds back for a few extra seconds, breathing heavily, before pulling out into the street, making a right at the same stop sign, following them.

CHAPTER TWO

With a strange intensity, Scott follows the Mercedes for ten miles. He keeps his distance in the wagon. Although the sites are mostly the same, some things have changed in ten years. Seeing only barbed wire and steel bars makes someone forget what it's like to be on the outside, and Scott is no exception. The back roads are still familiar to him, but the trees are overgrown and there are a bunch of new houses that he doesn't recognize. Even some of the houses that he does recognize look different in a way—many of them with worn out roofs or faded paint or cracked foundations. It all reminds him of how much he's missed.

When the Benz makes a left at Sunapee Drive, Scott thinks he has an idea where they're headed. If he's right, it will complicate matters, so he'll have to pick his spot carefully if he's going to get this done today. Now that Abby has seen the note, the longer he waits, the higher the risk is that the police involved. And if that happens, he'll never get the opportunity to do what he needs to do.

The mall looks the same as it always has. It's a little rundown and sits back from the street a bit, and the parking lot is jammed with cars and trucks and buses. Scott almost loses the Janis's while he searches for and eventually finds an open spot in the back, close to the edge of the parking lot. He spots them walking inside, so he runs to catch up to them, and eventually does when he tracks them down near the food court.

Inside and out of breath, Scott falls in behind the threesome. Abby and Kurt stand on either side of the little one as they walk in a line, not talking much. Even from behind, Scott can see the difference in Abby already—her slow movement and lack of grace—and he wonders how long it'll take her husband to realize it, too.

The little girl has long dark hair, jet black, which reminds Scott of his own, and it's held together in a tight braid. She's thin and has long legs, and from the back, she looks like a girl approaching her teenage years. Jitters take over as the anticipation of seeing her face is eating at Scott, but he's able to restrain himself. He reminds himself how important it is to do this right, how critical it is to not make a careless mistake. Patience, after all, is a virtue.

***

Abby is on the left, Kurt on the right, and they each walk in stride with Chloe in between them. Abby is still troubled by the note that's in her pocket and what it means, although she tries to put on a smile that doesn't look phony. She fears she's failing at it, though, as she notices Kurt continuously gazing over to her in her peripheral vision. She refuses to look at him for fear he might see right through her.

"Look! Can we go in there?" Chloe asks, pointing to the pet store. She takes off in that direction before her parents even have a chance to respond.

Abby yells after her, "Slow down, Chloe! Stay close!"

Chloe ignores her mother as she cuts between strangers and rushes into the pet store. She heads directly for the puppies behind the glass.

"Will you watch her, please?" Abby says to Kurt as she watches Chloe from across the corridor. Her abdomen grumbles as the all too familiar feeling approaches from somewhere deep inside. She stops on a dime, beads of sweat forming on her neck, and heads back in the direction they originally came from.

"Where are you going?" Kurt asks.

"Bathroom." Abby starts to walk in that direction, but Kurt grabs her hand and spins her back toward him.

"Hey, are you okay?"

Abby offers a frail smile, hoping to fool him. "I'm fine."

"Are you sure? You look like you've seen a ghost."

Abby suddenly notices the corner of the note in her pocket jamming into her thigh. It feels like a knife slowly carving out a chunk of flesh, leaving a trail of damaged goods in its wake. "I'm okay, really."

Kurt raises an eyebrow, but pushes no further. He pulls her toward him and kisses her on the cheek, then releases her hand. Abby smiles, glad it was her cheek and not her lips that he'd kissed, and backtracks toward the ladies' room. She swallows hard to keep the bile down.

***

Scott is like a hawk, his talons out, waiting for just the right moment, ready to attack. In front of him, the Janis's are his prey. The jitters in his hands are bad, the tightness of his chest worse. He's starting to doubt if he has what it takes to go through with this.

Suddenly, the tables are turned; the predator becomes the prey.

Abby stops, turns, and starts back toward him. Her head starts to turn, her eyes mere moments from finding Scott's. Scott searches for an escape. Lines of men, women, and children walk in groups in the corridor; employees pick their fingernails in the painted tiles in the front of empty storefronts; a nearby security officer twirls a keyring. Scott's wheels spin, his surroundings blur, his legs and feet frozen and unmoving. He tries to move, searching for somewhere to hide, but the tiles beneath his feet morph into quicksand. He pulls and twists until his joints hurt, but his feet only sink deeper. The harder he tries, the more it hurts.

Then something happens.

Kurt stops Abby and pulls her in close, giving Scott a second chance. Whatever its purpose, the quicksand relinquishes to the universe and Scott breaks free, turning quickly and rushing into the closest store before Abby spots him.

Scott crouches behind a mannequin wearing a visor and a tank top and a pair of shorts so short he'd never let his own child wear them. The saleswoman greets him, smiling, friendly, completely unaware of Scott's intentions. He ignores her and keeps his head down as he watches Abby rush past the store with a hand over her mouth. Once she passes fully, Scott exhales and moves out of the mannequin's shadow and past the dejected saleswoman. He rests a hand against a wall and catches his breath, once again questioning his ability to go through with this. Before he talks himself out of it, he slips in line with the crowd, keeping Abby at a safe distance, but still in his sight, and follows her down the corridor.

Behind the food court is a long passageway that wraps around the fast food booths and comes out on the other side. As far as Scott can remember, there are bathrooms and the mall management office and the security office in the corridor, and not much else. Abby disappears into the darkness, her legs almost at a run. Scott considers going in after her, but then thinks of what his goal is by being here and what he wants to accomplish, so he doesn't. Instead, with Abby temporarily preoccupied, he turns back and heads for the pet store.

***

Dismayed by her coldness, Kurt watches Abby scamper away, almost running. watches Abby scamper away, almost running. Something is off with her today, he admits, but he can't pinpoint what it is. There's a bit of an edge to her, a startle factor that he's never seen from her before, the culprit of which makes him curious. But it's Chloe's day today, so he brushes it off for now. Summer break from school has just begun, and Kurt is looking forward to spending some quality time with his daughter over the next couple of months. He crosses the corridor, dodging rowdy teens and tense parents, and joins Chloe inside the pet shop.

"Look how cute he is, Daddy," Chloe says to him when he enters, a smile on her face. An energetic yellow lab leaps toward them, a glass enclosure separating man from animal, with its tongue saturating and smearing the glass. "Can I keep him?"

"Your mother doesn't want a puppy around the house, sweetheart."

"I'll take care of him, I swear! I'm nine years old now, you know. You won't even have to do anything, I promise. I'll do everything by myself. I'll feed him and I'll—"

"We'll see. Maybe for your birthday."

"I just had my birthday like two months ago!"

"Maybe for your next birthday, then."

"But, Dad—"

Kurt raises an eyebrow at her, cutting her off. More than anything, he hates it when Chloe whines, and she's dangerously close to approaching that territory. Chloe understands her dad's expression and says nothing further. She crosses her arms and turns her back to him, sighing dramatically. Kurt knows he'll be getting the silent treatment for a while now.

"Chloe—"

"Kurt Janis, is that you?" an excited male voice says from somewhere behind Kurt.

Kurt turns and searches for the voice that sounded somewhat familiar. When he finds his old neighbor's smiling face across the way, he waves. "I'll be right back, sweetheart," he says to Chloe, then walks out of the pet shop to say hello to his old friend.

Chloe is left alone.

***

Back in front of the pet store, the firmness of a wooden bench digs into Scott's rear. It's sticky with warmth, with chipped paint and a split down the middle, and it separates the two sides of the corridor. In Scott's hands is a slushy, once chilled, now warm, that he'd found sitting on top of a trash can. He thought it might help him blend in to the crowd, but no one has even looked at him, so he's starting to doubt that. Or maybe that means it's working.

The little Janis girl and her father seem to be having some sort of disagreement inside the pet shop. Scott shields his face behind the jumbo plastic cup, a huge grin on his face. He's hopeful something will break in his favor soon, before Abby returns.

Behind him, a man's voice calls out Kurt Janis's name, making Scott leap, his heartbeat fluttering. Kurt Janis looks into the hallway, searching for the voice, and seems to locate it directly behind Scott. Scott doesn't know if Abby has ever told her husband about him; he bets not, but he can't take that chance. Scott pushes the cup higher, completely blocking his vision, doing all he can to ensure Kurt doesn't recognize him.

Kurt walks out of the pet store, head up, chin high, his bright teeth showing, and makes his way toward the bench. Scott curls his shoulders, making like a turtle hiding in its shell, and tries to shrink himself down to nothing. The jitters in his hands start up again, causing the melted ice to slosh around. The strong smell of sugar and plastic chemicals overpowers him, but he keeps his face covered until Kurt passes.

Kurt moves past the bench and engages in a friendly banter with the man who'd called his name. The little hairs on the back of Scott's neck rise as he feels Kurt's stale breath on his skin. The physical closeness of the two men—both in proximity to one another and in their connection to Abby, which, Scott suspects Kurt doesn't know about—makes Scott uneasy. There are so many secrets, yet, so much time has passed. So many questions still need to be answered, and so many uncertainties still hang in the balance. The meter in Scott's brain has redlined; he's overloaded.

Anxious, Scott pushes to his feet and sucks in a deep breath of whatever chemicals invade his airspace. He tosses the once icy beverage into the waste bin and heads into the pet store, not looking back, unsure what he'll say if confronted by Kurt Janis or anyone else.

Scott keeps his head down, his hands in his pockets, and makes his way around the perimeter of the pet shop. The girl's back is facing him, her attention directed to a handsome pup behind the glass. Scott stops in front of all the cages and glass habitats, checking out the tarantulas and ferrets and guinea pigs. One of the iguanas stares at him, taunting with his tongue, as if it knows what Scott is up to. Scott stares back, but ultimately ignores it and pushes on. The iguana wouldn't understand, he thinks, nor would any of the other four or eight-legged creatures out there. Scott doesn't think a two-legged creature would understand the pain he's been through, either.

Scott passes a hamster on a wheel as it trains for a marathon, the metal squeaking like a rusted hinge with each rotation, and makes his way closer to the girl. Every so often, he shoots a glance to the hallway, where he finds Kurt still engaged in a deep and animated conversation behind the bench, still distracted. Scott can sense the window of opportunity starting to open for him, but the hardest part, he fears, will be crawling through it.

Upon approach, Scott refuses to look directly at the girl, but he does sneak a glimpse out of the corner of his eye a few times. The voyeurism makes him feel uneasy, like he's doing something he shouldn't be, but he can't help himself. He needs answers.

The pattering in his chest is like a drum roll, the pleasure signals being sent throughout his body like an orchestra. Music plays in his ears—soft music, gentle music, with violins and a choir and a mandolin. Then it gets louder. There's a marching band and heavy, thumping bass and an electric guitar riff. Scott's world spins. Vertigo comes and goes, his knees weaken, his head wobbles on his neck as if it were too heavy and disproportionate like a mushroom. Fainting seems like a real possibility.

"Hi." It's a girl's voice, a young girl. The Janis girl.

Scott plants his feet firmly against the tile and steadies himself. He closes his eyes until the spinning stops, then opens them and looks back at the girl, who's facing the glass case. "Hi," he says. "Cute puppy."

"Yeah," the girl says, smiling. "My dad won't let me get him, but I think he really wants to come home with me."

Scott nods and wipes a dab of sweat from his brow. "Why not?"

The girl stops smiling and crosses her arms. She faces him. "Because he's stupid."

For the first time, Scott looks at the girl's face and into her eyes. They're dark and thick, and they complement her hair almost perfectly, as if her features were hand-picked. They almost take his breath away. Scott hasn't been around girls of her age since he was her age himself, and he wasn't expecting her to look so grown up. It makes him realize how much things have changed in the past ten years. Despite the dark hair and eyes, he sees a young Abby on the girl's face. The same high cheekbone structure is present, along with the same symmetry that Scott had once been so drawn into himself. She's already beautiful like her mother, and Scott wonders if Kurt treats her like the princess she is. Her reaction about the puppy makes Scott believe otherwise, and the thought makes his heart ache.

"Why is he stupid?" Scott asks as he tries to hold back a smile. He really just wants to listen to her talk.

The girl does talk. She tells him about the way her parents treat her—too many rules and not enough freedom—and how they won't even let her get a puppy, even though she promises to take care of it. Scott nods occasionally and frequently looks into the hallway to check on Kurt, who's still oblivious to what's happening inside the pet store.

"My name's Scott, by the way," Scott says once the girl stops talking. "I'm a friend of your mom's, actually."

"You are? I don't remember a Scott."

"I don't live around here, so I haven't seen your mom in a while. That's probably why."

The girl nods.

"What's your name?"

"Chloe."

Scott's cheeks burn, hardly able to hold back a smile. Abby had always liked the name Chloe, him too, but listening to the girl actually identify herself in her own voice is a whole different experience. The softening of his heart applies a stinging pressure in his chest.

Chloe glances out into the hallway for her dad, then Scott does too. Kurt now has his back facing them and is using the bench as a crutch, howling with laughter. The window, Scott realizes, is wide open now. The light on the other side is blinding. The draft chills his skin.

"I have a puppy just like this, you know," he says.

"You do! What's his name?"

"Benny. I actually have him with me in the car, if you want to go meet him."

Chloe bites her lip, suddenly looking uncomfortable. "I don't think my parents would like that."

Thinking fast, Scott says, "I saw your mom just a few minutes ago, actually. She was heading to the bathroom and she told me where I could find you and your dad. She said you might like to meet Benny since you love dogs."

"I don't know. I should go ask my dad first."

"Really, your mom said it was okay. She said to meet her back in the store in a few minutes, so we'll be coming right back. It'll just be for a minute."

Chloe looks at her dad again, but his attentiveness has long since been gone. She shrugs. "Well, if my mom said it was okay, then I guess I'll go meet him. But just for a minute."

Without saying anything further, Scott leads Chloe out of the store before she comes to her senses. His heart is pounding, his head aching with tension, the flowing adrenaline making him shiver. His hands again tremble with jitters. He and Chloe exit to the left. Scott pushes Chloe to the inside and against the wall, using his body to hide her. He keeps his eyes straight ahead, his head down, with sweat oozing from his pores, and pushes onward. An exit sign glows orange just up ahead.

"Should we tell my dad?" Chloe asks.

"I don't think we need to. Your mom will be here in a minute and she'll tell him."

Scott gently puts his arm around Chloe's shoulder and leads her down the busy walkway. They reach the illumination and push through. The door to the outside is at the end of a long, dark, and slightly eerie hallway. Scott doesn't exhale until they step outside and the dimly lit corridor is at their backs.

Once outside, Scott leads Chloe to his mother's station wagon at the far end of the parking lot. "Here we are," he says as they arrive at the wagon, the breeze still gusting, albeit not quite as hard as it had been earlier. It offers him much needed relief.

"Where's Benny?" Chloe asks as she looks through the rear windows of the station wagon, ignoring the hole of rust on the frame. She falls back on her heels and throws her hands on her hips.

Scott unlocks the door, slides his head into the back seat, and pretends to look for the puppy. "I don't know," he says. "He was in here when I left."

He pulls away from the car and faces Chloe to gauge her reaction. Her lips are pursed and she makes a clicking sound with her tongue; she doesn't buy it.

"You don't really have a puppy, do you?" she says. Then she takes a step back.

A nervous sweat covers Scott's back, drenching his shirt like a sponge. He should have had a plan.

Now what?

Chloe shifts her eyes to the side, drops her arms, and starts to twist her torso. But Scott recognizes what she's about to do, and he's quick too. He does the only thing he can think to do.

He panics.

In one smooth motion, Scott wraps his arms around Chloe's waist and lifts her off the ground, holding her parallel to the tarmac. Chloe kicks her feet and screams piercing screams at the top of her lungs, arms flailing, midriff showing. Her voice vibrates through the desolation of the parking lot. Bracing her torso and upper body between his thigh and rib cage, Scott stretches her legs out with his free hand and forces her into the back seat. She fights and squirms, but eventually loses the battle of strength and slips onto the floor between the front and back seats, still screaming, now crying. Scott slams the door and rushes around to the other side of the wagon. His entire body trembles from the shot of adrenaline. His eyes widen, scanning the parking lot to see if there are any witnesses. As far as he can see, miraculously, there are none.

He hops in and starts the station wagon as quickly as he can.

***

Chloe gathers herself and pushes from the floor onto the back seat, all kinds of thoughts running through her mind like scavengers. Her muscles tense and her breaths are short, but she's not hurt, only stunned. Once she comes to, the heavy burden of her own stupidity suffocates her.

As the old station wagon speeds away with its tires squealing, the momentum tossing Chloe back and forth on the back seat, she reaches for the door handle behind Scott's seat and yanks on it. It won't budge. She goes with the momentum of the vehicle and reaches for the handle on the other door, but that's locked from the outside too. As the car steadies and the hot smell of burning rubber starts to fade, Chloe realizes there's no way out. For the first time, she recognizes her life might be in danger. The noises around her are deafening.

***

Abby rushes into the bathroom and vomits into the toilet in one of the empty stalls. The combination of being in her first trimester and the shock of the delivery in her mailbox this morning has made her stomach churn. When emptied, she sits on the toilet bowl and rests her face in her hands, shaking and groaning from the pain of her aching guts. She wasn't ready to deal with this yet, not like this. She can't believe it's been ten years already.

Once she settles, Abby gathers herself and rinses out her mouth in the sink, spitting the acid against faded porcelain. Then she leaves the bathroom and heads back out to find Kurt and Chloe. She hasn't told Kurt about the pregnancy yet, and she's not sure why. They'd tried for a second child for years after Chloe was born, but after losing two fetuses around the eight-week mark, they stopped for a while. The pain simply hurt too much. Part of her is afraid she might jinx it. Or maybe she's afraid Kurt won't want another one after all these years. She'll tell him when the time is right.

In front of the pet store, Abby finds Kurt laughing with his old friend and neighbor, Fred. They haven't seen him and his wife in two or three years probably, despite living in the same town. Life tends to get in the way sometimes.

"There you are, Abby," Fred says as Abby approaches. "How are you?"

Abby leans in and accepts his polite embrace. "Good to see you, Fred. Where's Caroline?"

"Oh, she's down the hall looking for shoes, as always."

"Some things never change, I guess," Abby says, smiling half-heartedly.

"You got that right."

Noticing that Chloe isn't with Kurt, Abby peers into the pet store. She doesn't see her in there either, so she turns to Kurt with curiosity and says, "Where's Chloe?"

"She's looking at puppies," Kurt says.

"No, she's not."

"Of course she is, she's right over there." Kurt turns and points into the pet store. Except, there's no one there.

Panic sets in.

Abby rushes around a wooden bench that separates one side of the corridor from the other and hurries into the pet store, pushing past a group of teenage girls. A loud, repetitive pounding drums in her ears. She makes the rounds in the store and finds no one, no Chloe, so she yells out for the employee. Abby paces anxiously until a youthful looking woman appears from the back. She can't be any older than her early twenties.

"Can I help you?" the woman asks.

Abby is frantic. "Did you see a little girl in here? Dark hair, brown eyes, wearing denim shorts."

Kurt joins Abby in the store just as she finishes asking the question.

"There was a girl in here a few minutes ago. Why?"

"So, she left then?" Abby says.

"Yeah, she left with a guy."

"What!"

"What? What's the matter?"

"How old was this guy?" Kurt interjects.

"I don't know, about your age probably. He looked kind of like you, actually," the woman says, pointing to Kurt. "But I only got a quick glimpse. I was in the back."

"Oh, God," Abby says, now pacing more quickly.

"What? What's wrong?" the woman says, her face scrunched, her lips puckered. "It looked like he was her dad or something."

Stars spin, forcing Abby to grab a hold of the side of the counter to keep herself from falling. She squares up her feet so she has better support, and when she does, she can feel the note once again poking into her thigh through her jeans. It seems to have gotten sharper. She wants to scream, but knows she can't.

Still next to her and seeming oblivious to her pain, Kurt says to the store clerk, "That wasn't her dad."

"How do you know?" the woman asks, her voice quaking.

Abby glances up and notices how completely pale the woman's face has become.

"Because I am."

CHAPTER THREE

With Chloe sitting quietly in the back, Scott keeps his hands on the wheel and drives along the back roads that parallel the high-traffic areas. The jitters in his hands have disappeared, the sweats subsided, but he still senses his fuse could burst at any moment. He patters his thumbs on the faded leather wheel to try to distract himself, but he fears it's only making him more anxious. His mother's cabin is thirty-five miles from the mall and on the edge of the Tiadaghton State Forest. They're not even halfway there.

Although he knows it had to be done, Scott's struggling to comprehend what he's gotten himself into. He'd thought it was going to be easy to get the girl to agree to go with him, and initially, it was, but he hadn't really thought the whole thing through. That, he realizes, was his biggest mistake. But, in the end, he got the girl, and that's all that mattered, although it didn't make any of this easier.

Scott peers in his rearview mirror every so often to check in on Chloe. She's stone-faced and sitting tight against the door, as far away from Scott as she can be. He hates that she's afraid of him, although he can't blame her. He's given her no choice. Her back is pressed against the edge of the seat, her eyes scanning everything around her with a concentrated precision. Her fingers fidget with something in her lap, but even when adjusting the mirror to get a better look, Scott can't tell what it is.

"You should put your seat belt on," Scott says in the most harmless voice he can.

Without saying anything in protest, Chloe obliges. Scott readjusts the mirror again so he can see the full reflection of her face.

"I'm sorry about all this," he says as he switches his eyes between the mirror and the road. "You don't have to be scared."

Chloe's bottom lip starts to quiver, but she quickly stops it. She strong for her age, Scott can tell, and he's glad Abby has taught her how to be that way. Woman and girls, especially, must be strong.

"Where are you taking me?" Her voice is weak, innocent.

Scott smiles but ignores the question. "I really do know your mom, you know. She and I go way back. Way before you were even born, actually."

Chloe says nothing.

"Before even your dad knew her. We've known each other forever practically. We basically grew up together."

Chloe's lip starts up again, but this time, she doesn't fight it. Tears as thick as molasses begin to stream down her face.

Sensing he can say nothing that will help the current situation from the front seat, Scott lowers his eyes from the mirror and keep them straight ahead. Seeing Chloe like this makes him feel terrible about what's happened. He can only imagine what she's thinking, and he wishes he could explain to her what's going on.

Except, he can't. Not yet. Maybe not ever.

Scott sighs, questioning, but hoping he's doing the right thing. "We'll be there soon," he says. "Then you get to meet someone very special. I think you'll really like her."

***

Detectives Hank Berger and Melanie Chase have been assigned to the Janis case. Hank knows very little about what awaits him and his partner as they cross through the yellow crime scene tape, but he's ready to get to it. There's another missing girl, he's heard, and it makes his skin crawl with endless possibilities. He doesn't have the best track record with this type of situation, and everyone knows it.

He and Melanie approach the scene. There's an aura of anxiousness that surrounds the area, and Hank feels the pressure right away. The tie around his neck chokes him as if it were a python, forcing him to loosen his collar. Everyone, it seems, is on edge. The local cops already on the scene unfold their arms and jump to attention as he approaches, Melanie a step behind. The men put up a façade of being desensitized and unaffected by what's happened, but Hank knows better. He can tell by their slouched shoulders and moistened foreheads that they're glad to see him, thankful the situation at hand is no longer their problem. Hank's seen everything once and most things twice, and at his age, he didn't think he'd have to go through this again.

But, it turns out, he was wrong.

"What's going on here?" he asks.

After some initial stumbling from the locals, Hank and Melanie are debriefed on the situation. There's really not much to learn, which Hank was afraid of. In situations like these, things can get ugly fast—he, of all people, knows that firsthand. He and Melanie are pointed in the direction of the girl's parents.

"You the parents?" Hank asks as he approaches them from behind. He already knows the answer and their names from the debriefing, but it's a quick way to break the ice. Offering his sympathy for the situation they're in isn't his strength.

Kurt and Abby Janis turn around at the sound of Hank's voice, facing him and Melanie. Abby's face is saturated with dried tears, mascara smeared on her cheeks, her eyes puffy. Kurt is visually disheveled, his hair out of place, his fingernails bitten to nubs, and is clearly shaken by what's happened.

"Yes, we're the parents," Kurt says. "You are?"

Hank opens his badge open and flashes it. "I'm Detective Berger and this is Detective Chase. We're going to be the lead investigators on the case."

They all shake hands.

"Tell me what happened," Hank says. "Start from the beginning."

"We already told the other guys. You want us to tell you too?" Kurt says.

"They're just locals. I'd like to hear it from you in your own words."

Kurt looks to Abby for support, but she's unable to provide much of anything. She just stares blankly into space, her cheeks penetrated with a deep red flush that's reminiscent of overripe tomatoes. "Okay then," Kurt begins. "I was with my daughter—our daughter—in the pet shop—"

"And where were you?" Hank asks, looking in Abby's direction.

She makes eye contact with him, and the first thing Hank notices after the tomatoes on her face is the glazed look in her eyes. It's as if a pane of glass has burrowed inside her eye sockets, waiting to shatter at any time. Right away, it worries him.

"Bathroom," Abby says.

Hank turns back to Kurt. "Okay. Continue."

"Chloe, our daughter, was looking at the puppies. I ran into an old friend who was walking by and we were just talking, then the next thing I know, Chloe's gone."

"What were you are your friend talking about?"

"Just catching up. I hadn't seen him for a while."

"Must have been pretty important for you to leave your daughter alone like that."

Kurt raises an eyebrow. "Excuse me?"

Melanie clears her throat and steps in. "What my partner is trying to say is that it's really important you tell us everything. Anything and everything may help." She places a hand on Abby's wrist and offers a partial smile. "I know it's difficult."

Hank admires how caring and genuine Melanie seems, and he wishes he had the same way with people. Even in his younger days, he was never like that with the victims. But with only six months left until retirement, he's not motivated enough to learn a new skill, either.

Kurt looks to Melanie and says, "Come to think of it, we did have a bit of a disagreement."

"Who's 'we'?" Melanie says.

"Chloe. Me and Chloe."

"You didn't tell me that," Abby interjects, the glass in her eyes thinning.

"I didn't think it was important. It was nothing, really. She just asked about getting a dog, that's all."

"What did you tell her?"

"I told her I'd think about it. I said you didn't really want a dog around the house."

"So you made me out to be the bad guy?"

"It's not that, it's just—"

Melanie clears her throat again, which halts the banter for now.

"Sorry," Kurt offers, sheepishly.

"Is there anything else you can tell us?" Melanie tries.

Kurt looks to his wife for approval, then says, "I think we told you everything."

Melanie nods and reaches inside her coat and fetches out a business card. She hands it to Kurt, who takes and reads it. "If you remember anything else, please call me. Okay?"

"That's it?" Abby says. "You're not going to do anything?"

Melanie looks to Hank briefly, then says, "No, that's not it. We're going to do some work around here—talk to some people, look at some tape—then we'll see where to go from there. There's nothing else you can do at this point, though. We don't even know what we're dealing with yet."

"My baby is missing!" Abby says. "She was taken!"

"Mrs. Janis, I can't fully understand what you're going through as a mother, because I'm not one myself, but we don't even know what's happened yet. We'll find out, though, I can promise you that. We'll call you when we know something."

"I'm not leaving. No chance in hell."

Hank studies Abby hard. He gets a strange vibe coming from her, but he's unable to pinpoint where it's coming from. To him, it seems like she's forcing it. He says, "Do you have something else to contribute to the investigation? Something that maybe you've left out?"

Abby pauses and her face turns pale. "No. Nothing we haven't said to you or the other guys or the lady on the phone already."

Hank keeps his eyes on her for a second longer. Something definitely feels off; she's too defensive. "Okay, then. You don't have to leave, but stay out of our way. We have work to do."

"He's right, Mrs. Janis," Melanie says. "You're more than welcome to stick around. But, if you don't mind..."

Kurt nods. He gets it. He wraps his arm around his wife and moves her toward the bench.

"Thank you," Melanie says. "We'll be right over here if you need anything." She and Hank head toward the pet store.

The store is clean and tidy, but it's loud and smells like a zoo. Puppies bark, kittens whine, and some caged critter makes a high-pitched squeal that Hank doesn't recognize. Strong fluorescent lights reflect off the cages, forcing Hank to look away for a moment. A young woman who's teary-eyed and very pretty greets them as she stands behind the counter with her hands folded. Dark bags under her eyes tell Hank all he needs to know about her credibility as a possible witness. Ignoring the overhead lights, Hank scans the ceiling and quickly finds two cameras on opposite ends of the room, both mounted in a corner. He suspects their angles might suffice.

"Can you make a copy of the VHS for me?" Hank asks the woman as he points to one of the cameras.

The girl behind the counter lowers her eyebrows, almost frowning. "I'm sorry, officer, I don't know what that is."

"Detective."

"Sorry. Detective, I don't know what you mean."

"How old are you?" Hank asks.

"Nineteen. Why?"

"You're nineteen and you don't know what a VHS cassette is?"

The girl shrugs.

"A VHS, Hank?" Melanie says. "What is this, 1995?" She turns to the girl behind the counter. "Sweetie, the security cameras—do they work?"

"Yeah, they work."

"Do they record?"

"There's a DVD recorder out back."

"Will you grab the DVD for us, please? We'll need a copy."

The girl nods and disappears into the back.

Melanie turns to Hank again and puts her hands on her hips. "A VHS, Hank?"

"What?" Hank says, then he shrugs.

A moment passes. Hank stands with Melanie, anxiously shifting his weight from one foot to the other, while they wait for the girl to return. He whistles softly, tapping his toes on the tile under his feet. The noises from the animals have softened.

"So, what are you thinking, Hank?"

"I don't trust her."

"Who?"

"The mother."

"Mrs. Janis? Why not?"

Hank faces his partner. "Because she's lying to us, Chase. I have a feeling she knows more than she's letting on."

"Why do you think that?"

"I just do, Chase. I just have that feeling."

CHAPTER FOUR

After being forced to abandon the back roads and merge onto a two-lane highway, Scott pulls off the main strip and detours down a dead-end road. The station wagon is old and rusted underneath and isn't built for the off-road conditions, so he lets off the gas as he makes his way over exposed tree roots and around broken limbs. Despite the day being at its brightest, the thick forest eliminates all of the sunlight to give it a feel of nightfall. It heightens the intensity.

Scott's mother's cabin appears after a half mile of maneuvering around the uneven terrain. It's a log cabin made of a dark red oak and it sits surrounded by a bevy of shade-loving plants and shrubbery. It's well-kept and welcoming, even in spite of the eerie entrance. Scott proudly calls it home.

And now, Chloe can too.

Scott pulls the wagon in front of the cabin and kills the engine. It spits out an exhausted whirl as it comes to a stop, a layering of black smoke forming a cloud in the rear. Scott slides out of the wagon, his shirt pulling on the seat as if it were stuck with gum, and takes in the scents and sounds of nature: flowers blooming, woodpeckers pecking, trout jumping in the pond down in the back.

So peaceful. So isolated. So perfect.

With rocks scrabbling beneath his feet, Scott makes his way around the front of the wagon and looks through the glass at Chloe. Her eyes shift from side to side, scanning her surroundings, trying to gauge where she is and why. Scott can see the wheels spinning in her head, and he's impressed with her sense of awareness at such a young age. Abby really has done well. He leaves Chloe alone and heads into the cabin.

"Mother, I'm home," Scott yells out as he enters, the door scraping the tile behind him. He holds his position and waits for a response, but gets nothing. Only crickets.

A moment later, the floor creaks from down the hall, the sound of shuffling feet nearing. Just then, his mother appears, wearing her apron that's covered with black, charred holes from years of use. She's had the same one for as long as Scott can remember, and it reminds him of his childhood whenever she wears it. The warm aroma of freshly cooked blueberries fills the cabin, Scott tasting them as he licks his lips.

"Is she here?" Scott's mother, Diane, asks as she enters. She dries her hands on the belly of her apron using the same circular motion that she has thousands of times over the years. Her eyes widen and sparkle the way the pond does when the sun hits it just right, her face glowing with anticipation.

"In the car," Scott says.

Diane smiles a little, wipes it away, then covers her mouth to keep it hidden. "Okay, so what do we do now?" she asks.

"That's the same exact question I was going to ask you," Scott says. "I thought you knew."

***

Inside one of the offices of the local precinct, Hank sits with Melanie while they review the security tapes from the mall, frustration building. Unfortunately, despite the many angles, there's not much to work with.

Melanie controls the remote and rewinds and fast forwards at Hank's instruction. Hank rocks in place. They use the time stamp at the bottom to narrow down their search, but even with the targeted sections of video, they're practically worthless. The one thing the tapes do reveal, though, is that the man who has Chloe Janis might be a professional. The way he maneuvered around the pet store, looking so casual and carefully avoiding looking directly into the cameras, it's like he knew what he was doing. Either that, or he's one lucky son of a bitch. But no one can possibly be that lucky, Hank thinks. Bottom line, the footage is a dead end.

"Stop the tape," Hank says as he tosses a pen onto the table, huffing.

"See something?"

"Nothing to see, Chase."

Melanie nods in agreement. "What do we do now?"

Hank gets to his feet, slowly, as if it pains him to do so, and starts for the door. "Let's go talk to them."

Melanie grabs her steaming mug, the usual scent of roasted coconut and marshmallows following her. She slips a small bag, half gone, of extra marshmallows in her hip pocket, and follows Hank. They join the Janis's in the interrogation room down the hall, where they've been waiting since they insisted on following the detectives to the station.

Abby and Kurt both stand when the door opens and the detectives walk in, looking anxious and eager for some good news. Hank sits across from them, Melanie too, and wastes no time in getting down to it. There's no easy way to tell them what he and Melanie have found.

"Okay, so we've reviewed the tapes," Hank begins, "and I've got to tell you, there's nothing suspicious that jumps out at us."

"Nothing suspicious?" Abby says. "How could that be?" Her eyes are still red, but she seems more alert than she had been at the mall. The shields of glass have disappeared from her pupils.

"We still have to take a closer look, but all signs point to your daughter knowing the person she left with."

"That's impossible."

"Why do you say that? Is there something else should know?"

"Of course not," Abby says, looking away.

"Well, alright then," Hank says. He glares at her as a tense silence fills the room.

"But like Detective Berger said," Melanie interjects, "we still have to look at the tapes a little closer. We still don't know much right now."

"Do you have anything?" Kurt pleads. "Anything at all?"

"We do have a visual of the man in question," Melanie admits. "And we can confirm that your daughter did leave with him."

Kurt is wide-eyed and almost excited about this. "That's good news then, right?"

"It's a step in the right direction," Melanie agrees.

Kurt looks between the detectives and his wife, his sunken eyes showing his apprehension. "Why do I feel like there's a 'but' coming?"

Melanie looks to Hank, who gives her a subtle nod. "Well, it's just that..."

"What?" Abby says. "What is it?"

Melanie looks to Hank again, and this time, he fills in the rest. "Based on the criteria developed by the state of Pennsylvania, there's nothing else we can do right now."

Abby jumps to her feet, frantic, the legs of the chair scraping the floor underneath her. "What do you mean there's nothing else you can do? My daughter has been abducted!"

"According to what we can tell from the tapes, your daughter didn't appear to be in any kind of danger. They left the pet store together. She was just walking next to the man and he didn't appear to be threatening her in any way. Quite frankly, it seems as if your daughter went willingly."

Abby slams her hands on the table and leans across it with rage boiling in her eyes. "You son of a bitch!"

Kurt reacts quickly and wraps his arms around Abby's waist, pulling her back as if she were a toddler having a meltdown. Melanie jumps to her feet and puts a hand on her weapon, backing away a step. Hank stays seated and stares back at Abby, wondering where her outburst came from. He's been through this type of thing once or twice, and her overreaction seems out of line. Admittedly, and maybe foolishly, he wasn't expecting it. Her unpredictability is something to pay attention to already, he notes, and the investigation has only just begun.

When the dust settles and everyone sits back down in their seats, emotions in check, Hank clears his throat. Very calmly, he says, "I don't know what you think we're doing here, Mrs. Janis, but we're on your side, okay? We're doing everything we can, but you're not making our jobs any easier."

Abby breathes fire at him with her eyes, but says nothing. Kurt caresses her forearm to try to coax her back to reality. A bead of sweat on his forehead starts to move south, but Kurt refuses to address it. The pulsating veins in his neck tell Hank that Kurt's taken aback by Abby's abruptness, too.

"Our daughter wouldn't have run off with some guy, okay?" Kurt says. "She wouldn't do that."

"I've heard that before," Melanie says. "And in all honesty, we do believe that to be the case. It doesn't make much sense that a nine-year-old girl would run off with a guy like that."

Hank keeps a close eye on Abby, studying her, trying to determine who she really is. Her husband seems to have her adequately restrained.

"I don't understand then," Kurt says. "Why can't you do anything if you don't think she went willingly?"

With his eyes still locked on Abby, Hank says, "In order to file a missing person's report at this stage, the child must be in imminent danger, which she doesn't appear to be. Or she has to have been abducted, which she also doesn't appear to have been. And considering it's only been a couple of hours—"

"But, she just said—"

Hank holds up a hand to stop him. "Listen, I know. I get it. But since your daughter doesn't meet any of the criteria right now, we just have to wait it out."

"For how long?" Kurt asks, the defeat obvious in the softness of his voice.

"Twenty-four hours."

Abby jumps to her feet again and lunges at Hank. Kurt is slower to react this time, having let his guard down just a little, but he's able to pull her back before she does anything she might regret. Melanie is back on the defensive, quickly on her feet again, her hand back on her weapon. Hank only flinches and sighs heavily. He's starting to get annoyed at the whole scene developing in front of him for a second time.

"Twenty-four hours!" Abby exclaims. "She could be dead in twenty-four hours!"

"Listen, lady," Hank says with a fiery tone. He points a somewhat unsteady finger in Abby's direction and holds it there. "If you can't control your outbursts, then I'm going to have to ask you to leave. I'm sympathetic to how you feel, I really am, but there's nothing we can do right now. If your daughter doesn't return home in twenty-four hours, we'll be ready to go, full steam ahead." Hank lowers his finger, but keeps his hard eyes on Abby. "I'm sorry, but I don't make the laws, I just enforce them."

CHAPTER FIVE

Chloe doesn't try anything while Scott leaves her alone in the station wagon. He'd locked his door from the outside before he went inside the cabin, so Chloe realizes there's no way out. Each of the windows are rolled up tight and sealed, and Chloe has no intentions of trying to break a window either. Even if she did, where would she go? She has no idea where she is. It's probably best if she waits and does what Scott tells her to do, she decides, so she stays buckled.

Scott reemerges from the cabin in a matter of minutes and walks back toward the wagon. The warmth is trapped behind the seals, making the air heavy inside the wagon, forcing Chloe to break out in a sweat. She tenses up as Scott approaches, a casual smile on his face, and she wraps her sticky palms around the seat belt over her chest. Outside the door, Scott fumbles with the keys on his keyring, eventually finding the one that fits. When he finds it, he opens Chloe's door, letting fresh air rush inside the wagon and invigorating her lungs. Chloe breathes it in and gets some relief.

Without saying anything, Scott leans across her chest and reaches for something near her waist. Chloe pushes herself back against the seat and clenches her teeth together, frightened, waiting for something to happen. The sweat on his neck tickles her nose, his aftershave making her eyes water. She steadies herself and holds her breath, unsure what to expect, and braces for pain.

But the pain never comes.

A click of metal and plastic pops and the seat belt loosens in front of Chloe. She stays unmoving, letting it be as it twists its way around her shoulder and slides back into its stationary resting position. Her tensed core muscles relax and she exhales, suddenly realizing how trapped she'd felt buckled in.

Scott backs out of the wagon, and holds his hand out for Chloe. She looks at him with apprehension, unsure what to think, unsure if she can trust him. He smiles at her again and pushes his hand closer. With the same degree of uncertainty, Chloe gives in and takes Scott's hand, not knowing what other option she has. She lets him pull her to her feet, thankful to have flat ground underneath her. Together, they walk hand in hand toward the cabin. The moistness of Scott's hand threatens to allow Chloe to slip away.

But, regretfully, she doesn't.

Scott leads Chloe into the cabin and closes the door behind them. They enter into a small kitchen, complete with a rectangular table close to the middle of the room and old nonpatterned tiles under foot. On the other side of the kitchen, wearing an old apron covered with streaks of grease and small tears and what looks like writing from a child's marker, an older woman is waiting. She's older than Scott, but not quite old enough to be a grandmother. She does have a motherly look to her, Chloe thinks, and Chloe wonders if she might be Scott's mother. The resemblance isn't immediately clear to her, but Chloe never has been very good at that type of thing. The woman stands halfway across the room with her hands over her mouth and tears in her eyes. Her eyelids are sunken and her cheeks are thinner than they should be, but she looks otherwise happy.

"Mother," Scott says, his voice shaking. "I'd like you to meet Chloe."

A hollow, muffled squeal protrudes from underneath the cupped hands over the woman's mouth. It's the recognizable sound of joyousness.

Scott turns to Chloe and says, "And Chloe, I'd like you to meet my mother. You can call her—"

"Didi," the woman says tearfully. "I'd like you to call me Didi." She clutches her hands to her chest slowly makes her way across the room, tiptoeing like she's approaching a wild animal. She makes her way toward Chloe and stands in front of her, studying her, searching for approval. Chloe doesn't react as the woman crouches down, her arthritic joints making it visibly painful to watch, and gazes directly into Chloe's eyes. "You are so beautiful. You are absolutely perfect." Didi gently places her hands on Chloe's bare arms and slides them up and down.

The hairs stand up on Chloe's forearms, receptive to Didi's gentle touch. Chloe stares down at the strange woman, confused, unsure what to think. The woman has a warm and welcoming presence about her which Chloe is drawn to, but it all feels so wrong. Part of her wants to give the woman a hug to find out if the spinning is real or not, but even just the thought feels inappropriate. Because she's never been so confused in her entire life, Chloe starts to cry too.

"Don't cry, Chloe," Didi says, wiping her own tears away. She pulls Chloe into her chest and squeezes her. "Everything will be okay. I promise. Everything will be fine."

Chloe just stands in place with her arms dangling at her sides, feeling mostly bones, as the woman's soft breath tickles her ear. She doesn't offer up any resistance when Didi rubs her back, but she doesn't give her anything in return either. She just lets the warmth tingle all throughout her body. She closes her eyes and pictures her mom, imagining it was her pressed against her chest instead of this stranger. It makes her cry even more.

Didi releases Chloe after a generous thirty seconds of awkward embracing, and she pushes to her feet, wincing. She wipes away the tears from Chloe's cheek with her thumb and washes them away on her apron. "Are you hungry, Chloe? I bet you're hungry."

Chloe shrugs.

"I've made a fresh blueberry pie. Handpicked blueberries. We have our own bush in the back near the pond, you know. Maybe we can do that together sometime—pick some berries, that is. Do you like blueberries?"

Chloe nods.

Didi exhales a bit and smiles. "Good. Now, let's go get us a piece of pie, shall we? It's still warm even, and that's the best part." Didi puts her arm around Chloe's shoulder and leads her toward the giant rectangle across the kitchen.

***

Jordan Huff wanders around the walkways of the mall in Mifflinburg, alone, with his hands in his pockets, twirling a loose thread between his fingers, enjoying his freedom. He's been willingly sober for thirteen months, two weeks, and five days. That's also how long he's been out of prison for.

He doesn't often make the trip from the double-wide he shares with his girlfriend in Montgomery to Mifflinburg, but something inside him told him to get out of the house for a while today. So he did. He could use a new pair of steel-toed boots for work, so it gave him an excuse to make the trek. Mindy, his live-in girlfriend, works all day on Saturday's and half days on Sunday's, so Jordan spends a lot of time by himself. He often gets tired of cleaning the trailer and preparing meals, so he thought some exercise to clear his mind might help to break up the monotony.

He just wasn't expecting the mall to be a crime scene.

Jordan's generally reserved. The daily pressures of prison life were of high-intensity and stressful, and since he's been out, he's mellowed. He learned what life was like on the inside—the struggle to stay alive, the struggle to trust your surroundings enough to get a good night's sleep - and now that he's out, he's doing all he can to keep a low profile. He just wants to keep his head down and stay out of trouble.

Drugs are what did him in, got him, put him away. It got out of hand so quickly. One day he was sixteen and smoking a little pot with his friends, and the next day he was twenty-seven and hooked on the hard stuff. Although he hated it at the time, him going to prison was the best thing that'd ever happened in his life. It got him sober. Rehab failed twice prior to that, so he's thankful he's getting a second chance at life. And now, he's determined to make the best of it.

The yellow crime scene tape that creates a barrier from one part of the mall to the other was not something Jordan had expected to see today. He hasn't been inside a mall very many times in the last ten years, but he'd always remembered them as being safe havens for teenage girls and single moms. The police tape tells him otherwise now. Things, apparently, have changed.

A young police officer with a baby face and huge biceps stops him as he approaches the tape. "You can't come any further than that," the officer says.

Jordan looks past the strange-looking man and sees a swarm of officers moving in and out of the pet store further down the corridor, some carrying black duffel bags, others holding their hats. "I just wanted to get some new boots," Jordan says, motioning to the men's shoe store that sits adjacent to the pet store.

"Sorry, no can do. Come back another time. We'll be busy here for a while."

"What's going on?"

"I can't really say. Police business."

"Did something happen?"

"Like I said, I can't really say anything at this time. An investigation is ongoing."

Jordan nods, feeling unsatisfied.

"Sorry about your boots," the officer says, "but you'll have to come back another time."

Jordan bobs his head up and down for a while and turns his back to the officer. The mystery intrigues him, and he wonders what's being hidden that the public can't know about. He figures it'll be public knowledge soon enough; everything always is.

With his hands still jammed deep in his pockets, the loose thread being stubborn, Jordan makes his way back toward where he came from. He'll gladly save the money for now.

Mindy Jacobs owns her own business—a hair salon—so most of their disposable income is reinvested back into it. Jordan doesn't mind. Mindy accepted him for who he was and what he'd gone through early in his life, and he's forever grateful for that. Without her taking a chance on him and seeing the good, there's no telling where he'd be. Probably still in Pittsburg with his old friends and old temptations.

Aside from his imprisonment, which was responsible for his sobriety, Mindy moving from the city to the more affordable town of Montgomery to open her salon was the best thing that'd ever happened to Jordan. He jumped on the opportunity to move in with her, and everything's been great. It's been over a year already. Jordan found employment at a steel factory almost immediately after moving to Montgomery, and although he works with other released convicts, he hasn't once been tempted to relapse. Mindy has made it clear to him that if he ever did, he's out. No exceptions. That motivation alone has been enough to keep him straight. And for all she's done for him, for her acceptance of him and his wrongdoings in his past, he's going to make it up to her one day. He's slowly saving his pennies, and once he gets enough saved to do it properly, he's going to buy her a ring. He's had his eye on one for quite a while, and he's never met a woman more deserving than Mindy. When the day comes for him to cash in, Jordan just hopes she'll say yes.

***

"I'm going to kill him," Abby says to Kurt, his Benz hugging the road that leads them back home. She's still steaming from the results of their conversation with the detectives, and Kurt doesn't blame her. He feels the same way. He's just more understanding than his well-meaning wife; the detectives' hands are tied.

"I know," he says.

"Can you believe they're making us wait for twenty-four hours before doing anything?"

"I know."

"What is this world coming to?"

Kurt doesn't know how to respond, so he says nothing. He knows Abby won't understand the position the detectives are in, as a mother. A hostile silence overwhelms the Mercedes that's already without a vital cog. Kurt peeks in his rearview mirror to where his baby girl should be sitting in the back, but she's not there. Her absence makes his heart ache, the guilt strangling him like a noose. As he looks back to the road, pain everywhere, he can suddenly feel the elephant in the car with them. As much as he tries to ignore it, its burden is crushing him, suffocating him, sucking the life right out of him. He can't help but think this is all his fault.

"Listen, Abby, about what happened—"

"It wasn't intentional."

"I know, but if I was paying more attention—"

"It could have happened to anyone."

"Will you give me more than that, please? You can't possibly understand the guilt I feel about what happened."

"What do you want me to say, Kurt?" Abby shuffles around in her seat and faces him. "Do you want me to tell you it's all your fault and that if you weren't ignoring her and talking to Fred that this wouldn't have happened? Is that what you want?"

Kurt lets the words sink in. He's not sure what he'd been expecting, but he doesn't feel any better having heard it aloud. He sighs. "I guess you're right. I don't know what I was hoping to accomplish." He takes Abby's hand in his own and massages a knuckle with his finger. "I'm sorry."

Abby squeezes Kurt's hand and drops her head slightly. "I'm sorry too," she says.

"We'll get through this. We'll find out who took Chloe and we'll get her back. Whatever it takes."

Abby nods in agreement, but looks away.

"We just have to stay by the phone," Kurt says. "If the detectives find something else on the tapes, maybe we can file the report sooner."

Abby nods again, keeping her eyes averted.

"And if not, twenty-four hours from now we'll hit the ground running—just like they said. We'll find out who did this and what they want. We'll get our baby back."

Abby doesn't respond, but Kurt can hear her sniffling as she stares out the window. He's failed her more than he thought possible, and it's out of his hands to fix it. Relinquishing control of the situation is going to be difficult, he knows. But he also knows if he doesn't empower the detectives to do their jobs, he may never see his baby girl again. He wishes there was something more he could do.

CHAPTER SIX

With a belly full of blueberries and doughy pie crust, Chloe is led to the den off the rear of the kitchen for the first time. The den, just like her bedroom at home, is filled with toys. There are dolls, a plastic kitchen set, puzzles, containers of crayons and markers, and a bookshelf full of miscellaneous knickknacks in colored bins. The walls are covered with narrow windows that allow natural light to fill the room.

Chloe walks over to one of the windows and looks outside. Unlike the front of the house, which is heavily shaded by the sagging trees overhead, the backside is wide open and bright. There's a clearing with far fewer trees and a small pond not far from the window. A plump blueberry bush is on the edge of the forest, standing alone, seemingly lonely. Chloe watches a flock of ducks paddling in the blue ripples of the pond. One leans forward and dives down, coming back up with a catch. Chloe smiles with hopes that the duck, like herself, will soon have a full belly too.

Suddenly bored with nature, Chloe turns from the window and makes her way over to the shelves of toys. She shoots a glance over her shoulder at Didi and Scott, both of whom are standing in the doorway, nodding and smiling at her. Chloe flashes a smile back, thankful for having some space between them, hoping they believe the smile is genuine. She digs into the colored bins on the bookshelf and sifts through the options. In the first one, she finds an old slinky, a couple of Barbie dolls, and some

Matchbox cars. There are lots of toys scattered amongst the bins in an organized chaos, and Chloe can't help but wonder if they're all for her. She wonders where it all came from. Some of the stuff is for little girls, she realizes, and not someone her age, but she doesn't say anything. She keeps the smile on her face and pretends to like everything.

She grabs the largest doll she can find, its red hair unnaturally curly, its eyes beady and blue, and starts to stroke the ginger-colored curls with a plastic brush she's found. She doesn't look back to Scott and Didi, but she can feel them both watching her, their eyes sharp and penetrating. It makes her uncomfortable, but this time, at least, she doesn't have to taste Scott's sweat as she breathes in. At least now, she has some space to think about what her next move might be.

***

Scott and Diane stand in the doorway that leads back to the kitchen and observe Chloe sorting through the bins of toys. Scott takes pleasure in seeing Chloe so happy, and it helps to ease his mind about what it is that he's done. He can see now that he's made the right decision by bringing her here—the smile on her face tells him as much.

Scott shifts his eyes toward his mother to gauge her reaction. The top of her closed fist is pressed against her mouth and nose, as if to keep whatever's inside in. Scott can see the smile on her face underneath her fingers, which makes him smile too. She absolutely loves this, and it's about time she has some joy in her life. Scott's brother, Tommy, doesn't bring his two girls around to see their grandmother very often, so Diane has never had the chance to spoil a child like she's always wanted. She was unable to provide Scott and Tommy with much growing up, so now that she's able to, Scott is more than happy to allow her to experience it. She deserves it. This moment is as much hers as it is his.

Scott puts his arm around his mother's shoulder and pulls her in close. Diane accepts and leans into his chest, the smell of lilies following. Her body is frail and cold to the touch through her loose clothing that once fit perfectly, but Scott doesn't let his mind go there. Instead, he closes his eyes and allows himself to enjoy the moment while it lasts.

It's so nice to have this woman in my life again, even if it's just for a little while.

Diane takes ahold of his hand and kisses it, sending shivers through his fingertips that reminds of him his childhood. The dryness of her kiss feels like the wrinkled lips of an old woman, but Scott ignores it. He wants to forget about her impending demise for as long as he can. For now, there's so much joy in their lives to take in.

"This is so great," Diane whispers as she keeps her gaze on Chloe, who has discovered the bin of plush Disney figurines.

"It's been a long time coming."

"After all these years," Diane says, "we can finally be a family."

Scott nods and forces a smile. He knows this is only just the beginning of what's about to come. And he knows there's still something else he has to do to make this all work. Without it, everything will fall apart. He would hate to break his mother's heart and have this all taken away from her. It's already damaged enough.

***

Once the Janis's leave the station, Hank and Melanie spend the afternoon in the same private room as before, thoroughly reviewing the tapes again. Hank is convinced they've missed something—he can't accept the man's perfection; he had to of made a mistake somewhere. Melanie's already on her fifth cup of marshmallow-filled coconut coffee, and the smell of it is starting to make Hank nauseous.

"So, what are you thinking, Hank?" Melanie asks between sips. "Where's your head at?"

"Pardon me?"

"The tapes we've been studying here all day—what do you think?"

"I have my opinions, but why don't you tell me what you think?"

"Okay, Melanie says, "the little girl, the victim—"

"I'll stop you there. Victim? Why do you call her a victim? We're watching the same film, aren't we?"

"You know what I mean, Hank."

Hank looks at her blankly. "No, in fact, I don't know what you mean."

"Fine, Hank. You tell me then. What do you call her?"

"She's a girl, just a girl. There's been no crime as far as I can see, so there's no victim. Not yet. Do you want me to tell you what I see, Chase? Do you want me to tell you what I think is happening here?"

Melanie nods.

"I think a young girl left with an older man on her own accord and didn't appear to be in danger in any way. I saw a girl who was familiar with the person she left with. I saw a girl who wasn't afraid. And you know what else I saw? I saw a girl who was mad at her father for telling her no and left with someone else to piss him off. Daughters tend to do that, you know."

Melanie rolls her eyes. "It doesn't bother you that a nine-year-old girl has run off with some guy old enough to be her father?"

"We don't know that. There's no shot of his face anywhere. We don't know how old he is."

"No, but based on the eyewitness—"

"The eyewitness was confused and shaken. And she only got a glimpse of the guy. That's hardly a reliable witness. She doesn't know what she saw."

"Fine, take her out of it. You can also assume, based on—"

"No assuming. Not in this line of work. It gets us nowhere. No one has ever solved a case by assuming anything."

Melanie sighs. "Fine, Hank. I get it. Take detective work out of it for a second, okay? As a father, can you sit there and tell me this doesn't bother you?"

"I never said that. It irks me to the bone, matter of fact. If it was my daughter, I'd be scared shitless."

"Okay, so what's the problem?"

"The problem is we don't have any snapshots of this guy's face and the video feed loses them in the parking lot. We don't know if they walked somewhere or if they drove off. We don't know if someone picked them up or if there was a car waiting. We don't know if they went out for ice cream and are back at the mall as we speak. We don't know what happened after the video feed lost them. Quite frankly, Chase, we don't know shit."

Melanie sighs again, sounding exhausted already, defeated. "But think about it for a second. What good could possibly come out a grown-ass man leaving with a girl her age? Haven't you ever seen those child predator shows? They're all over cable."

"I don't watch television. But I have seen these cases up close. More than I can count."

"And it doesn't worry you?"

"Of course it does. I thought we already established that. But things aren't always as they seem, Chase. You'll learn that. We can't assume anything at this point. Besides, you're forgetting one thing."

"What's that?"

"We don't even know if this guy likes girls. It could all be one big misunderstanding. You of all people know what it's like to be misunderstood. Don't you, Chase?"

Melanie rolls her eyes again.

CHAPTER SEVEN

Scott spends much of the afternoon watching Chloe play, and he does eventually work up the courage to join her once she seems to be more comfortable. She appears to be settling in. She's talking more, albeit not as much as she did in the pet store, but Scott can tell she's starting to loosen up. That helps him loosen up some too.

In the evening, Diane puts together a nice dinner for the new threesome and they gather at the table to eat together. Chloe doesn't each much, but Scott doesn't press the issue. She mostly eats away the middle of the plate and spreads the rest around the perimeter, giving the visual effect of having eaten most of it. Scott knows the trick himself, but he lets it go. He can understand why Chloe may not be very hungry tonight.

Diane heads to bed before the sun goes down, being wiped out from an emotionally charged day. Scott goes in to check on her a while later, and for the first time he's seen, she's fallen asleep with a smile on her face. Scott knows she had a good day today, despite everything. And if it all works out like he's planned; every day going forward should be a good day. Diane needs all the good days she can get.

***

Chloe stands by the window in the den and looks out over the pond again. The flock of ducks has disappeared, but a soft ripple still vibrates on the surface of the water where they once were. There's a magnificent sunset starting to form over the treetops, and Chloe can't keep her eyes off it. The array of oranges, yellows, and reds are complimented by some spots of purple that remind Chloe of lilacs. The sunset doesn't get this pretty at her house.

Chloe can sense Scott approaching her from behind—she can smell his aftershave again. She tenses up when it hits her nose, but she relaxes once Scott clears his throat and announces himself. He's really trying not to frighten her, she recognizes, and she's pleased about that. But she's confused too, as his motive is as clear as mud. He's been acting like a totally different person than he was at the mall as the day's gone on. It seems like it was so long ago already.

"Pretty out there, isn't it?" Scott says.

Chloe nods, not looking at Scott.

"Want to go get a closer look?"

Chloe turns to Scott now and says, "At what?"

Scott points out the window. "The pond. I've seen you looking out at it all day. Do you want to check it out?" Scott smiles and holds out his hand for Chloe to take.

Chloe looks at Scott's hand with uncertainty at first, but then she takes it, not wanting to upset him. It's not nearly as clammy as it was earlier—a sign, perhaps, that he's not as nervous as he had been. For some reason, that makes Chloe feel a little better, too. She lets him lead her out the front door, down the wooden steps on the porch, and around the side of the house to where the pond is in the back. The grass leading up to it is little dry, brown in some spots, the blades snapping underneath her sneakers like twigs as she walks. It hasn't rained in a while.

When in front of the pond and hovering over the top of it, looking down, Chloe can see her reflection in the water. Her eyes are a little red still and her hair's a mess, but she doesn't look as sad as she thought she might. A ripple distorts and washes her face away, so she turns and looks up to Scott, who nods his head in approval. Chloe lets go of his hand and explores around the banks of the water. The lonely blueberry bush on the brink of the forest catches her eye.

***

As much as it feels so right, Scott releases Chloe hand and lets her explore the pond up close. He keeps his distance behind her but does follow as she makes her way around the perimeter of the pond. He's happy to show her she has some freedom when she's with him, unlike what her dad allows.

Nightfall is rapidly approaching and the crescent moon is forcing the sun behind the tree line. A light evening breeze gives Scott a chill, and he wonders if Chloe feels it too. Cold pimples cover his arms with dots, forming a maze on his skin. The birds overhead are starting to flock to their nests and the bats and owls are starting to wake. It won't be long before the bears and foxes and coyotes start roaming these woods.

The first woodstove fire of the season will be the first one Scott's seen in a long time, and he's been looking forward to it for years. He hopes Chloe learns to enjoy the pleasure of it too; it's the simple things. He closes his eyes and imagines himself sitting in the rocker in front of the woodstove with a blanket and a cup of coffee. He can almost smell the crackling of the woodchips and feel the warmth of the flames already. He swallows and the taste of hazelnut lathers his throat.

"You know," Scott says, opening his eyes, Chloe intently studying some movement at the bottom of the water, "your mom and I—"

"Is she coming here?" Chloe asks, suddenly excited and looking at him. "When can I see her?"

Scott pauses for a moment and thinks. "I don't know. I don't know if she's coming here or not. We still have to figure all that stuff out."

Chloe drops her head and turns away. "Oh."

Scott stares into space, not knowing what to say. Although he should have, he hasn't prepared a response to that inevitable question. Despite all of the things he has, some things he just hasn't considered thoroughly enough. "You'll see her soon, though, okay?" Scott eventually says. "I promise."

Chloe nods and starts walking back toward the cabin, suddenly disinterested in whatever it is she was looking at in the pond. Scott can tell she doesn't believe him, and he supposes he can't blame her. He's not sure if he believes himself. Chloe stops and tosses a handful of pebbles she'd gathered from the muddy bank into the pond. They all land in the same area and splash like hail hitting the water.

An hour or so later and back inside the cabin, once the sun has gone down, Scott shows Chloe her new bedroom. It's adjacent to his own, which is adjacent Diane's, keeping them all close at night. Chloe's room is furnished with a twin bed with a purple bedspread that's pushed against the far wall. Similarly colored curtains hang from the single window at the foot of the bed. The hardwood floor is warm now, but Scott will soon have to pick up an area rug to cover it during the winter months, much like the one he has in his room.

"It's not much right now," Scott admits, "but you can decorate it anyway you want. If you want to paint the walls or put some of those toys in here, you can. We'll get you someplace to put your clothes too. I guess you're going to need some more clothes too, huh? And a toothbrush. We'll have to make a list and take a trip to into town. Maybe tomorrow. It'll have to do for tonight."

Chloe nods, but doesn't say anything.

Scott stands awkwardly in the doorway, not sure what to do with his hands, while Chloe looks around her new bedroom. "I guess that's it then," he says. "If you need anything, the bathroom is down the hall and I'm right next door, okay?"

Chloe turns to face Scott and says, "Okay."

"Goodnight, Chloe."

***

Once the door closes and Scott disappears to the other side, Chloe walks across her new bedroom and sits on the edge of the bed. She tries to figure out what this all means. Talk of new clothes and a toothbrush and decorating worries her. This doesn't sound like a temporary arrangement.

The bedsprings are inexpensively made and not very supportive, so she bounces up and down when she sits. The bouncing eventually subsides, but then reality hits. Tonight is the first night in her life that at least one of her parents won't be there to tuck her in. It's the first night in her life that no one will be there to tell her they love her. The thought of that, the thought of the new life she doesn't want, brings Chloe to tears.

She kicks off her shoes and slides under the covers, desperate for the warmth. The sheets are freshly cleaned and unwrinkled, smelling of flowers. Outside the window, the now dark sky is filled with stars and a bright moon, lighting up the trees. They all look the same to her—intimidating and burly and never-ending. As she stares at them through the darkness, she has no idea how she's going to get out of here.

Chloe pulls her knees up to her chest and wraps her arms around them, hugging herself. She clenches her eyes closed and lets the tears fall onto the sheets, forming droplet marks where they land. If only one of those stars were a wishing star, she thinks as she stares out the lonesome window and into the night, she would wish for her mom and dad to come rescue her. She holds out hope that her wish will be heard while she sleeps. Or maybe she'll wake up and this will all have just been a bad dream.

Until then, she keeps the light on and snuggles up with the pillow. The smell of spring fills her airways and offers her some comfort. She ignores her growling belly that reminds her she should have eaten more for supper, and she closes her eyes and cries herself to sleep.

***

Scott waits outside Chloe's bedroom for a moment, one ear toward the door, just listening, before heading down the hall and checking the front door in the kitchen. He secures it with the deadbolt that locks with a key, then jams the key back in his pocket where it'll stay. Each of the windows in the cabin are sealed from the outside and don't open at all from the inside. This way, even if she wanted to, Chloe can't try to sneak out during the night. There's simply no way for her to escape.

Before heading off to bed himself, Scott grabs the landline from the kitchen counter and dials the number he's had memorized for as long as he can remember. After all these years, he hopes it's still in service. He hadn't planned to do this quite yet, but he also hadn't expected for the subject to be brought up so soon either. He walks toward the den so he can't be heard, twirling the stretched coil around his fingers, and waits while the call tries to connect. He's not quite sure what he'll say if the call does go through, but he really hopes it does.

***

Night has fallen. Abby and Kurt are in separate rooms on the opposite side of the house. Kurt thinks Abby has gone to bed because she's too depressed to do anything else—that's what she told him anyway. Whether he believes her not is a different question, but he's left her alone, so he must. Although Abby's depression is part of it, that's not the entire story. The stress of the day has put a strain on the growing fetus inside her belly, so she's feeling under the weather. And the truth is, Abby can't face her husband right now. The guilt she feels for allowing him to take the blame for what has happened is far heavier than the guilt he could possibly feel for thinking it's all his fault. In reality, it's actually all her fault and she knows it. Worst of all, she already knows who it is that has Chloe, and she knows what it is that he wants. She just won't give it to him. There has to be another way.

Although Abby's supposed to be in the bed, resting with a cool cloth on her face, she's actually sitting on top of it and doing some research on her laptop. The sound of the cooling fan from her computer is the only noise in the room. The overhead lights are off and the screen brightness on her computer is at its lowest setting, so she's prepared to easily fake it if Kurt were to come upstairs to check on her.

Abby scours the web for any news article, press release, or for any mention of the recent parolees or released inmates from the state prisons. She doesn't find the name she's looking for. She thinks back to when he was sentenced and recalls it being fifteen to twenty-five years that he was supposed to serve. She doesn't remember anything about him being eligible for parole after ten, but it was such a crazy day that it's possible she just missed it.

They had regular communication initially. Abby would visit when she was able and she'd write letters every few days. She'd send pictures of Chloe. Over time, the letters became less frequent and eventually stopped altogether. Scheduling time to visit became almost impossible with a newborn and then a toddler who was starting to understand her surroundings more. Chloe had said something about visiting a jail to Kurt once when she was three, but Abby dismissed it by convincing Kurt it was just a wild imagination. He bought it, as usual. After that incident, though, Abby stopped completely. She stopped visiting - with or without Chloe—and she stopped paying for the private post office box downtown. Even if he wanted to write to her, she'd never get it. All the letters would be sent back and he'd get the message.

At least that's what Abby thought.

Even now, after all these years, she gets a blank envelope in her mailbox with a handwritten note addressed to her. How he found her, she has no idea, and how he pulled off what he did is terrifying. He must have been watching her and followed them to the mall, Abby concludes. He was probably walking right behind them the entire time. They probably shared the same air, walked on the same tiles, touched the same door handles. The thought gives Abby chills. The realization that he might have been so close to her and she was completely unaware makes her wonder what else he's capable of.

Disappointed in finding no mention of his name in any recent news articles, Abby shuts off her laptop and puts it back on the desk across the room. She hides the note from the mailbox in between a couple of pages in the paperback she's been reading and closes the drawer of the nightstand. She strips off her pants, slides under the covers like silk, and closes her eyes, letting the exhaustion take her away into her subconscious. Just as she feels herself starting to drift away into the blackness, the vibration of her phone on the wooden nightstand next to her brings her back. She reaches over and checks out the caller ID. It's an unregistered number.

She considers not answering and letting it go to voicemail at first, but then it hits her. A phone call from an unregistered number at this time on a Saturday night while her daughter is missing can only mean one thing. Abby pops up into a full state of awareness, the blood rushing to her head making her vision blur, and answers the phone before it stops ringing and she loses what could be her one and only opportunity. Her heart begins to pound so hard that she fears her ribs might crack. She inhales sharply and brings the phone to her ear.

"Hello," she says, being sure to speak at just above a whisper so Kurt doesn't hear anything.

There's some heavy breathing from the other end of the phone, but no response. She can hear whomever it is chewing on the inside of their cheek. It stays that way for a long moment.

"Is anyone there?" Abby presses.

After another moment of awkward chewing and heavy breathing, a male voice finally says, "Hello, Abagail."

Abby drops the phone in her lap and puts her hands to her mouth to muffle the sound of her gasp. Every muscle in her body tenses.

It's him.

She quickly gathers herself and picks up the phone again before they get disconnected. Despite her heart now beating so hard that the t-shirt she's wearing from Kurt's drawer is moving in rhythm with the thumping, she keeps her composure and musters out a response. "Hello, Scott," she says.

"It's nice to hear your voice."

Abby pauses for a moment to allow herself to catch her breath. She can tell Scott is smiling on the other end. "What do you want?" she says. "What did you do with Chloe?"

Scott ignores the question. "I told you I'd find you."

CHAPTER EIGHT

Sunday morning. Melanie lays awake in the bed next to her lover, their feet touching, and waits for the alarm to sound. Her internal clock has told her to awaken at sunrise, and it's spot on as always. Her alarm sings next to her less than a minute after she opens her eyes. She dismisses the chime, turns over, and wraps her arms around her partner, digging her face into the warm space between her neck and shoulder. Melanie kisses the exposed skin until she opens her eyes too. When she does, she turns and faces Melanie, and they share a morning snuggle.

Melanie has been on and off with Bree Berger for a couple of years. Recently, they've been going strong, and it's starting to get serious. Bree can be just like her father—combative, hard-nosed, and stubborn at times—and Melanie sometimes struggles to balance the similarities of the personalities between her personal and professional lives. Bree Berger is Hank Berger's daughter—the same Hank Berger that Melanie sees at the office every day, the same Hank that she's partners with—so the relationship can be complicated.

"Morning, baby," Melanie whispers as she gazes deeply into Bree's hazel eyes. At first glance, it looks like Bree's pupils are in the shape of hearts, but then Melanie realizes it's the reflection of her own. She's falling hard for her.

Bree smiles but doesn't say anything.

"Sleep well?"

"Mostly. You?"

"Always when I'm next to you."

Bree smiles again and leans in for a kiss.

"I don't know why I just thought of this now," Melanie says as she stretches and yawns, her muscles flexing, "but your dad went on one of his rants again yesterday. I meant to tell you last night."

Bree leans up on her elbows. "What did he say?"

"The usual. He went off about how I of all people should know what it's like to be misunderstood."

Bree scrunches her face and lowers an eyebrow. "What brought this on?"

"Who knows? We were just talking about this case we're working on, then all of a sudden he just went off on this tangent."

"He can be such a jerk sometimes." Bree tosses the covers to the side and slips out of the bed. She scampers across the carpet, her feet close together like a tiny mouse, and disappears into the bathroom. Melanie can't help but stare at her bare backside with a grin.

"I think you're being too hard on him," Melanie yells out so Bree can hear from the bathroom. Sitting up, she continues, "He's not that bad. He's a little hard to get along with sometimes, but he just needs to be treated a certain way. He's not much different than you in that way, you know."

Bree reappears from the bathroom with a toothbrush in her mouth, her breasts uncovered. "Why are you defending him?"

"I'm not defending him, I'm just saying."

Bree disappears back into the bathroom and finishes her quick brush. "Whatever," she says when she reemerges, the toothbrush gone. She makes her way back over to the bed and sits on the edge. She pulls her jeans up from the floor and onto her thighs. She stands and jumps as she yanks them up so they make it over her hips.

"He would love to see you, you know," Melanie says.

"He told you that?"

"Not directly, no. But I can just tell. I see the guy almost every day."

"Yeah, well, the phone works both ways. You can tell him that." Bree tosses a shirt over her head and heads for the door.

Melanie slips out of the bed and follows behind Bree as she leaves the bedroom and heads for the breakfast nook. She grabs Bree's bra from the floor on the way. "You can't avoid him forever. How long has it been?"

"Six months. Maybe longer. I'm not sure."

"Don't you think it's been long enough?"

Bree stops, turns around, and faces Melanie. "Let's not do this today, okay? I have to go."

"You don't want to stay for breakfast?"

"I can't. I have to work in a couple hours. I'll get dressed and eat at home before I go."

"Bree, you can shower here."

"Stop, please. I don't want to do this right now."

Melanie crosses her arms and looks away, a strap of Bree's bra tickling her skin.

Bree takes Melanie's face in her hands and spins it so she's forced to look back at her. "See you tonight? I'll be late remember, I'm working a double."

Melanie doesn't react. Still with Bree's soft hands on her face, she lets Bree pull her in close and accepts a peck on the lips. The fullness of Bree's lips dominate Melanie's thin ones, wetting them with a natural moisturizer that Melanie lacks.

"I'll think about what you said, okay?" Bree says.

Melanie smiles, finally.

"But I have to go right now." Bree turns and heads for the door.

Melanie follows and lets her out, handing her the bra. Bree takes it and smiles, tossing it over her shoulder like a satchel. Melanie watches her go, making her way down the corridor and toward the elevator, which she disappears into. Once it dings and the floor starts to vibrate underfoot, Melanie turns and heads back inside, where she prepares herself mentally to get ready to spend the day with the other half of the dysfunctional Berger family.

***

Scott wakes shortly after sunrise to the sound of the bathroom fan humming and the shower running. He slides out of bed and checks on Chloe right away, slightly panicked. He finds her sound asleep and wrapped up in the blankets on her bed, looking like she belongs. A sharp exhale leaves Scott's body, releasing some tension he didn't know was there. He squeezes the doorknob and pulls it slowly to avoid it creaking, then he tiptoes away and heads toward the kitchen.

On the table, he finds an empty coffee cup along with a short pencil and yesterday's paper with the crossword puzzle completely filled out. The coffee pot is half-empty and the counter in front of the toaster is covered with crumbs. The smell of melted peanut butter makes his mouth salivate. Scott checks the time and steps outside.

The morning air is already a little humid, but it soothes the dry skin on Scott's face. The razor burns on his neck from yesterday are still painful, but the slight breeze helps. He looks up and admires the sun trying to break through the trees overhead, knowing it always fails to do so completely, and starts down the dirt path on foot.

The conversation he had with Abby last night, albeit brief and direct, hasn't left his mind. He hardly slept at all, his thoughts rummaging through his mind nonstop like a freight train running late for a deadline. Hearing her voice again after so many years without it was magical. He missed her more than he even knew. In case it wasn't obvious enough before—with the letter and the sequence of events that followed thereafter - he made his intentions as clear as crystal to her, and he thinks she understands. The bottom line is the ball's in her court now, and what she does with it will depend on what happens going forward. It's simple: with her participation, she'll see Chloe again; without it, she won't. Scott just has to wait for her to make her choice.

The newspaper delivery driver brings the daily paper about halfway down the beaten path, so Scott's in for a half-mile round trip. It would be faster to use the station wagon, he realizes, but he prefers to walk to help wake himself up each morning. He'd gotten in the habit of walking the grounds every morning when he was locked up, so his body needs the physical activity in the morning now. Without it, his legs are as stiff as a board—he found that out on day one on the outside.

Right about where it usually is, Scott finds the newspaper in the middle of the path, wet with dew and wrapped in its customary clear plastic bag. He tears it open and starts making the trek back toward the cabin, crinkling the wrapper into a ball and shoving it in his pocket. While walking, he flips the paper open and holds onto the crease. When he sees it, he nearly chokes on the same air he'd found so soothing just a few moments ago.

Chloe's face is on the front page.

CHAPTER NINE

Melanie arrives at the station before eight o'clock and settles into her space. The mug on her desk is steaming and full of slowly melting mini marshmallows, the mist warming her nose. The Janis case files are stacked in a pile on the corner of the desk, a thin layer of dust already developing on the top.

According to the law as established by the state of Pennsylvania, an Amber Alert may be registered to Chloe Janis twenty-four hours after the incident. According to the time stamps on the tapes from the mall, that means that sometime early this afternoon the report can be officially filed. Until then, all Melanie can do is and keep busy and hope that little Chloe Janis is safe.

And wait for Hank.

Where is Hank?

The glass door that separates the cubicles from the reception area is kicked open with a thrust, bouncing on its hinges like a swinging door at a saloon. Melanie looks up from her coffee, expecting a cowboy with a pistol ready to duel, but only finds Hank. For some reason, she's not surprised to see him.

Hank finds the nearest table, scanning the room with dark, angry eyes, and slams a folded newspaper on it. Melanie rests a hand on her mug to stop it from rattling, the impact like a small earthquake. Hank puts his hands on his hips, strain on his face, and waits until he has everyone's attention.

"Which one of you leaked this out to the press?" Hank calls out to the roomful of detectives.

The men and women in their cubes look around at one another with uncertainty. Lots of shoulder shrugging, lots of hushed murmurs, but no answers.

Hank grabs the folded newspaper from the table and spreads it open for the group to see. He pans it to each side of the room so everyone can get a glimpse before saying anything, his hands not completely steady. When it makes its way to Melanie's attention, she squints to see it, but when she does, her eyes bulge and she gasps softly. She knows instantly that this is trouble.

"This is the pretty face of a nine-year-old girl," Hank begins. "Her name is Chloe Janis and she went missing from the mall yesterday afternoon. Detective Chase and I haven't even been able to file a missing person report yet. Now, somebody tell me, if that's the case, how the hell did this get out to the press?" Smoke leaks out of Hank's ears like a chugging locomotive.

Nobody says anything. If there was a bird in the room it could be heard chirping. If a pin were to be dropped it would echo in the emptiness. Melanie can hear herself swallow, and from across the room, she thinks Hank probably can too.

Hank scans the room again and nods. "I see how it's going to be. When I find out which one of you opened your big mouth and gave this confidential information to the press, I'm going to see to it that you never work in this state again. You got that?"

Everyone ignores him and goes back to their work. No one seems concerned with the threat, which, to Melanie, says something. Hank scoffs and shakes his head, huffing, then walks toward Melanie. She looks down and tries to avoid eye contact, flipping through some papers to look busy. His desk is adjacent to hers near the back corner, so she prepares herself for his wrath—she knows it's coming. Upon approach, he slams the newspaper on her desk and throws himself into his chair, a puff of air exploding beneath him. He ignores the ringing phone on his desk and turns to face her.

"Can you believe this shit?" he says.

Melanie grabs the paper and reads through the article, slightly panicked. There aren't a ton of details printed, to her relief, but it's more than enough to piss off whomever Chloe is with if he sees it. The article makes him out to be a monster. Melanie hates to defend the guy, but even she admits it's too much too soon for this. They still don't even know if he abducted the girl or not. "A $20,000 reward?" she says, shocked, reading. "Who's offering a reward? Did the Janis's say anything about a reward to you?"

Hank shakes his head. "Not to me."

Melanie moves her attention back to the article and reads aloud, "Police say that the nine-year-old Chloe Janis might be in imminent danger and that the abductor may be armed and dangerous." She looks up. "Jesus Christ, Hank. This is on the front page of the Sunday news. What a fucking mess."

"No shit."

Melanie tosses the paper down and shakes her head, trying to figure out what it means and where the information might have come from. She draws a blank. With a slight nod of her head, she motions to Hank's phone, realizing it's still ringing. "You going to answer that?"

Hank grunts. "Probably just a reporter."

Melanie nods, and the ringing stops.

Then Melanie's phone rings. She reaches for it, not hesitating. "Detective Chase." She doesn't say anything to the man on the other end, but after a moment, she presses a button on the phone and hangs up the receiver, calmly, trying to keep herself neutral. "Hank, you're going to want to take this. Line one."

"Who is it?"

"It's the mayor."

***

The first thing Abby does when she wakes up is sneak into the bathroom and throw up. Her stomach is empty to begin with, what with not having eaten for more than twelve hours, so it's mostly bile. Luckily for her, Kurt is already up and downstairs, so she can hide her situation for another day. Her first trimester with Chloe was difficult too—lots of morning sickness and hormonal changes—so Abby knows she won't be able to keep it from Kurt for much longer. One of these days, Kurt's going to catch on and ask about it, and she'll be forced to confront it head on. But until then, she'll keep pretending like everything is fine.

Once she cleans her face and rinses her mouth with mouthwash, Abby joins her husband downstairs in the kitchen. When she walks in, she notices Kurt's skin has paled and that dark bags have formed under his eyes, which she assumes is from the lack of sleep. He doesn't acknowledge her right away.

On the table in front of him, the newspaper catches Abby's eye. The bright colored photo sticks out immediately, so clear and vibrant that it could be framed. In fact, Abby realizes, it is framed; the same photo is hanging up on the wall near the stairs, along with other family photos and memories. Chloe—her daughter, her pride and joy, her only daily reminder of her past—stares back at her from the front page of the newspaper, smiling cheerfully, obliviously, having no inclination of the danger she'd be facing just months after smiling for the camera that day at school.

Abby covers her mouth with her hands and gasps, nearly stumbling backwards.

She quickly grabs the paper and reads the article, not saying anything to Kurt, her knees weakening. Her heart is pounding by the time she reaches the end and she can feel the wetness of her own perspiration starting to form on the back of her neck. She's suddenly lightheaded and nauseous and is forced to sit down before being overcome by the sensations. The printed words from the article pierce her heart like a lance puncturing a jouster's chest during a match. If Scott sees this, he's going to lose his—

that's her first reaction. There's no telling what he might do then.

"What the hell is this?" Abby asks after she catches her breath.

"What's wrong?" Kurt says, sensing his wife's displeasure. "I thought you'd be thrilled."

"Did you do this?"

"Of course. I called in a favor last night. You were pissed yesterday when the detectives said we'd have to wait twenty-four hours before doing anything. Now everyone knows and we can get Chloe back. What's the problem?"

Abby hands tremble with jitters. "It's just...what about what the detectives said? Maybe we should do what they say. They'll know what the best path forward is."

"What are you talking about? Yesterday you were so angry. What happened?"

"It's just...I don't know." Abby looks away. She wants to tell him what's going, but she just can't. She can't tell him that he's just made the biggest mistake of his life.

Kurt slides his chair toward Abby's and grabs her arms with a softness that only a romantic would understand. He lowers his head so he can look directly into her eyes, which he does. "Abby, what's the matter? Something's wrong."

Abby looks up and into Kurt's eyes. A deep hurt swims in them, drowned by the sadness and guilt he feels for what's happened. Abby knows it, she sees it, but she can't find it in herself to respond to him, to tell him what's going on. She can see her husband means well, but he has no idea what he's up against. And telling him would only make it worse.

"What's wrong?"

"I just wish you would have talked to me about this first," Abby says, desperate to keep her true feelings hidden. "This is a big step to take on your own. We just need to be careful here. We don't know what this guy wants from us."

Kurt pushes back in his seat and considers this. His expression turns from defensive to fearful, then to devastation.

At first, Abby thinks she's been caught in a lie, and she quickly tries to retrace her words so she can correct it before Kurt calls her out on it. But then she realizes it's not that at all. Kurt has suddenly turned a soft shade of white, droplets of sweat beading on his forehead. "What?" Abby says.

Kurt pauses for a moment, scratches his throat, and says, "Well, if that's how you feel, then you're going to be really pissed about what else I did."

***

Reluctantly, Hank picks up the phone from the base unit on his desk. He shoots a glance at Melanie, who has a look of concern on her face. He hits the button that connects the call and holds the speaker up to his ear and engages. "Detective Berger."

"Hank, it's Mayor Thomas."

"What can I do for you, Mayor?"

"I need you to explain to me what the hell you were thinking?"

Hank is taken aback. "I'm going to need more than that, sir."

"Stop joshing with me, Hank. I'm serious here."

"So am I."

Mayor Thomas sighs. "The article about the Janis girl, Hank. Explain."

"I'm just as surprised as you are, to tell you the truth. I grabbed a paper on the way in and that was the first I saw or heard of it. I'm still working on finding out where the leak came from."

"That's not what I'm talking about."

Hank is puzzled, not sure what else Mayor Thomas could be referring to. "I'm not following."

"It's not the article I'm upset about. It was my idea, in fact."

Hank's guts wrench inside of him. He can feel his blood pressure rising. "What do you mean it was your idea?"

"Tell me, Hank, do you know who the Janis's are?"

Hank says nothing.

"I didn't think so. Mr. Kurt Janis is a vice president of Mifflinburg Bank and Trust. He's in charge of overseeing all the loans that the bank offers. Three-quarters of the homeowners in this county have their mortgages from his bank."

Hank considers this new information for a moment. After not connecting the dots, he says, "What does that have to do with anything?"

"It means your theory that the Janis girl just walked out with this guy is bullshit. The guy obviously has done his homework, unlike you, I can tell, and he knows what the Janis's are worth. Could this not be more obvious? This is a kidnapping. This is about ransom."

"That's not what the surveillance tapes are telling us."

"The hell with the tapes! The hell with everything." Mayor Thomas pauses, reels himself in a bit, and takes a deep breath. "Hank, listen. Kurt Janis is a personal friend of mine, okay? I've known his daughter since she was a baby."

"All due respect, we're following protocol here."

"I understand that, I do."

"But?"

"But, I'm giving you the go ahead to bypass protocol."

"How do you expect me to explain this? People are going to ask questions."

"I know that, and I've got you covered. I'll explain everything."

"Meaning what?"

"I'll be there in a couple hours."

"You'll what?"

"I'll be there along with the Janis's and a bunch of cameras."

"Excuse me?"

"We're holding a press conference before lunch today. All you have to do is stand there and look pretty. You can handle that, can't you? I'll do all the talking."

"You're shitting me, right?"

"I don't shit anybody, Hank. See you soon." Mayor Thomas hangs up before Hank has a chance to respond.

Hank sets the phone down and thinks, trying to figure out what just happened.

"What was that all about?" Melanie asks.

Hank rubs his face, hard, for a long second. Eventually, he stops, turns to Melanie and says, "You were right, Chase. This is about to be a goddamn shit show."

CHAPTER TEN

With the newspaper in hand and the humidity at his back, Scott stops in his tracks, right in the middle of the dirt path about a half mile from the cabin. He stares at the ink on the page, both at the menacing written words and the full color photo of Chloe's face. While initially dumbfounded and shocked that the news has made it in the paper already, the displeasure quickly vanishes. As he starts reading the article, his heartrate slowing, he comes to the realization that it's not as bad as he initially thought; it's not as bad as it could have been. In fact, he sees some good in it.

The language used by the reporter is stern, aggressive, and less than flattering. Terms such as *predator*, *terror*, *nightmare*, and *villain* are all used loosely. It almost seems as if the article was written to garner attention as opposed to reporting unbiased facts, Scott thinks. He doesn't know how to feel about that. The individual words do hurt, he admits. But through it all, in spite of the carefully selected tone and purposeful writing that's been shared with four out of five homes in the county this morning, there's no mention of the name of Chloe's abductor; there's no mention of Scott's name at all. That, of course, is a good thing.

It also means two other things. First is that the police don't know it was Scott—if they did, they most certainly would have announced it to the world in an effort to find him sooner. Second is that Abby hasn't told the police anything—that's either because she's scared of what the consequences will be if she does, or she's considering her conversation with Scott from last night. If Abby is still the same person Scott thinks she is, he bets it's the latter. He has to assume that's what's going on here, and it actually excites him.

Scott gathers his thoughts and allows for multiple scenarios and endgames to run through his mind as he makes the trek back to the cabin. He feels energized. Walking faster, as he considers the idea that maybe, just maybe, this is all going to work out. The newspaper is wrapped in between his fingers like it's precious cargo, and that's because it is—it's imperative he keeps it away from Chloe. If she finds out the whole county is looking for her, then there's no telling how she might react. He doesn't know her well enough to trust her, nor does he know what girls her age are capable of.

After thinking hard about it, Scott decides he's not at all upset about what he's read. If it were him in the same situation, he'd want to spread the news to anyone who would listen too. That's what every parent would do. That's what every parent should do, even if it's just a front. People would be more suspicious if the news somehow got out that a little girl was missing and it was being withheld from the public. Scott strongly considers it, and he thinks Abby is doing the right thing. And by the way she's playing the game so far—playing both sides like a real pro—Scott likes his chances. His decision to bring Chloe here is looking better and better.

By the time Scott makes his way back into the cabin, the shower has stopped and the fan has idled. He can hear distant shuffling coming from down the hallway, so he heads in that direction with the newspaper in hand, in search of his mother. Inside her bedroom, Scott finds her swaying in a rustic rocking chair that sits next to the window and overlooks the corner of the pond. Diane sips on a steaming cup of tea that smells of cranberries and honey. Scott stands in the doorway and watches his mother for a moment, wishing she was well, hoping she takes the news okay. She doesn't seem to notice his presence.

Despite Diane not yet even being in her sixties, she looks older than most people her age. Scott suspects it all stems from the years of heavy stress and constant worrying she'd endured while raising him and Tommy. Although that may be part of it, the truth is that heart disease is killing her. Scott doesn't want to admit it, but he knows it's true; the proof is staring him right in the face. The disease isn't in the advanced stage yet, but it's still pretty severe.

Diane had open heart surgery five years ago to replace her leaking aortic valve, which appeared suddenly. One minute she was fine, planting and weeding her garden, and the next she'd found herself uncomfortably short of breath with an aching chest. She had the sense to drive herself to the hospital.

In many cases, the doctor had said, the aortic valve can wear out over time to the point where it can be controlled with medication, but in other situations—and this is what happened in Diane's case—the valve deteriorated so suddenly that emergency surgery was needed. She went under the knife the next day.

Scott didn't hear of the news for a few days. He was right in the middle of what turned out to be a ten-year prison sentence, so it took a call from the hospital after the surgery had been ruled a success to finally let him know. He was crushed, of course, knowing his mother had to go through it alone. Even though he was locked up and was unable to be there to support her, he doesn't think he can ever forgive himself for that. Nobody should go through that alone, and he let her down in that regard.

He's let her down so many times.

It took six months, but eventually Diane was in good enough health to finally go visit her son. Scott remembers the day vividly. Although still in recovery at the time, his mother had lost a significant amount of weight—so much so that her already trim frame had become frail and boney—and she'd lost much of her color. She looked sickly, almost cancerous.

Eighteen months after the first surgery, it happened again. Diane underwent a second open heart surgery to replace the same valve, but when the surgeon got inside her chest, he'd found more damage than originally thought. The surgeon used a manufactured valve the second time around, which was supposed to last longer than the natural replacement, and so far, it has. The valve has held up, but the heart disease hasn't slowed down. In fact, it's destroying her heart even faster than her doctor had expected.

The only way to keep Diane alive long term is to find her a replacement heart. She's on the transplant list along with thousands of other people, but she may never get one. Considering her age and general poor health, her doctor doesn't think she'd even survive the surgery if one became available. She will inevitably succumb to the disease—it's just a matter of when, not if. Diane is the epitome of a ticking time bomb.

Diane's declining health has been a turning point in Scott's life. Seeing his mother slowly dying has made him realize how precious life is. Scott stayed out of trouble after seeing her unwell, and peaceably served the rest of his time behind bars until he was granted parole on the first attempt. Him being released on parole has been a blessing. Not only does he get to be with her for what's remaining of her life—which her doctor has said is a year or two at most—but he also gets the chance to give her the two things she's wanted more than anything in her life. That's what Scott is trying to do for her, granting her last dying wish.

Thinking about his mother and her unavoidable fate, Scott wipes a tear from his cheek and walks into her bedroom. He feels so sorry for her. He would take her place in a minute if he could, and she knows that. The wooden floor creaks as Scott steps into the room. Diane turns to investigate. She smiles behind the steam from her teacup, but Scott can see the weakness behind it. He recognizes how much she's forcing it.

"How are you feeling?" Scott asks.

Diane shoos him away with her free hand. "We're not talking about that. Did I not make myself clear? I don't want to talk about me dying. It gives me the creeps."

"You're right. I'm sorry," Scott says. He quickly changes the subject to the matter at hand. "Are you sure you're up for this?"

"Of course, don't worry."

Scott's hesitant, but he sees no other way. He hadn't expected she'd get worse so quickly. "Okay," he says. "Call the house if you run into any trouble."

Diane smiles playfully. "And what is it you'd be able to do for me? I'm taking the one car."

Scott considers this, shrugs, and concedes that she makes a valid point. "Just call me if you get into trouble, okay? I'll figure it out."

"Okay, Scotty." Diane leans across her chair and pats Scott on the knee.

Scott takes his mother's hand and kisses the top of it. For her being so young, her skin is awfully wrinkled. If he didn't know any better, he'd think he was holding the hand of an elderly woman. Feeling it slipping, Scott releases Diane's hand and grabs the newspaper from under his arm. She looks at it as he drops it in her lap, the smile disappearing from her face, the lines on her cheeks fading. When she gasps, the teacup slips from her grasp and falls to the floor, shattering into a hundred pieces and spilling hot tea all over the hardwood. Scott is sent back on his heels, frantic, scrambling to avoid the penetrating liquid heat as if it were magma.

***

With Mindy already gone to work and Jordan left alone, he wakes up late and makes some toast. Mindy is already gone for the day, so he keeps his pants off, instead choosing to lounge around in his underwear. The toast is burnt, and the charred crust sticks to the pits of his molars. He searches for a toothpick in the cabinet by the fridge.

The note Mindy left for him on the table makes his heart smile, and he looks forward to having her home this afternoon so he can show her how much she means to him. He falls in love with her more every day.

Through the screened-in porch past the living room, Jordan spots something sitting idly in the driveway. The morning sun gleams down on the blacktop and makes it difficult for Jordan to make out what it is. His initial reaction is that it might be a cat, as it looks to be about the appropriate size. He watches the figure for a moment, curiously, waiting for it to move along. But it's not moving.

Is it dead?

Jordan pops up and carries his charred toast over to the window to get a better look, his tongue trying to dislodge a chunk of wheat that's stuck in his teeth. Whatever the object is in the driveway, Jordan still can't tell. He squints directly at it, using his hand to shield his eyes from the sun. A blanket of clouds overhead glides across the sky and moves in front of the sun, a shadow forming over the object in the driveway. Through the umbra, the object becomes clearer, and it's not a cat. It's not alive and never was. It's just the daily newspaper, wrapped in plastic and covered in dew.

Jordan steps out onto the porch and into the sun. The toast stuck in his teeth tastes like charcoal and is as hard as stone, so he tosses what's left of the piece to the crows. Further down the driveway, Jordan scoops up the newspaper and tears off the plastic wrapping, the wetness latching onto his fingers like a suction. The front page has an eye-catching headline about the incident at the mall in Mifflinburg yesterday, something he'd almost forgotten about. The little girl mentioned in the article was apparently abducted, which explains the heavy police presence there yesterday.

Jordan reads the article standing in the driveway, uncaring about his vulnerability to his neighbors. The little girl's name is Chloe Janis, which means nothing to him. He doesn't know anyone in the area aside from Mindy and his coworkers, so that doesn't surprise him. And he knows nobody in Mifflinburg. There aren't any photos of the girl's parents in the article, although neither name means anything to him either.

What Jordan does find strange, though, is the little girl herself. Although he's not around children much—or ever, really—and her name doesn't sound familiar, something about her look does. He tries to place the face, tries to think of where he might have seen her, but he draws a blank. Her features are familiar—the high cheekbones, narrow face, and long forehead—but he doesn't know from where. All he knows is that he's seen her before, in some form or another.

Jordan is stumped. His bare shoulders are being warmed by the sun now that the clouds have moved past, and the soles of his feet are a little hot on the blacktop, so he heads back. He tucks the newspaper in the waist of his boxers and walks back toward the double-wide. Near the door to the porch, a trio of crows have found the burnt toast and are squawking at one another over it. Jordan watches them tussle for a while before heading inside with the snapshot of the little girl still entrenched into his mind. He can't get over her familiarity, yet, he can't figure out where he's seen her before. And he knows, until he figures it out, it's going to make him crazy.

CHAPTER ELEVEN

Abby hasn't spoken a word to her husband since first thing this morning at the breakfast table. That was hours ago. It's five minutes before eleven now.

A press conference? For real? What the hell was he thinking?

His explanation had been that after talking to the mayor—with whom he also considers to be a personal friend—they had decided it was the best path forward. Mayor Wesley Thomas said he'd talk to the detectives himself and give them the go ahead to officially make Chloe's case an Amber Alert. In doing so, a press conference would be held in front of the police station to announce it to the world this morning. The idea is to put a scare into Chloe's kidnapper so he'll let her go unharmed. The case should be national news by supper, according to Wesley.

The problem with that—and it's the issue that nobody except for Abby knows—is that Scott isn't going to just let Chloe go. Abby knows there's only one circumstance under which he'll do so, and that, in reality, isn't truly even letting her go. But Abby doesn't want to go down that path. Not anymore. That bridge has long since been burned. So that means Abby has to pretend to be genuine to the cameras even though she knows it's useless. But it also means she has to play both sides so that Scott doesn't freak out either. If he sees the press conference and thinks Abby's truly desperate and hopeful that he'll return Chloe unharmed, he'll know of Abby's true intentions.

And she can't have that.

Abby needs him to think he still has a chance for his plan to work. She's desperate for that, really, as it's probably her only chance to get Chloe back.

The press conference is about to start. Abby stands next to Kurt and behind the mayor and two detectives, sweating heavily, her stomach churning. Both she and Kurt are dressed in their Sunday best—a hip-hugging black dress for her and a dark suit for Kurt. With all the darkness behind the podium, it's like they're preparing for a funeral. It makes Abby sick, but she knows deep down that she'll never let that happen.

Scott wouldn't go that far, would he?

A large crowd of reporters with notepads, handheld tape recorders, and news video cameras gather in front of the podium, some pushing, other less aggressive ones giving in and fading to the back. Microphones from each of the local and state news stations sit crookedly in the holders in front of the podium in preparation. Mayor Thomas tests the audio quality with the folks in the back, and once they give their approval, he prepares to start.

Abby thinks she might be sick.

Kurt grabs her hand and squeezes tight, the moisture on his making it feel slimy. Although she refuses to look him in the face, she doesn't fight him. She reminds herself who she needs to pretend to be. She must act like she would if she knew Scott was watching. The red bulbs let her know the cameras are rolling, so it's time for her to play along.

Mayor Thomas introduces himself, the Janis's, and the two detectives working the case, then thanks everyone in the media for showing up on short notice on a Sunday. He wastes little time and offers up a summary of the article that has garnered so much attention locally. He uses some of the same language that was written in the article, almost as if he were reading directly from it. He raises the newspaper and pans it to the crowd, showing the cameras the photo of Chloe for dramatic effect.

Abby blocks out the noise and is temporarily blinded by all the flashbulbs, which make her eyes water. Tears fall and she's forced to wipe away them away from her cheek, her eyeliner smudging. *This is good*, she says to herself, *the effect of the tears is good*. She has to be believable. She has to play the victim here.

Before she knows it, Kurt releases her hand and steps forward, toward the podium. She shakes herself and tries to remember to maintain her persona, but she suddenly feels like she's on an island, alone and unsure what to do with her hands. Lights flash in her face, one after the other, burning her eyes, but she tries to ignore them and watches as Kurt steps up to the podium. He shakes the hand of his longtime friend and Mifflinburg mayor, Wesley Thomas. Abby listens in to what her husband has to say.

"Thank you to everyone for being here," Kurt begins, his voice already shaking as it echoes through the amplifier. "As Mayor Thomas mentioned, my name is Kurt Janis, and I'm Chloe's father. My wife Abby and I are overwhelmed and saddened by what has occurred to our daughter."

Abby cringes. *None of this would have ever happened if Kurt had been...*

"But with your help, and with the help of everyone in and around the Mifflinburg area, we pray we can bring her home safely." Kurt pauses, covering his mouth and looking away while more flashbulbs go off. "My wife Abby and I would like to offer a reward of $20,000 to anyone who may have any information that leads to the safe return of our daughter."

Abby cringes again. The money that's another thing Kurt didn't consult with her about. She'd forgotten all about it after reading it in the paper earlier this morning. All of her attention had been on how she was supposed to act during this press conference, so somehow twenty grand slipped her mind. Do they even have twenty grand? She doesn't know. Money management isn't her thing. All she knows is that Kurt brings home six figures, plus a bonus, and that she and Chloe have anything and everything they could ever want. That's all she cares about.

"That's all we want," Kurt continues. "Whoever did this and why, we don't care. We just want our daughter back." His voice quivers. "Please, we just want our Chloe back."

Abby's stomach violently twists, the pain arching her back. She feels a sudden urge to heave and does all she can to stop it. Her insides wrench. The pain reminds her that she'd forgotten to eat again this morning. It's now been almost twenty-four hours since she has. The growing fetus inside of her is not happy, and she's the one who's paying the price for it.

Kurt retreats from the podium and returns to his position next to his wife, weeping. He takes her hand again and squeezes it. Tears stream down his face like rain. All the while, Abby can only concentrate on the twisting that's going on inside of her. She doesn't once look Kurt in the face or offer him her shoulder to cry on. All she can think about, in this moment, is herself.

***

Hank listens quietly as the mayor opens up the floor for questions. He's standing offstage left, Melanie at his side, and at an angle so he can see what's going on in all directions: the Janis's to his left, the crowd of reporters to his right, and the mayor straight ahead. An empty street is the backdrop. Hank digs his heels into the pavement and tries not to look directly into anyone's eyes. He wants to avoid having to answer any questions at all costs. These people can be brutal.

Hank looks over to his partner to gauge how she's doing when he notices her staring. He follows her eyes. She's locked in on the Janis's. Abby holds onto Kurt's hand, but she looks to be distant and disengaged while Kurt struggles to compose himself after his heartfelt speech. Hank finds it odd. Usually, it's the other way around—the mother breaking down while the father tries to comfort her. But Abby isn't doing either. She's just standing there, seemingly staring into space, completely unaware that her husband is having a difficult time. Kurt wipes his eyes with a tissue while Abby looks almost ill with boredom.

To avoid any of the cameras catching on to what he's seeing, Hank coughs quietly to clear his throat and to gather Melanie's attention. Melanie turns away almost immediately, then shifts her eyes to Hank's. Subtly, he moves his eyebrows ever so slightly as if to say to her, "I told you so." He knew there was something Abby wasn't telling them.

"Detective Berger," Mayor Thomas says as he turns to face Hank, "this one's for you."

Hank unexpectedly looks into the crowd at all of the eyes staring back at him like vultures ready to claw at his throat. He hadn't been prepared for questions—the mayor had told him not to be. He starts to sweat, his belly knotting. As slowly as he can, Hank makes his way to the podium, feeling like he's approaching a plank. He gives the mayor a look of discontent and stands near the edge of the plank, his hands tied, and faces the crowd. With a dry throat, he says, "Will you please repeat the question?"

There's a hushed murmur that comes from the back of the crowd. Eventually, a microphone makes its way back to the rear and winds up in the hands of a familiar face. Hank recognizes her immediately. It's Marie Washington, and she's one of the fiercest reporters in the county.

"Detective Berger," Marie begins, "it's my understanding that you have yet to move this case through the system and proceed it to the status of an Amber Alert. Is that correct?"

Hank looks to Mayor Thomas, who'd said he was going to handle this. But the mayor is whispering something in the ear of an armed security guard offstage. Hank's on his own. "There are certain protocols and procedures that need to be followed in order to move a case to that stage."

"So, you haven't moved the case along then, correct?"

Hank shuffles his feet and readjusts his belt, his toes curling over the edge of the plank. He's becoming uncomfortable very quickly. "Not at this time."

"May I ask why? The mayor has made it clear that he's authorized an Amber Alert to be issued."

Hank looks uncomfortably to the mayor again for some backup. Mayor Thomas does eventually meet his eyes this time, and he makes his way back over to the podium.

Mayor Thomas steps in and says, "That's enough questions for now, okay? Let's let the detectives get back to work. Thank you, everyone, for coming."

A buzz comes from the crowd. It's the sound of unsatisfied reporters.

Hank steps away and wipes his brow. Melanie offers him her verbal support, but it doesn't help. Before getting out of the lights and heading back into the station, he searches for Marie Washington in the crowd. She's standing in the back, still holding the microphone and staring back at him, tapping her pen against her lips. This is the exact reason why he didn't want to make this public and hold a press conference—people like her. The case is cold enough as it is, never mind reporters like Marie Washington adding unnecessary heat. He turns his back to her and storms off. She's just doing her job, he realizes, but that doesn't make him feel any better either. The man he really wants to talk to is Mayor Thomas, for he is the one who's made empty promises. Hank barely notices Abby Janis vomiting into the bushes as he rushes past.

CHAPTER TWELVE

While yesterday had been such a good day for Diane—one of the best days she's had, perhaps—today isn't going nearly as well. She's fatigued and her chest aches, and general muscle weakness overwhelms her, but she presses onward. She has a job to do. In addition to the physical limitations, she's also scared to death about what Scott had showed her earlier—the newspaper article. The anxiety from that only worsens her situation, the burden heavy. She does believe Scott when he says he has everything under control, as he did after she'd read the article, but even a dummy can recognize when things aren't going according to plan. And Diane's no dummy.

She'd recognized the restlessness in Scott's eyes when he'd told her his thoughts about the article. He'd tried his best to downplay it by telling her it wasn't all bad and that it shows Abby's willingness to play the game with the media, but Diane knows better. Chloe's face—her wonderful, already beautiful, innocent face—being on the front page of the Sunday paper is not good, no matter how you spin it. Especially not this quickly. She doesn't care what Scott says; the cops are going to be on to him soon.

They're going to be on to both of them.

The thought of it all ending so abruptly after all the planning that went into it is torturous for Diane, the possibility making her restless. She imagines that's how she'd feel if she was told there was a new heart available, just to have it taken away at the last minute. It's almost not fair. Life can be that way, she's learned.

The drive from Diane's cabin on the edge of the Tiadaghton State Forest to Mifflinburg will take her just shy of an hour, which she hopes will give her enough time to rid herself of her worries. It might be wishful thinking, though, as already she's finding the more she thinks about it, the more worrisome it becomes. There's something in the pit of her stomach that tells her things are going to end badly, and she typically has a good sense about things like this. Much like with the failing heart in her chest, it's only a matter of time before the walls cave in and everything comes crumbling down around them.

The traffic on route 44 is almost non-existent at this time in the morning, so Diane makes good time. When she gets into town, she stops off at the only pharmacy downtown and picks up some toiletries for Chloe, plus a little something for Scott. The clerk behind the counter looks at her strangely when ringing up the collection of items, but Diane only smiles. There's nothing else she can do—the clerk wouldn't understand. The real reason for coming into town, though, is in the mall. That's where Diane heads to next.

The corridors inside the mall are hushed. Mothers hold their children close and husbands wear their heads on a swivel, keeping an eye out for danger. The storefronts are quiet and mostly vacated, the employees tucked inside. The scattered uniformed police officers roam around the corridors, their shoulders squared and firm, their chins up. Diane can smell the fear.

She avoids eye contact with everyone, keeping her head down, concentrating on her walking. There's a silent buzz about the place that looms around every corner, a reality that no one wants to acknowledge. They never thought it would happen in their town—no one ever does. But it could, and it did, and Diane has a difficult time holding her head up high, knowing she's played a part in it.

Diane isn't supposed to strain herself physically—doctor's orders—so although she can see the pet store at the far end of the corridor, she paces herself and walks slowly toward it. Her chest is still tight, her breathing labored, the pressure of being back at the scene of the crime building within her. Her health is starting to slow her down and has been increasingly worsening for a while. She knows she's dying, and she's learned to accept it, but it's the whole slowing down part that eats at her the most. She used to be on her feet for twelve hours a day or more while she waited tables for all those years, and now she's exhausted after an hour of light activity. It's amazing how quickly her body has given up on her.

Finally reaching the end of the corridor, Diane slogs into the empty pet store, greeted by a young woman without much enthusiasm. She looks to be of college-age, unhappy and lacking confidence, a blankness on her face. Diane wonders if it's the same girl that was manning the store yesterday, the same girl Scott had mentioned. Based on the deep bags of exhaustion under her eyes and uncared for blemishes on her face, Diane assumes it might be.

Just as was described to her, there's a sheet of glass across from the register that separates the window shoppers from the prized possessions of the shop. One puppy in particular stands out, the golden one, and Diane has her eye on it. The puppy's paws hopelessly slide down the glass as it tries to climb its way to the other side, barking cheerily, its tail wagging like a propeller. Diane bends down to the pup's level, her everything hurting, and it lets out a little squeal that would make even the most brutal man's lip quiver. The pup's tongue is too long for its mouth and it unravels as he smiles with joy, the moistened tip nearly touching the floor. The blind happiness makes her forget about the pain.

"How much for this guy?" she says as she struggles to get back to her feet, her joints pulsating.

The girl from behind the counter walks around it and slowly makes her way toward Diane, her energy still far lower than it should be for someone of her age. "A thousand."

Diane winches and faces the girl. "Yikes."

"He's a purebred."

Diane sighs, but not out of frustration. She has a smile on her face while she does it. The money, she knows, will be well worth it. "Okay," she says, "let's do it."

An hour later, equipped with detailed instructions on how to care for a new puppy and five hundred dollars' worth of supplies and accessories to get her started, Diane leads him out. She fights to restrain him as he yanks on the leash, thankful for the employee who helps her carry the supplies. A nice older woman stops them in the corridor and admires the pup and offers some friendly advice on how to train him. Diane smiles, nods, and forgets everything by the time she gets outside.

Once they get to the station wagon, the pup sniffs everything, still tugging, emptying what's left of his bladder on the grass surrounding the pavement. The pup thanks the store employee for helping by slobbering all over her hands one final time, yelping with excitement, and leaps onto the front seat of the wagon like he's done it before.

Before accelerating out of the parking lot, the pet store employee gone, Diane takes a rest and catches her breath, leaning against the headrest. All the excitement has gotten her overheated, her heart thumping in her ears, her neck wet with perspiration. She cracks the window, letting cool air flow through the cabin like a wind tunnel, providing her some relief. The pup leans his head toward and glass, his oversized, floppy ears slapping against the breeze. He looks a little silly with those ears and that tongue, Diane thinks, but he'll grow into them. She's looking forward to it.

The pup stumbles around on the seat for a while at each stop, start, and turn, but he does eventually get the hang of it and sits. He lasts only a few minutes before exhaustion takes over and his eyes start to roll back in his head. He eventually lies down, curls up in a ball, and closes his eyes, allowing the vibration of the balding tires against the pavement to put him to sleep. Diane's wounded heart melts as his tail smacks against the cloth while she pats his head. She looks at him and smiles, the strain on her body being worth it, knowing Chloe is going to absolutely adore him.

***

The sun creeps its way through the window underneath the curtain at the foot of Chloe's new bed, penetrating her skin with heat. Chloe rolls onto her side, still half-sleeping, and gets a face full of sunlight. She shields her face with a blanket and tosses the pillow over her eyes, trying to enjoy her final moments of blackness. The fresh linen still smells clean and the sunlight warms her dried skin. She feels rested.

Chloe's belly grumbles as she turns over and starts to stir, rubbing away the crust from her eyes. The first thing she's going to do is go downstairs and see if her dad will make her pancakes. He usually makes a big breakfast for everyone on Sunday morning, which Chloe always looks forward to. She thinks she might be able to eat an entire jumbo stack this morning; she's pretty hungry. Her mouth salivates just thinking about it—the sweetness of the chocolate chips, the smoothness of the melted butter against her tongue, the warmth of the maple syrup washing it all down her throat, a tingle of bitterness remaining on her lips.

Chloe pushes herself out of bed, her toes curling around the cotton on her feet. She scans her bedroom. She looks for her desk, but doesn't find it; she looks for her laptop, but doesn't find it; she looks for her tablet, her bookshelf, her bureau, her basket of shoes, but doesn't find any of those things either. She doesn't find anything of hers. She doesn't recognize anything.

Then she remembers where she is.

Her heart sinks. She sits back on the bed, feeling defeated, and drops her head. Suddenly, the grumbling in her belly subsides and turns to pain instead, pinching from the inside out. She stays sitting on the edge of the bed for a moment, wondering to herself how she'll ever be able to get out of this mess. Those tall trees don't look as intimidating during the daytime as they did during the night, but she's not sure how deep the forest is. It seems like it goes on forever. She could get lost out there.

Chloe gets to her feet again, feeling depressed, holding onto the hope that her parents will come rescue her. She makes her way across the hardwood and opens to the door, the doorknob cool to the touch. The hallway is silent, the rooms next to hers unoccupied. Somewhere down the hall, a metal spoon clanks against something porcelain. Reluctantly, Chloe heads toward the sound.

***

Scott sits at the kitchen table with a mug of cold coffee and a half-eaten English muffin in front of him, stirring a spoon through the brown liquid, making a whirlpool in the mug. He has a lot on his mind. He's read the article on the front page over and over, and he still doesn't fully know how he feels about it. He's conflicted.

Down the hallway, the floorboards creak and soft feet shuffle toward him. His attention turns to the sound immediately, and he's a little unnerved. Facing day two with the newspaper article floating over his head makes him uneasy. He hopes his mother will be back soon.

Chloe appears in the doorway and leans against the doorframe, all of her weight trusting the stability of the wood. Her hair is a mess—frizzy and sticking up in all directions, the braid from yesterday long since gone—and her eyes are sunken. Scott quickly scrambles to find the front page of the newspaper and hides it underneath the other sections before she notices. His elbow knocks against the coffee mug, nearly toppling it from the table.

"Good morning, Chloe," Scott says, his voice shaking, as Chloe makes her way into the kitchen.

Chloe rubs her eyes and doesn't say much. She mumbles something under her breath, but it passes Scott by. Just now, looking at Chloe, Scott realizes she's wearing the same outfit she did yesterday—a purple graphic T-shirt with some light-colored casual shorts—and he kicks himself for not asking his mother to pick up some new clothes while she's at the mall. He'll have to find another way since going back himself isn't an option. He won't ask his mother again either—she's not well enough. She shouldn't have even gone today, he admits.

"Are you hungry?" Scott asks as he slides the chair back and gets up from his spot, the felt pads on the underside of the legs gliding across the floor with ease. He walks over to the sink and pours his cold coffee down the drain. The pipes guzzle it out of site, but the pleasant aroma still stays the same. "What would you like for breakfast? An English muffin? Cereal? Toast?"

Chloe says nothing, but takes a seat at the table. She rubs her eyes some more, yawning. Scott nervously watches her, hoping she won't shuffle the newspaper around and see her face staring back at her. He wants to say something to distract her, anything to take her attention off the paper, but he can't. His mouth goes dry.

Chloe pushes the paper aside and looks elsewhere, making room in front of her. She eventually tells Scott that toast with butter will be fine, and he gets right on it, relieved she's not old enough to show an interest in the daily news. He waits to exhale until his back is to her and the bread is in the toaster, the heat inside turning the leftover crumbs to ash. He doesn't know how long he can do this for. The anxiety, already, is killing him. He's starting to doubt whether he's cut out for this lifestyle.

Scott taps his fingertips on the counter, waiting anxiously, his nails clicking, desperately hoping he'll find something in common with Chloe. Excluding the original trip from Mifflinburg to the cabin, this is the first time they've been completely alone since the pick-up happened, and he's not totally sure what to do or say. He'd never envisioned it would be so difficult to connect with her.

After a couple of minutes, the toaster releases Chloe's breakfast, the metal snapping like a mousetrap. Scott jumps at the sound and welcomes the distraction. He grabs a knife from the drawer and spreads a thin layer of butter on top of the toast. He finds some orange juice in the fridge and pours Chloe a small glass without asking her if she wants it first.

Chloe accepts them both—the glass and the plate—and takes a bite of the toast, chewing it slowly, shifting her eyes like she's contemplating something. She turns and looks Scott in the face, chews some more, and says, "Why am I here?"

Scott's heart leaps. Chloe's boldness surprises him, catching him off guard. Although he's been expecting a question like this since he brought her here, he hasn't come up with a good answer yet. Chloe seems to know very little about the dynamic between himself and Abby, so he treads lightly. "Well," he begins, stammering, "remember how I said I'm an old friend of your mom's? Well, it's true. In fact, your mother and I—"

A car door slams outside. Scott finds the clock on the stove and nods—the timing makes sense. He breathes a sigh of relief as he knows Diane is here to rescue him from having to go any further for now. He needs more time to figure out how to say what it is he wants to say. Moving quickly, he walks over to the window above the sink and peeks outside. In the driveway is his mother's station wagon, tired and whirling to a stop, the drive belt squeaking as the engine lets out a little cough. He tells Chloe to stay put as he steps onto the porch.

In the driveway, Diane clips an oversized leash to the new puppy's collar and puts him on the dirt. He urinates where he stands, his golden coat shining, and lets his nose explore his surroundings, his tail wagging nervously.

"Everything go okay?" Scott asks.

"I got everything, if that's what you mean," Diane says as the puppy tries to force her toward the woods.

Scott recognizes a look of trepidation on his mother's face and he can't help but suspect it's something more than just the puppy trying to pull her. "What's the matter?"

"You haven't heard?"

"Heard what?"

"It's all over the news. TV and radio. Every outlet is covering it."

"What, Mother? What?"

"What do you think?"

Scott shrugs.

"You! Us!"

Scott shakes his head in confusion and places his hands on his mother's arms. He can feel her muscles tensing. "Mother, what are you talking about?"

"Abby and her husband held a press conference this morning. It just ended a few minutes ago. The mayor was there, plus the two lead detectives."

"What?" Scott says, perplexed.

"I know. Every news station in the region is running press about it and every radio station played the press conference live."

"Oh, God."

"I heard every word, Scott. This is bad. This is really, really bad."

Scott makes a small circle around his mother, flexing his fingers, the jitters returning. "Did they say my name?"

"No. They don't know who you are yet. But it's only a matter of time, I'm telling you."

"Christ. That didn't take long."

"What are we going to do?" Diane says, her voice trembling. "This is getting worse by the minute."

Scott places his hands on his mother's arms again and stares directly into her eyes. His breath is quick, but he slows it so his mother won't sense his worry. "Just relax, Mother. You're getting flush."

"The newspaper is one thing, but now TV. This is bad, Scott. This is so bad."

"It's alright," Scott says. "It'll be alright. I know what I have to do. I'll take care of this."

"Scotty—"

The front door swings open and a sharp gasp sounds from the porch. Scott whips his head around and looks in the direction of the sound. There's Chloe on the porch, her mouth open and hands on her cheeks, staring awestruck at the puppy.

"It's a puppy!" Chloe yells, her eyes wide, her voice high.

The puppy turns at the sound of Chloe's voice and takes off running toward her as if he recognizes her. The leash is torn from Diane's grip and the handle bounces around in the dirt as it chases the puppy toward the porch. Chloe opens her arms and lets the puppy tackle her and slobber all over her face, shrieking with joy. She laughs from her belly like every kid is supposed to, and it makes Scott completely forget about the conversation he was having with his mother. He's not even mad Chloe disobeyed him; he's just happy she's surprised.

"Can I keep him?" Chloe yells out through giggles, her back planted flat against the porch.

"Of course you can!" Diane hollers back. "He's for you!"

Scott grins from ear to ear.

It takes Chloe a while to move the puppy off her chest so she can sit up, but she eventually does and wipes off her face. She grabs the handle of the leash that has since retracted and is sitting at the bottom of the steps, and she runs over and wraps her arms around Scott's waist. Scott is knocked back on his heels, shocked at the gesture, and barely has time to even process what's happening before Chloe lets go and does the same to Diane.

"I love him!" Chloe says, the puppy at her side, its rear end swinging so fast it looks like he might topple over. "What's his name?"

Scott looks to his mother, who already has tears in her eyes. He wraps his arm around her shoulder and pulls her in close, tears welling in his own.

My girls.

"Whatever you want," he says. "You can name him."

Chloe scrunches her face and looks into the sky, thinking. When she's thought of the perfect name, she moves her head back down to Earth and looks at Scott. She smiles and says, "How about Benny? That's a good name."

Scott holds on to his mother as his knees almost give way. He squeezes her so firmly that he's afraid he might fracture her feeble bones. He can do nothing else but smile at Chloe's suggestion while his heart slowly begins to melt away.

So, this is what it feels like?

CHAPTER THIRTEEN

Hank storms through the front doors of the police station, his fists balled, and darts toward the cubicles in the back. There's a cluster of pent up anger trapped inside of him that he needs a release for, and bad. It's not that Marie Washington's questions pissed him off, because he respects what she does as a reporter. She wouldn't be doing her job if she didn't ask those questions, Hank admits, but it's how she asked them that irks him. She was confrontational and ruthless and was just outright nasty, but that's still not the root of Hank's anger. No, he's not upset with Marie Washington. It's the mayor Hank needs a word with, the same mayor who threw him to the wolves out there.

Melanie yells out to him from somewhere behind, but Hank doesn't stop. He plows his way around the tables and maze of cubicles until he finds his desk, where he throws himself down. Pockets of air dispense from the many holes that have formed on the seams of the leather chair, deflating like Hank so badly needs to do.

"Slow down, Hank," Melanie says once she approaches, out of breath. "What was that about back there?"

Hank only grunts, too heated to do anything else.

"Seriously, Hank. You look like an amateur running away from the podium like that. The reporters are having a field day out there."

Hank finally looks at his partner. "Let them."

Melanie sighs heavily, her muscles visually releasing tension. She takes a seat, sliding her chair in close so Hank still has plenty of personal space, yet she's close enough so only he can hear when she whispers. "Hank, what's going on?"

Hank inhales one long, deep lungful of freshness and holds it, exhaling only when he can't stand the pain any longer. He sinks into the leather, feeling a little defeated, betrayed maybe, and finds his partner's eyes. The dark brown of her irises are warm and welcoming, and it helps Hank to relax. Through her unblinking eyes, Melanie looks attentive and ready to listen, which Hank appreciates. He hasn't had someone to talk to since his wife left him, and that was quite a while ago.

"I'm getting too old for this shit, Chase," Hank admits. The press conference has him feeling drained. "Can you believe what the mayor did to me out there? Seriously, what kind of—"

"Careful what you say, Detective Berger," Mayor Thomas says, suddenly appearing in the office. He straightens his necktie and walks toward Hank and Melanie, shoulders squared, making no effort to conceal his arrogance. Melanie swivels back toward her desk as the mayor approaches and hovers over them, his entourage of men on his heels. "If you have something to say to me, detective, I expect you'll say it to my face."

Hank rises up and stands close to the mayor, ready to give him a piece of his mind. Hank is slightly taller and a lot thicker than the mayor, giving him the appearance of towering over him up close. But Hank has no illusion of where he stands on the totem pole regarding the mayor's position on the community. Physical size is one thing, but a man with power is another. And a man with power who stands on the top of the totem pole is something completely different.

"Do you have something you want to say to me, Detective Berger?"

"What happened out there?"

Mayor Thomas crosses his arms. "I don't know what you're referring to."

"You said you were going to have my back. Did you forget about that? What you did—throwing me to those animals—"

"Don't be so dramatic, Hank. It wasn't that bad."

"It was hell, Wesley! They made me look like a fool. The papers are going to crush me for this. It could put the entire investigation at risk."

"Well, don't let that happen. Stop it before it starts. That's what I pay you for, isn't it, detective?"

"You don't pay my salary. The taxpayers do."

Mayor Thomas very calmly uncrosses his arms, shifts his weight back on his heels, and says, "Do you forget who you're talking to? Do you not know what I'm capable of? If my memory is accurate, I believe you're due to retire soon. Isn't that right, Hank?"

"What does that have to do with anything?"

"I'd hate for something to happen to your pension. You know, with you being so close and all."

Hank is taken aback, the mayor's words attacking like a torpedo. He swallows hard. "Is that a threat?"

"Of course not." Mayor Thomas looks over his shoulder at a couple of men from his entourage and shrugs. "I didn't hear a threat, did you?"

"No, sir," one of the men says. "I didn't hear a threat."

The mayor turns back and faces Hank, offering a crooked smile that Hank knows is meant to incite him. Hank bites on his tongue, desperate to stop himself from saying something he might regret.

"No threats here, Hank. I'm just saying I'd hate if something were to happen, that's all. That would be all too unfortunate."

Now Hank is the one to cross his arms, his tongue aching. He knows he's at the mayor's mercy. "What do you want me to do?"

"I want you to listen good, listen real good." The mayor takes a step forward and puts his face close to Hank's so they're only a few inches apart, the mint on his breath burning Hank's eyes. "I want you to keep your mouth shut and do as I say. I want you to do your job and find that little girl. Alive! I will not have this hanging over my head. I'm due for reelection in a couple of months and I will not have this be a black eye. Do you understand me?"

"That's why you're doing this? For political reasons? To make yourself look good? Is that the message you want to convey to the public? That all it takes is a little bit of money for someone to go above our heads. Not a good look, if you ask me."

"Watch yourself, Hank."

"What did Kurt Janis pay you? Five, ten grand?"

Mayor Thomas raises a finger and shoves it in Hank's face, his own face reddening. "That's enough."

"Oh, come on, Wesley! We all know his bank was one of the biggest supporters of your last campaign. Do you really expect me to believe this is because Kurt Janis is your friend? It's bullshit. You know it and I know it. This is about him scratching your back, and now it's your turn to scratch his. This is all about money and politics. You're just another politician playing the game."

"Hank, I'm warning you." The mayor is trying to keep his voice even, but it's a struggle. The redness on his face is darkening, his pointed finger now trembling.

"Where were you when the Corey girl was kidnapped the winter before last? What, there wasn't enough money involved, was that the issue?"

"That's enough! They're totally irrelevant! Completely different circumstances." The mayor pauses, takes a breath. "Did you ever consider that perhaps I don't want what happened to her to happen to the Janis girl?"

Hank shifts his weight, having no response.

"I'm done talking about this with you, Hank. Stay out of the news, follow orders, and find the girl." Mayor Thomas nods to his entourage.

Hank says nothing as he watches the mayor turn his back to him and follow his men out of the office. Hank's exhales, the tension releasing from his balled hands. He knows the stakes have just risen even higher. Not only is the girl missing, but now that money and politics are involved, his livelihood is on the line too. He has no choice but do what the mayor says and when, as he knows all it takes is for a termination due to misconduct for his entire pension to be gone. All he's worked for, compiled through more than thirty years of service in the state of Pennsylvania, could be lost in an instant. Mayor Thomas holds all the power.

Hank sits back down and slouches into the faded leather, his head spinning. He leans forward and flips through the calendar hanging next to his computer until he finds the big red X that covers the twenty-third of December - that's the last day he'll ever come back to this office. It's the last day he'll ever go to any office. It's the last day he'll work for someone else ever again. He's left counting the days in his head until he can get the hell out of Dodge.

***

Kurt tends to his wife as she throws up in the bushes, her entire body shaking violently. He holds her hair back in a knot while she groans in pain, obviously experiencing a great deal of discomfort. The whole scene has come out of nowhere, shaking Kurt up pretty good.

Behind him, a flashbulb goes off, intruding in on the private moment. Kurt repositions himself so he's directly behind Abby, her dress riding up as she hunkers over the bush, her bile strangling the green of the shrubbery. A second flashbulb goes off, sending Kurt into a frenzy, screaming at the reporter to go away. The man with the camera takes off running, his pants drooping, childish laughter escaping from him as he disappears around the corner.

"Jesus Christ, Abby," Kurt says, turning his attention back to his wife. "Are you okay?"

Abby spits, wiping her face on her wrist. Tears pool in her eyes, black makeup smearing her face, a mucus bubble in her nose. Through it all, she nods and says, "I'm okay."

"Are you sure? Do you feel ill or something?"

Abby shakes her head. "No, I'm okay. It must have just been the shock of the whole thing. First Chloe, now all these people. I'm just overwhelmed."

Kurt pulls his wife in toward him and wraps his arms around her. He can smell the acid on her breath, the vomit in her hair, but he kisses her forehead anyway. "I'm sorry," he says. "I should have mentioned this all to you first. You were upstairs last night and I found myself fighting with insomnia, so my mind was running wild. I remembered Wesley owed me a favor, so I gave him a call and told him what was going on. He suggested we do this and told me he'd personally talk to the detectives. I'm sorry for not telling you earlier. I should have." He kisses Abby's forehead again, his lips dry.

"It's not your fault," Abby says as she pulls away. "You're doing the right thing. I'm just a little shaken up, you know? I'm sorry for being so short with you."

"If it's about the twenty grand, don't worry about it. Between savings and investments, we have more than enough. We can take out an equity loan on the house or take some cash out of the retirement account if we need to. Money's not the issue. We'll find the money."

Abby nods and throws herself back into Kurt's arms again. "I just want my baby back."

"I know, me too. We'll get her back."

***

Abby lets Kurt rock her back and forth for a moment, his hands clutching her back as if to tell her he's never going to let go. Although it does feel natural, part of Abby wishes some of the reporters were still around to see it—except for that one straggler, all of them had rushed off right after the presser ended. It would definitely help her look more genuine about the situation. After Kurt's heartfelt apology, Abby feels even guiltier than she had before. While she was upstairs last night trying to come up with a way how she could lie her way out of this, Kurt was downstairs trying to come up with ways to legitimately resolve it. She knows Kurt is only trying to help and he's doing what any logical father would do, so she can't be upset at him for that. If he had any idea what this all meant and how much more difficult he's making it on her, he would surely be acting differently.

But she can't tell him the truth yet. The timing still isn't right.

After her tears dry up and Abby feels steady enough to walk, she takes Kurt's hand. He leads her around the back of the police station and toward the car, their fingers interlocked like they were made for each other. Abby's stomach has settled. Up ahead, Mayor Wesley Thomas and his security crew exit the police station through the side door, descending the stairs, and approach a dark limousine that idles just a few meters away.

Kurt stops and releases Abby's hand, noticing it too, and retrieves the car keys from his pocket. He hands them to her. "Take these," he says. "I'll meet you in the car. I'm going to catch up to Wesley and thank him again."

Abby takes the keys and nods. Kurt takes off toward the limo as Abby disappears around the opposite side of the building and makes her way to the mostly vacant parking lot. She finds Kurt's Mercedes parked in the front row, glistening as the sun hits it just right. The car beeps as Abby approaches, letting her inside.

Just as she drops into the seat, her phone buzzes from inside her wristlet, a soft vibration rattling against the zipper. Abby fumbles around inside the portable bag, feeling for her phone, and grabs it. The LED on the front flashes green, telling her she has a new message, so she unlocks the device and opens the text. It's from a number that's unfamiliar to her, but considering the circumstances, she has only one guess who it's from. The message is concise, to the point, and makes her heart leap.

WE NEED TO TALK.

CHAPTER FOURTEEN

Jordan has been glued to the television all afternoon. There was a press conference in front of the police station in Mifflinburg not long ago, and all the news has been talking about is the missing girl. Her face has popped up on the screen hundreds of times, and each time Jordan has seen it, it makes him crazier. He still can't place where he's seen her before.

Chloe Janis's face is definitely familiar to him, but the more the news anchors and field reporters talk about her, the less likely it seems it's possible. The family is from Mifflinburg and has lived there all of Chloe's life, so that all but rules out that Jordan might have known them from somewhere else. The girl's father gave a speech during the press conference, so Jordan got a good look at his face. He doesn't know Mr. Janis—there's no doubt about that. The cameras only panned to the mother a couple of times, but her head was turned away from the cameras each time, probably in anguish. Jordan can't imagine what she's going through, and he feels for her. Mothers usually deal with these types of situations the worst.

Across the room, the screen door on the porch squeaks and Mindy walks in, looking exhausted. Jordan didn't hear her or see her pull in, so seeing her surprises him. Time has passed him by in a flash. Mindy walks over to him, plants a wet kiss on his lips, and flops down on the sofa next to him. She's wearing heavy makeup, but all Jordan sees is her.

"Hi," she says.

Jordan licks the cherry flavor from his lips. "Hi."

Mindy's perfume is a little overpowering, her hair stiff with hairspray, her blouse cut a little lower in the front than Jordan would like, but it's all part of the persona. When she worked in Pittsburg, the short skirts and blouses that showed off her bust worked well. The city was filled with younger guys who would go to her so they'd get a free show with their cut, and the tips were great. But out here, Jordan thinks, with the woods at their backs and rural streets and dirt roads weaving through them, he's not so sure that'll make a difference anymore. He hopes she recognizes that soon, too.

"What are you watching?" Mindy asks, her eyes already shutting from exhaustion.

"Just the news. Have you heard about this?"

"Heard about what?"

"A little girl was abducted from the mall in Mifflinburg yesterday."

Mindy opens her eyes and sits up a little. "One of my clients mentioned something about it, but that's been it."

Jordan grabs the newspaper from the table next to him and hands it to Mindy. She straightens completely and reads the article.

"Wow," she says once she finishes. "That's scary."

Jordan nods. "Do they look familiar to you?"

"Who?"

Jordan points to the television. The press conference is being played again; it must be on a loop. "The family—the parents or the little girl. Do you recognize them?"

Mindy studies the screen, then shakes her head. "I don't think so. Should I?"

"I don't know. I feel like I've seen that little girl before. I just can't remember where."

Mindy shrugs. She tosses the paper on the arm of the couch, stretches out her back and yawns. She kicks off her heels and gets up.

"Where are you going?" Jordan asks.

"I'm going to jump in the shower. Do you want to join me?"

Jordan takes a second to consider it, and it takes only a second. He flips off the television and jumps to his feet. Mindy takes his hand and leads him toward the bathroom, smiling. Jordan hopes that by taking his mind off the Janis's for a while, maybe he'll be able to figure out where he knows the girl from. Sometimes all it takes is a cleared mind to find the answers you seek, and he's hopeful that'll be true for him. Jordan closes the bathroom door once he and Mindy step inside, the fan humming overhead once the light switch is flipped. They both start to undress.

***

Once they're all back inside the cabin—Scott, Diane, Chloe, and Benny the puppy—Scott segregates himself in his bedroom with his mother's mobile phone. He knows what he has to do. The situation has soared out of control a lot quicker than he'd projected, so he's going to have to rush his plan into action.

That's not what he wanted to have to do.

He hopes it doesn't lead to mistakes, but he has no choice but to move forward. He had planned to wait a few days or a week even before doing what he plans to do now, but he doesn't think he has that much time anymore. If feels like everyone is starting to close in on him already.

He needs to arrange a meeting with Abby.

Scott sends Abby a text message. Realizing she may still be around the press, he doesn't dare to call. It'd be too risky. Instead, he'll sit back and wait for a response.

Scott puts the phone on vibrate, pockets it, and joins his mother and Chloe in the living room. Chloe and Benny are getting reacquainted with one another, and Diane is practically in tears watching. Chloe doesn't seem to notice it's the same puppy she'd seen in the pet store just a day earlier, but it doesn't matter. A puppy is a puppy, and she finally has one.

"Do you like him?" Scott asks as Chloe tugs on one end of a knotted rope while Benny chews on the other, growling playfully like a ferocious beast.

Chloe looks up, glowing and smiling. "I love him! I've always wanted a puppy!"

Scott looks to Diane and smiles at her. She pats the top of his hand and smiles back, her touch warming. They both watch Chloe and Benny play together for a while.

It takes nearly an hour for Abby to finally call. The vibration against Scott's thigh startles him, his heart leaping in his chest. He excuses himself, sneaking down the hall and into his bedroom. He closes the door, locks it, and flips open the phone before the vibrating ends, pressing his back against the door. "Hello," he says with a partial whisper.

"Scott? It's Abby." Her voice is muffled a bit by the sound of water hitting an empty bathtub.

"You getting wet?"

"What do you want, Scott? I only have a few minutes."

"You sound stressed."

"Scott, please!"

Scott takes his time walking over to the bed, which he sits on. "Do you want to see her?"

"You know I do." Abby's tone suddenly brightens, her voice rising. "Just tell me where, when, and how."

"We can't meet anywhere in public now, thanks to you. You have to come to me."

"It wasn't my fault, you have to believe me. I had no idea until this morning."

"About which part—the paper or the press conference? Are you trying to have me disappear with her forever?"

"You have to believe me! I didn't know!"

"Which one was it?"

"Which one what?"

"The newspaper or the press conference—which one did you not know about?"

"Both."

Scott bites his tongue, not believing Abby has the guts to lie to him in a time like this. She must be out of her mind. "You know what, this was a bad idea," he says. "I don't have time to play games with you. Kiss your daughter goodbye."

"Wait! Scott, please! Please wait!" Abby's pleas are desperate.

Scott sighs. "What?"

"Please. Just tell me what to do."

Scott pauses for a moment and thinks. Disappearing with Chloe is not what he wants; he knows that and Abby knows that. But he will if he has to. "Fine, I'll give you last chance. One more chance, Abby, that's it."

Abby exhales heavily. "Thank you."

"Meet me here tonight after dark."

"Where's here? Where are you?"

"I can't give you that information right now. Nice try. At dark, take route 44 north for twenty-five miles. There's a Texaco at the intersection where route 44 intersects and branches off. When you get there, pull into the gas station and call this number. I'll give you further instructions then."

"Will I see Chloe?"

"If you don't try any funny business, then yes. I'll have eyes watching you, so if there are any cops, I'm out. I'll take Chloe and you'll never see or hear from us again. You got that?"

"I just want to see my daughter."

"Good, then. I guess we'll find out how badly."

"But, Scott, how do you expect me to get out of the house? My husband's going to ask questions."

"You're a smart girl. Figure something out."

There's a long silence before Abby finally concedes, although it's not without hesitation. Scott is confident she'll come up with something; she doesn't have a choice. It's her first and only chance to see Chloe again, after all.

"And one more thing before I forget," Scott says. "Bring a bag of Chloe's clothes, will you? She's been in the same outfit since yesterday."

CHAPTER FIFTEEN

Chloe Janis isn't the first child to go missing from Mifflinburg. Hank was lead detective on a different case the winter before last, and it completely consumed all of his time for over a year. It ended badly. Her name was Leanne Corey, she was six-years-old, and he'll never forget her.

Leanne was abducted from the local park and was never seen alive again. It all went down in the middle of the day during February vacation from school. It was a Wednesday. Hank remembers it well. It was surprisingly warm for being in the middle of winter and there was no snow on the ground. There wasn't a cloud in the sky.

Lots of other parents had the same idea as Mrs. Corey did that day, so the park was crowded. It happened in the blink of an eye. Mrs. Corey was watching Leanne from across the park, but when she turned her attention to her six-month-old son for just a second, Leanne disappeared. A handful of witnesses saw a white van speeding from the area, but no one caught the plates or a glimpse of the driver.

After seven months with no solid leads to pursue, Leanne Corey's body was found. She was discovered by a retired couple who were hiking the trails of the Rocky Mountains in Colorado, fifteen hundred miles away. She was completely naked. Her body was immediately extradited back to Pennsylvania, where the coroner ruled the cause of death to be suffocation. Thankfully, there were no signs of sexual assault.

Hank spent the next six months trying to answer the most important questions. Who took her and why? He didn't have much success. A career criminal did eventually confess to the kidnapping while already serving a life sentence in a California prison for an unrelated first degree murder conviction. Hank dropped everything and flew across the country to meet with the guy in prison himself, but he refused to admit to killing Leanne. Hank all but pleaded on his hands and knees for a full confession, but the full confession never came. He was tried and eventually convicted of kidnapping and killing the little girl, but Hank was never fully satisfied. Despite the conviction, the guy still denied his involvement in her murder and wouldn't give up the names of any possible accomplices. Hank believes the guy did indeed murder Leanne Corey, but he never found out why. Even to this day, Hank doesn't know, and he never will, since the convicted killer died during a prison fight earlier this year. It still keeps Hank up at night.

The timing of it was all wrong on a personal level for Hank. He and his wife of thirty-two years had just recently filed for divorce and his family was in turmoil. Although his lone daughter, Bree, was grown, it was still difficult for her. Everything she'd ever known had changed.

Bree was going through some dramatic changes in her life that she was afraid to tackle by herself at the time, and Hank wasn't there for her like a father should be. The case of the Corey girl completely took over his life, ten to twelve hours a day, six to seven days a week. That's what he dreamt about, that's what he thought about, and that's what he lived. Bree still hasn't forgiven him for it.

They had a blowout. Bree felt that Hank cared more about the dead girl than his own daughter—she told him as much. Hank, of course, rejected the accusation. But when challenged further about all the time he'd been spending working on the Corey case, he had no choice but to back down. Then Bree broke down. Bree screamed at him, told him she never wanted to see him again, and stormed out of his new apartment. But before she left, she turned to him with mascara running down her face and tears in her eyes and told him what she'd been holding inside for so long. She'd been trying to tell him for weeks, but he was never around for her to talk to him about it. And somehow he was unable to figure it out on his own. During the time in her life when she needed his support more than ever, he was completely absent. Hank had already known she was gay and struggled to accept it, but the fact she was dating his partner made it even worse. Melanie had never said anything about it to him—that she and Bree had broken up—so he had no idea. They got back together later on, after all this had passed. Bree was trying to talk to him about it, trying to get his fatherly guidance, but he wasn't there for her. Their relationship hasn't been the same since.

***

Hank and Melanie have been swamped all day with phones ringing off the hook and their voicemail and email inboxes getting flooded with messages. A permanent blinking red light blurs Hank's vision, identical to the one that's illuminated on the phone on his desk. Reporters who were unable to attend the press conference from earlier have been calling requesting statements, but Hank has told none of them anything. The story is spreading like wildfire. News stations and independent journalists from as far as New Hampshire have called already, although Hank hasn't heard from any of the big guys in New York City yet. It's only a matter of time.

A few tipsters have called in with details Hank and Melanie already know. Multiple eyewitnesses saw Chloe leaving with a man, not appearing to be distressed, but no one saw where they went. No one has seen anything that happened once Chloe and her abductor stepped outside. Sometimes families of victims of crimes like this feel that offering reward money will entice eyewitnesses to share what they know, but Hank has seen the other side over the years. He's learned that people will call in—sometimes the same people over and over—with even a minor detail that does nothing to further advance the investigation. Some people will do just about anything to get their hands on some of that reward money. It's so obvious to Hank, and the idea of the reward altogether is something he wouldn't even consider if he was in this situation, because money is the root of all evil; he's seen it. The worst of the worst come out of the woodwork when free money is on the table.

By early afternoon, the phone calls start to die down. Hank takes inventory of the details they've compiled and works the state databases for any details on the backgrounds of Abby and Kurt Janis. Neither one of them has a criminal record. Hank learns that Abby's maiden name is Weston and she was born in Connecticut, and also that Kurt was born in Virginia but grew up in northeast Pennsylvania. Both of their juvenile records are clean of any wrongdoings and neither one of them appear to have any demons in their past at first glance. On paper, they both seem like genuine victims.

But Hank doesn't believe everything he reads.

There is something strange, though, that Hank notices immediately upon seeing it. There's a five-year gap between when Abby was Abby Weston and Abby Janis, and Hank can't figure out how that could be. Without having the time to dig further into it and track her social security number with the federal government, he has nothing but suspicion at this point. He makes a note to check more into it later, when time permits.

Hank hasn't trusted Abby from the moment he met her yesterday, and her antics at the press conference earlier today make her look even more suspicious. Something is off about her, this latest information all but confirming that, but it can be difficult to judge someone for how they act during a time of grief. Hank knows that. But he also knows innocent people don't have to try so hard.

"Did you see the way Mrs. Janis was acting during the press conference today?" Hank asks his partner during a moment of silence from ringing phones.

Melanie removes the pen from her mouth and says, "Strange, right?"

"There's something off about that woman."

"I don't know about that. She's a grieving mother. Her daughter was just abducted."

"You ever see someone act like that before? She was distant during the whole thing and acted like she didn't even want to be there. Yet, yesterday she was hyper aggressive. That's just not right. Something's not adding up here."

Melanie shrugs and puts the end of the pen back in her mouth, sliding it between her teeth. "I don't know, Hank. I agree her behavior has been strange, but everyone acts differently during times of trauma. It'd be unfair to judge her while she's in her current state of mind."

Hank says nothing. Melanie might be right, but he can't ignore the feeling he has in his gut. The combination of his experience and intuition tell him there's something more sinister going on than just a grieving mother. He just can't prove it.

At least not yet.

Staring at his computer screen, his eyes aching, the muscles on the back of his neck strained, Hank clicks the mouse a few times, sending the document to his printer. He grabs it once it's ejected from the printer, inspecting it for ink smudges and streaks. When satisfied with the result, he spins in his chair and faces Melanie, handing her the document.

"What's this?" she asks, taking it. She reads it quietly, taking her time. "What am I looking at?"

"Look at Abby's maiden name."

"Weston. Okay?"

"Now look at her married name."

"Janis." Melanie looks up. "What's the problem, Hank? Where are you going with this?"

Hank grunts and pushes himself up from his chair, his knees cracking, and climbs around the desk until he's behind Melanie. He can smell roasted coconuts when he gets close, along with a soft pomegranate in her hair. "Look," he says, pointing at the page. "Look at the dates. Look at the gap."

Melanie studies the details and seems to find what Hank has brought to her attention. She pauses, crosses her arms, and says, "Well, shit."

CHAPTER SIXTEEN

Abby and Kurt have received instructions from the detectives to go home and wait. Wait for what, nobody can say for sure. Abby has other things on her mind to keep her occupied. Kurt thinks she's taking a shower, so it gives her some time to make a phone call. After she hangs up with Scott, she does stand under the water for a couple of minutes, letting the water run over her shoulders and down her back while she weeps, the frustration finally boiling over. She keeps a hand on her growing belly, reminding her of all the things that still remain unsaid. Even after she gets Chloe back, things are never going to be the same again.

She's conflicted. One part of her thinks she should tell the detectives what's going on so they can formulate a plan to find Chloe, but the other part of her realizes there's no chance of that happening. If she doesn't show up tonight, alone, Chloe's gone forever.

With wet hair, dry eyes, and a glimmer of hope, Abby forces herself downstairs. The growing fetus inside of her is screaming for some nutrients, so Abby knows she has to eat something, even though she's not hungry. It'll be dark in less than five hours, so Abby has until then to find a way to get out of the house with a bag of Chloe's clothes. Kurt can't know what she's up to.

Behind her, Abby senses Kurt enter the kitchen. She can tell he's just gotten out of the shower himself, based on the smell of fresh musk that fills the room. Instead of the warm cinnamon from her oatmeal, all she can taste is the musk. While spooning a serving of mush into her mouth, Kurt puts his hand on her shoulder and pulls up a seat next to her. Everything inside her tenses up at his touch, which is colder than ice.

"Glad to see you're eating," he says with sincerity. "Are you feeling better?"

Abby puts her spoon down and looks deep into the dark brown of her husband's eyes. Some people have doubts that their partner loves them, but not Abby. She can tell by the softness in which Kurt looks at and talks to her that his love is genuine. She loves him too, but not the way he loves her. It should be every woman's dream—to have a man look at you the way Kurt looks at her—but it just makes Abby sick with guilt. She's desperate to find a way out of this without him ever knowing the truth about her past, but that's getting more difficult with each passing moment.

"Yeah, I'm feeling better now," Abby says. "It must have been a little stomach bug or something."

Kurt smiles, but then doesn't. "A stomach bug? You told me earlier you were feeling fine. You said you were just overwhelmed."

Abby considers this, then remembers what Kurt is referring to. It was when she got sick in the bushes after the press conference. She quickly backtracks. "Yeah, no, I know. It was just the combination of the two things, that's all."

Kurt gazes into Abby's eyes and nods. He seems to accept the explanation as truth, but it's hard to tell either way. "Okay, babe. But are you sure you're okay? You've been acting strangely lately."

"Of course I have. Our daughter's been kidnapped."

"I know. It's just that you've been...inconsistent."

"What is that supposed to mean?"

"It's just that you were initially really upset and angry when we were talking to the detectives. Then you were upset at me for trying to do something to help. And at the press conference you were distant and absent. I'm just worried about you."

Abby takes a bite of her oatmeal to buy herself some time. She ponders what to say as the mushed oats roll over her tongue, stimulating her mouth with heat. As she thinks about it, she realizes a window of opportunity might be opening. This might be her only chance, so she swallows hard and says, "I'm not sure what to tell you, Kurt. I'm grieving. I'm sorry if you don't agree with my methods of grief. I'm not sure how you expect me to act."

"I don't know, Abby. All I can say is that your antics have been overshadowing this whole thing. People are starting to notice."

Abby drops the spoon and crosses her arms, the metal noiseless as it falls into the oatmeal. "Who's noticing?"

"Everyone. There was a reporter who got a picture of you afterwards, did you know that?"

"Let them. What the hell do I care? I was sick to my stomach."

Kurt sighs. "Listen, Abby, I don't know how to say this, but—"

"Am I making you look bad, Kurt? Is that the problem here? You have an image to uphold in this community and I'm embarrassing you—is that it?"

Kurt looks away, but not before Abby recognizes the guilt in his eyes. She knows he won't say it aloud, but she also knows it's the truth.

"You don't embarrass me."

Abby scoffs at the half-hearted effort. "Okay, Kurt."

Kurt slides his chair closer to Abby and takes her hands in his own. The first thing Abby notices how smooth they are, then again how cold. "Abby, listen. This is difficult. I know it is. I'm struggling too. But the detectives are doing their jobs and the mayor—"

"That's who's telling you all this, isn't it? Mayor Thomas. He's the one whispering in your ear that I'm making you look bad. That prick."

"Wesley's my friend."

Abby rips her hands from Kurt's grasp, pulling it away so quickly she wonders if the ice might cause her hand to bleed. "He's not your friend! He never has been. He's just a fraudulent politician like all the others. He's just using you."

"Abby—"

Abby pushes herself away from her chair, leaving the mostly untouched bowl of oatmeal steaming on the table. She can feel herself getting genuinely upset now, and that surprises her. It also makes it easier for her to leave after dark to meet Scott. "No, Kurt," she says. "You listen to me. I don't know what you and the mayor are up to, but if Chloe gets hurt because of your publicity games, I'm going to kill you. I mean it. I will literally slit your throat. How dare you use my daughter as a prop?"

"Our daughter."

Abby winces. "Whatever."

"You should know me better than that, Abby. I would never do anything to hurt Chloe."

"Yeah, well." Abby brushes past Kurt, her heart thumping, and walks toward the doorway.

"Where are you going?" Kurt says, stopping her.

"Upstairs where I can't embarrass you. Come get me if the detectives call. If they don't, then don't."

Abby leaves, already conceding she's been too rough on him. She was downright mean. Although the last thing she wanted to do was fight with her husband, she saw the opportunity to engage him, and she took it. But she may have taken it too far. Accusing Kurt of sabotaging the investigation is pitiful. She feels like such a hypocrite. She knows Kurt wouldn't do anything to hurt Chloe. She knows he wouldn't use her for publicity, good or bad. And she knows everything he's said to her is the complete truth. Now, based on what the mayor has said to Kurt, she fears she's not being careful or convincing enough. She has to be better. But the most alarming thing of all, what worries her the most, is she fears they're starting to catch on to her.

***

Kurt throws his head in his hands out of frustration. He wants to pull his hair out. He didn't want to broach the subject with Abby like that, but he felt he had to. Mayor

Thomas had expressed concern about how she was acting during the press conference when they spoke afterwards, and he convinced Kurt to have the conversation with her. Reporters see things like that, the mayor had said, and when the papers run photos of Abby acting the way she was, people are going to start asking questions. Nobody wants that. Especially not now. Not with the election coming up in a couple of months.

He hasn't even told Abby yet, but Kurt is toying with the idea of running for public office. Mayor Thomas has been encouraging him to be his running mate, and Kurt would work directly underneath him if they were to win. And with this new and unexpected situation with Chloe, Wesley thinks it could help the campaign. Kurt can't bear the thought of Chloe's abduction being used as a tool to gain a political advantage, but the mayor knows what he's talking about—he's been elected and reelected three times now for various positions. Wesley keeps saying the publicity could set them apart from the other candidates. He keeps referring to it as the sympathy vote. They could get it either way, regardless of what happens to Chloe, but only if voters can empathize with Kurt and Abby. And as of right now, Abby isn't doing them favors, but Kurt can't tell her that.

Although it seems as if she already knows. It seems as if she's on to him.

Chloe's safe return home is the highest priority, of course, but the free publicity could be just what they need to get an edge. The mayor's public approval ratings have been steadily declining in recent months, so Kurt's presence on the campaign trail would help—he's a likable guy who has a lot of clout with the locals because of his position at the bank. And if Chloe is returned home safely on the mayor's watch, it would all but ensure his position as a shoe-in for the nomination. Kurt at his side would make it a near certainty.

Kurt's not so sure about the whole thing—he's not sure politics is for him—but he has a hard time saying no to the mayor. Wesley has a type of dominating presence about him that makes a man fold when pressured, and that's what Kurt has done. He'd promised the mayor he would be his running mate if he pushed the issue about Chloe's disappearance up the ladder. And with the Amber Alert now issued, Kurt feels it's his duty to follow through with his end of the deal. He just hopes it's all worth it in the end.

***

Scott can't stop looking at the analog clock hanging above the refrigerator, each click of the rotating hand taking longer than the last. It's getting close to being that time, and he's getting anxious. He knows he's in the driver's seat with Abby, but he can't help to be cautious still. What if she doesn't show? She's already proven the need to involve the police, so there's no guarantee she'll play along nicely even if she does. He hopes having Chloe's wellbeing at stake will keep her honest. He would never harm Chloe, of course, but Abby doesn't know that.

Scott thumbs a small box on the kitchen table, spinning it like a top. His mother had picked it up for him when she went into Mifflinburg earlier this morning. The instructions on the back seem pretty self-explanatory, but Scott's never done anything like this before. He wishes there was an easier way, even though he knows there isn't. Part of him doesn't even want to open it.

For his situation, this particular brand claims 99% accuracy. For some reason, he doubts the figure should be that high, but if it's printed on the box, it must be true. He has no choice but to trust them. He uses a kitchen knife to open the package, tearing away the plastic wrapping, then he sorts through the contents. There are a couple of small colored envelopes, each with two test swabs and a larger return envelope. A small instructional booklet written in the smallest possible font accompanies them, the critical steps highlighted in bold. All Scott has to do is two swabs each, label and seal the tiny envelopes, and mail them to the lab together in the larger envelope. Results will be known in two or three days.

This little box holds all the answers.

With the plastic seals removed and the colored envelopes ready for quarantining the swabs, Scott joins his mother and Chloe in the living room. Benny is asleep on the floor and snoring softly, his golden tail twitching every so often. An exhausted Chloe is doing the same thing right next to him, her arms tucked tightly into her chest, her body still. They've worn each other out.

Scott walks past his mother as she sits in the corner and looks out the window, swaying gently in a rocker. Scott looks out the window too and sees the pond providing a flock of birds with a late lunch as the sun starts to fade behind the trees. Diane doesn't say anything to him, she just observes, not smiling, but not frowning either; her expression is neutral and calm. This part is his responsibility.

Scott crouches down next to Chloe, the earthy smell of two-day-old clothes and wet dog hitting his nose. His breathing is heavy and his hand is less than steady, but he feels somewhat in control of himself. He needs to work quickly and carefully so Chloe won't wake up. The last thing he wants to do is frighten her.

Chloe's mouth is opened slightly while she sleeps, and it's more than wide enough for Scott to do what he needs to do. Her breath is stale and warm, and her tongue has a layer of thick saliva covering it with white bubbles. Scott makes a mental note to get her some water when she wakes up, the dog too. Wiping a bead of sweat from his brow with his shoulder, Scott pulls out the first of the two swabs from one of the colored envelopes and works the tip into Chloe's open mouth. She flinches at the touch of the cotton to the inside of her cheek, shifting her weight, her eyes twitching underneath her eyelids.

Scott jolts, clutching the base of the swab with both hands to keep it steady. He holds his breath.

A few seconds pass.

Chloe stays asleep.

Scott exhales.

Backing one hand away, Scott works up the courage to continue. He doesn't like the fact he has to violate her in her sleep like this, but there's no other way. He'd do it if there was—they just don't have the time to visit a clinic. He rolls the shaft in between his fingers and saturates the tip of the swab with her saliva, just as the instructions outline. He repeats the process with the second swab and backs away before she wakes up.

Back in the privacy and isolation of the kitchen, Scott feels a sense of relief. Chloe will never even know what he's done. He fills out the registration form and return envelope that came inside the box. He can't use his information, especially not now, so he writes down the first name and address he can think of. It's the only one besides his own that would even make sense. When that's taken care of, he seals up the first colored envelope with the two swabs from Chloe. Then he removes the two additional swabs from the second colored envelope and does himself. He drops them both inside the larger return envelope.

One envelope for Chloe, one envelope for him. Two samples each.

Ninety-nine percent accuracy.

Scott will drop the package in Monday's outgoing mail to be delivered to a lab somewhere in Canada. The lab will look at the samples under a microscope and do what they do to compare them to one another. He'll know the results by Wednesday at the latest. After all these years he'll finally know the truth, and the results could change his life. Check that; either way, the results will change his life.

CHAPTER SEVENTEEN

It's late afternoon and the phones have finally stopped ringing, the last of the messages have been listened to. Hank sends Melanie home to rest up while he stays back and waits for a fax from the Connecticut State Police. After finding the discrepancy in Abby Janis's file earlier, Hank's been digging into her background and doing his due diligence. The mayor would be pissed if he found out Hank is spending his time looking into Abby and not following up on every lead that comes in about Chloe. The truth is, there's nothing to follow up on—the leads are non-existent.

Hank is waiting for confirmation from Abby's home state about a thought he has. He's expecting a response at any time now, and he's been pacing anxiously. His fingernails are down to nubs, dried blood crusted to the edges of them. He hasn't told his partner much about his suspicion yet—it's a control thing—but he will in due time. If he's discovered what he thinks he has, he can't wait to break the news to her.

Finally, the fax machine beeps and automatically accepts the incoming message from Connecticut. Hank rushes to it and hovers while the machine warms up, his excitement level higher than it should be. It takes a couple of long and unsettling minutes, but the noisy fax finishes and ejects the paper into Hank's waiting hands. He scans the document quickly, looking for key information, and is giddy once his suspicion is confirmed. That's the thing about his job that's made him stick around all these years—the little things still do excite him. He finds exactly what he was looking for. Just as he suspected, Abby is hiding something. And now he's got her.

Instead of overreacting to the new information and doing something drastic, though, Hank sits and ponders his next move, his belly grumbling. At the end of the day, Chloe's safe return is the first priority, so Hank decides it makes the most sense to wait and address Abby's situation separately. The first forty-eight hours are the most critical when dealing with abductions and missing person's cases, so that needs to take precedence. And Abby's not going anywhere, so she can wait. He doesn't think his psyche can handle another Leanne Corey.

Instead of calling his partner and consulting with her first, Hank grabs his keys and heads for the door, killing the lights behind him. Instinctively, he knows what the right thing to do is. He has to go over to the Janis house, but not to confront Abby. Not yet. He just has to watch. He has to learn more about her as a person, not just as a piece of paper, and observe her when she thinks no one is looking. Her antics have been unorthodox throughout their interactions thus far, so Hank needs to see what she's like in her own environment. It might be difficult in the middle of the night, he admits, but anything he can see might help. And quite frankly, he just doesn't trust her, so he'll feel better knowing where she is tonight. Even if it means he doesn't sleep himself. It wouldn't be the first time.

***

Darkness has arrived. The moon has risen. Bright stars line the horizon in rows of gold. It's go time. Abby has spent the afternoon hiding upstairs and doing everything she can to avoid seeing her husband. She still feels awful for their argument, but she's decided she'll apologize when she comes back home later. After she sees Chloe. She'll explain everything then. Tonight is about her baby.

With Kurt busy downstairs—Abby can overhear him talking on the phone—Abby makes her move. There's a leopard print backpack in Chloe's closet that she'd used during the last school year, so Abby grabs that. As quickly and as quietly as she can, she opens up each of the drawers in Chloe's bureau and tosses some of everything inside the bag. Abby packs enough pairs of socks, underwear, t-shirts, and shorts to last for three days. Then she tosses in a sweatshirt and a pair of jeans, just in case. Three days' worth of clothes may not be enough, Abby realizes, but that's all she can stomach. She can't bear the thought of Chloe being away from her for that long. It's been too long already. Abby considers the idea of tossing in one of Chloe's electronic devices so she has a way to communicate with her—maybe her tablet that allows for GPS tracking—but she decides against it. It's too risky. Abby will find out for herself where Scott has been keeping Chloe soon enough anyway. She zips the bag and tosses it over her shoulder.

Across the hallway and in the bedroom, Abby gets dressed. She finds the most casual and unflattering outfit she can—mom jeans and a loose blouse—so Kurt doesn't get suspicious that she's sleeping with someone else. The last thing she can afford is to have him get upset and try to follow her. She's to come alone—Scott has made that much clear.

Downstairs, Kurt's voice has hushed, so Abby quickly finishes up. A brush with vertigo forces her to slow down and sit on the edge of the bed for a minute, her hand on her belly, but she quickly regains her composure. The thought of her straining the precious baby inside of her over this makes her sick. She doesn't know what she'd do if she lost another one. No woman should have to go through losing one baby, never mind two. And if Abby was to lose a third because of this, she might not ever be able to forgive herself.

With her car keys in hand and Chloe's backpack tugging at her shoulder, Abby starts for the door. She keeps one ear open and one eye peeled, trying to locate where her husband is in the house. She hopes she can sneak out without him noticing.

But she can't.

Abby runs into Kurt in the hallway near the stairs as he was on his way up. The surprise makes her gasp, her guts wrenching into unexpected pain. Now she has to try to explain herself.

"Where are you going?" Kurt says.

Abby says nothing initially. She hadn't planned what to say if she saw him—she naively didn't think she'd have to.

Kurt places his hand, palm down, against the wall as if to put up a roadblock. While it's an effort to get her to talk to him, all it does is piss Abby off. She grabs his forearm and pulls so his hand falls off the wall, almost stumbling. Then she walks past and starts down the stairs.

"Abby?"

She stops when she gets to the bottom, turns, and looks up to face Kurt. His eyes have fallen, his features tired. He looks truly hurt. "What?"

Kurt doesn't respond. He just stares at his wife with sheepish eyes.

"I'm going out for a while. I need some time to think. Don't wait up." Abby turns back around and heads toward the front door. Her heart is pumping, fearful of being held back for any longer. She doesn't want to make Scott wait. But before she can open the door, Kurt stops her again.

"Why do you have Chloe's bag?" he says, still sounding equally as hurt, even after Abby's brief explanation.

Abby stops. She'd hoped he wouldn't notice. Without having previously prepared a justification for having it, she looks over her shoulder and says, "I'll explain everything later. But right now, I have to go." She grabs the door handle, cold in her hand, and turns it. Then she steps out into the darkness.

CHAPTER EIGHTEEN

Headlights from the Janis's driveway stir Hank from his haze. He had nearly fallen asleep while waiting for something to happen—it's been an uneventful night. He reaches for the foam cup in the cup holder next to him, but it's bone dry. There once was coffee in it, but that was hours ago. Hank is exhausted.

An SUV backs out of the Janis's driveway and speeds away from the house like it has somewhere to be. Hank is suddenly jolted back into full awareness as the headlights approach where he sits between a couple of houses across the street from the Janis's. He ducks down in the seat, making himself small, and waits for the vehicle to pass. When it does, he tracks it out of the neighborhood, cracking the window to get some air.

After he gets close enough to capture the license plate on the target, he backs up and keeps his distance from it so he's not seen. He's able to thumb through the box of files next to him while he drives until he finds Abby Janis's vehicle registration information. Once he confirms the information on file with the state does match the license plate of the SUV in front of him, he backs up further and puts a safe distance between them. Abby Janis is definitely up to something.

Hank follows her for a while. He drives in silence, running through the various scenarios and reasons why Abby could be heading north at this time of night. He stays five or six car lengths behind her at all times to be cautious, although chances are she won't recognize him anyhow, not at night, even if she does realize someone is following her. But based on her actions up to this point, Hank feels confident she won't even notice. She's probably too preoccupied with whatever she's up to realize she's being followed.

Just as Hank is beginning to lose patience—he's been following her for twenty-five miles now and is quickly running low on fuel—Abby pulls off route 44 and into a Texaco station, its lights shining bright. Hank follows. It's the first gas station he's seen since leaving town, and it's a big one. There are three rows of pumps, lots of parking, and a well-lit convenience store in the center of the lot. The lights could be trouble, Hank realizes, so he drives around the backside of the store and to the other side of the building. When he gets to the other side and scans the pumps for Abby's SUV, he sees nothing.

She's gone. Vanished.

Hank can sense himself starting to overreact—he's already a bit irritable and flustered for having trailed Abby so long—so he puts the car in park and takes two deep breaths. The parking lot isn't that big, so he figures he must have just overlooked her. She couldn't have just disappeared into oblivion.

Once relaxed and ready to think rationally about the situation, Hank jams the transmission into drive and moves his car forward. He sweeps the parking lot again, taking his time, this time seeing the entire property and not just the rows of gas pumps. There's no one at the gas pumps and two parked cars in front of the building. Both appear to be empty. He doesn't recall having seen any other vehicles around the backside—just some dumpsters—so he doesn't bother rechecking. He drives around the perimeter of the parking lot, behind the gas pumps and close to the road, the speedometer on his dash barely above zero, then he spots her. Abby's SUV is parked on the opposite end of the store—the one section he couldn't see from where he was—with her lights on and a swift cloud of white exhaust spitting out the rear. Hanks stops when he sees her, feeling relieved, yet a little foolish for initially overreacting. Abby has him twisted in knots.

In an effort to ensure he doesn't get caught, Hank pulls his car up to one of the fuel pumps and hides behind it. It's unmarked, so he suspects he'll blend right in. Hank creeps forward slowly, cautiously, until he has a clear view of Abby. Although her window is closed and slightly tinted, he can see that she's on the phone. Hank rolls down his window and holds steady, trying to listen to Abby's conversation, but he can hear nothing. He steps out of the car and leans in closer.

***

Scott leaves the cabin shortly before nine o'clock. Chloe is still awake when he leaves, but just barely. Diane has agreed to stay up until after Chloe lets Benny out for the last time and brings him to bed.

It's a quick drive to his hideout location off route 44, but he ensures he leaves a few minutes early to allow himself to get in position. He's battling many emotions. He's excited about seeing and talking with Abby again, but he's also fearful of how she might react. The fear of her betraying him and using herself as bait while the cops ambush him is a legitimate one, but he's prepared for that possibility. With the seclusion of his hideout location, he should go unseen. But in case he is, he's prepared for a fight. Although unarmed and unequipped for a physical altercation, he's ready to confess all of Abby's dirty little secrets.

If he's going down, Abby's going with him.

Ten minutes later, Scott arrives at his destination.

There's a large Texaco station on the corner of route 44 where it branches off to go north or east. It's one of the only places to fuel up in this part of town—much of the 146,000 acres of the surrounding Tiadaghton State Forest are wildlife preserves—so it's a public hotspot. It also makes it an ideal meeting place—lots of possible witnesses in case Abby tries to make a scene.

Across from the Texaco is an open field with nothing but scattered bushels of hay and rusted farm equipment.

Scott waits for a break in traffic before pulling off the pavement and heading into the field. The farmland is unmaintained and the terrain is uneven, so he slows the wagon down to a crawl. The high beams bounce around as Scott maneuvers through divots and tall grass until he's far enough into the field where he can't be seen. He finds a good spot behind a rusted tractor and swings the rear end of the wagon around so he's parallel to route 44. He turns off the lights and kills the engine, pressing his back against the cloth of the seat. After resting for a second, he cranks down the windows in the front and pulls out his binoculars, their weight heavy in his hand. The sounds of the nearby vehicles screaming past are drowned out by crickets and the howling of the coyotes from deep within the forest. Only the stars will be a witness tonight.

The night has turned chilly, but Scott is still covered with heavy perspiration, his neck and back wet. He checks the time on his mother's mobile phone and drops it in the cup holder in the center console. A final sliver of doubt creeps into his mind about whether he should turn back, but it might be too late for that now. Abby should be arriving soon.

Across the street, the Texaco station is magnified through the oversized lenses of Scott's binoculars, and he keeps his attention on the entrance. As he does, a dark SUV crosses the path of his lenses and enters the parking lot. Scott tracks it with his binoculars, and he sees a tentative Abby sitting behind the wheel, her hands not visible. As far as Scott can tell, she looks to be alone.

Abby pulls the SUV into one of the empty parking spots on the south side of the convenience store and parks there. Scott sets down the binoculars and grabs the mobile phone again. He holds it in his hand and waits for the call, his palms sweating with anticipation.

So far, so good.

After a few seconds, Scott picks up the binoculars again and scans the parking lot and surrounding street one more time, just to make sure. The parking lot is empty besides the one employee's car in front of the store that was there when Scott arrived, and the street is empty.

But not for long.

Just as Scott puts his attention back on Abby—who now appears to be fumbling with something in her lap—a second vehicle passes through his line of sight, slows down slightly, then disappears around the backside of the store. Then, just a moment later, a third vehicle pulls in and heads directly for the parking spots in the front and parks next to the idle vehicle.

Son of a bitch.

The last of three vehicles to pull in—the one parked in the front of the store—dims its lights, but Scott's not fooled. The driver stays in the car, the back of their head sinking below the headrest. Scott can't tell if it's a man or a woman. Scott grinds his teeth, fury burning hot inside of him. He knows exactly what's going on here, and he's not pleased about it.

This is a set-up. Abby has just made a big mistake.

Scott's mother's phone vibrates in his hand. He squeezes it hard, hoping to snap it in two, trying to decide if he's going to let Abby explain herself or not. She really must have lost her mind this time. To humor himself, he decides to answer the phone, just so he can hear what Abby has tried to pull this time. Her explanation should be interesting. "Hello, Abagail," he says.

"I'm here. I'm at the Texaco station, just like you said. Now what?" Abby is calm and collected on the other end.

Scott, however, is not. "Do you think I'm stupid?"

"What are you talking about?"

"Answer the question, Abby."

"Of course I don't think you're stupid, Scott. What's wrong?" Abby's voice is starting to get shaky and edgy—a sure sign she's about to tell an untruth.

"Who are they? Local cops? FBI?"

"Who?"

Scott drops the binoculars and slams his open palm on the steering wheel, the rage still burning hot. "Goddamnit, Abby! Don't lie to me!"

"Please, tell me what's wrong!" Abby pleads. "I don't know what you're talking about."

Scott sighs and grabs the binoculars again. He looks through them and finds Abby. Her face is flushed, her lips puckered, but her eyes are looking straight ahead. She doesn't have the look of someone who's done something wrong.

"Scott, please," Abby says, her voice shaking.

"You were followed here," Scott says. "By two people. Are they cops?"

"That's impossible."

"There's one car parked in the front. The lights are off but the engine is still running with the driver inside." Scott searches around the rest of the parking lot through his binoculars until he finds the other vehicle that had trailed Abby in. He finds it parked next to one of the gas pumps and looking mischievous. The driver, a man, is out of the car and facing Abby, his hand on the hose of the pump. "And the second one is at the far pump to your left."

Scott watches Abby turn to her head to the left and look out at the pumps. She doesn't seem to react. "It looks like he's just getting gas to me," she says. "No one followed me. I would have noticed."

"I saw them, Abby. Stop with the lies."

"Wait, how do you know all this? Are you around here? Where are you? Where's Chloe?" Abby spins her head around and scans the parking lot, her gaze staring out over the field across the street. To Scott, it looks as if she's staring right at him, but he knows that's not the case. He knows she can't see him through the night.

"Stop looking, Abby. You won't find me. I can see you but you can't see me. Trust me. Was I not clear enough before when I said if you brought along cops I'd disappear?"

"You have to believe me. I didn't know I was being followed. I swear!"

"It's too late for that. You blew it."

"Scott, wait!"

"Goodbye, Abagail." Scott hangs up and powers his mother's phone off. It's just a prepaid phone, of course, so even if Abby brings the number to her cop friends they won't be able to trace it back to Scott or Diane. Scott keeps his binoculars on Abby and watches as she frantically plays with her phone—trying to call him back, he assumes. She pushes some buttons and puts the phone up to her ear a few different times, then she tosses it on the seat next to her in frustration.

Scott moves his attention to the sedan at the gas pump and to the one parked in front of the building, expecting one or both of them to approach Abby, but neither do. Scott finds this curious.

Could she have been telling the truth?

Eventually, Abby backs out of the parking spot and heads back to the main road. Scott watches as she slows down in front of the car at the gas pump, stops, then takes a left back onto route 44 and heads back the way she came. Moments later, the car parked in the front of the building suddenly comes back to life, lights and all, and reverses out of its spot. It, too, takes a left on route 44 and heads back the way it came. Scott learns the driver is a woman, but no one he recognizes. After a few more minutes, the third vehicle leaves after pumping some gas and also goes back the way it came. All three vehicles go in the same direction.

Then it hits him.

His mother had told him earlier that during the press conference she'd heard, there were two detectives—a man and a woman—who were introduced to be working on the case. It must be them who were with Abby. Scott is offended at her lack of subtlety—this proves how little she thinks of him. But now that he knows, Scott has no choice but to conclude one sinful thing about the woman he once knew so much about: Abby is a liar.

Scott is ashamed of her.

Scott starts the wagon's engine, the belt squeaking, turning on the high beams once it comes to life. He's never felt so down in his life. His anger has morphed into something less sinister, but the pain doesn't hurt any less. He feels taken advantage of, made a fool of, or something worse. Everything he thought he knew about Abby has been a lie. She's definitely changed over the years.

Scott takes a moment to reflect on where to go from here. It's clear Abby's not ready or willing to be a part of the life he has planned for them, so that leaves him with only one option, and it's not something he'd expected to have to do. Nor is it something he'd wanted to do. Nothing really has gone the way he'd planned, he realizes now. He feels like an amateur for thinking it would. While he needs some more time to process what has happened here tonight, he does know one thing for certain: tomorrow he and Chloe are to leave the cabin and never return. Tomorrow they will disappear forever. And it's all Abby's fault.

CHAPTER NINETEEN

The music is loud and the treble is high. The blinds are closed. The lights are dim. Melted wax masks the smell of sweat and body oil. Electronic bass rumbles through Melanie's bare thighs and adds to the ecstasy she's already experiencing. No man has ever made her feel this way, and she doubts any of them could. She feels like she's flying. She pulls a pillow over her face and screams into it while Bree teases her with her tongue, her toes curling into the softness of the mattress.

Then something chimes.

Melanie thinks it must be in her head—her brain sending the rest of her body a warning signal that she's about to explode. Except the chime doesn't stop and the climax isn't close. Melanie recognizes the chime and knows of its importance. The timing, literally, couldn't be worse. She removes the pillow from her face and looks for the source of the sound, the tingling between her legs subsiding. Bree is beneath her, her hands on her kneecaps, aware of her sudden change in concentration.

"Hang on a second," Melanie says, breathing heavily.

"Excuse me?" Bree says, looking up, raising an eyebrow.

"Phone's ringing."

"So what? Leave it."

"It's work. I have to take it."

"How do you know?"

"The ringtone. It's your dad."

Bree makes a face and pushes herself away from Melanie. “Ugh, don’t call him that.” She uses Melanie’s knees to push herself all the way up.

“I’ve got to grab it.”

Bree motions toward the ringing phone on the dresser with her eyebrows and Melanie rushes across the carpet to grab it before the ringing stops. She’s completely nude.

“Hank, what’s going on?” Melanie says, still with heavy breaths.

“Where are you?” Hank says, his voice muffled.

“I’m at home. Why?”

“What are you doing? Are you busy?”

Melanie looks to Bree and gives her an awkward smile. She’s a little embarrassed.

“What’s he want?” Bree shouts from across the room, covering her naked body with the bed sheet.

Melanie covers the microphone of her phone with her palm and hushes Bree, but it’s too late.

“Who was that?” Hank says. “Was that Aubrey? Is she there with you?”

Realizing she’s been caught, Melanie tries to change the subject. “What’s going on, Hank? Why’d you call?”

“Right, well, I’ve got some news about Abby Janis.”

“Oh, you do? Like what?”

There’s a brief silence while Melanie waits for Hank to respond. When he doesn’t right away, Melanie considers asking him again, but she knows he’s probably deep in thought. Eventually, he says, “I’m on my way over. I’ll tell you about it then.”

“It’s ten o’clock.”

“I know. It can’t wait.”

Melanie sighs. “Fine. When will you be here?”

“I’m pulling in now.”

Melanie sighs again, harder this time. “Thanks for the warning.”

Hank says nothing.

“Give me five minutes.” The call disconnects and Melanie turns back to Bree.

"What's going on?" Bree asks, her voice low, almost worried.

Melanie bites her lip and doesn't say anything right away. She knows Bree is not going to be happy with what she has to tell her.

***

Abby cries the entire drive back home. Somehow she's blown what might be her only opportunity to get Chloe back, and now she's forced to face the reality she may be gone forever. She's befuddled about how this even happened. Although Scott has put a fear into her that no mother should have to feel, part of her does think he might be bluffing. He has made it clear what he wants, and him disappearing with Chloe isn't it. But she can't take that chance. She has to do something.

Maybe the worst part of all of this is she doesn't even know who was following her. If she had the police with her and she was caught, that's one thing. But being followed without her knowing it is a completely separate issue, and it worries her.

Who could it have been?

Scott will never believe she didn't know. Not again. Not with what happened with the press conference earlier. Despite trying after Scott pointed them out to her, she was unable to see the face of either person who followed her. Whoever they are, she hopes they realize they may have completely ruined her life.

Now that everything important in her life has been flipped upside down and is about to be taken away from her, she has to decide where to go from here. Sooner or later she's going to have to confess to Kurt, she knows that. Everything she's done in her past, all her sins, will have to be aired out and put on the table. He'll probably leave her. But then there's his unborn child growing inside of her that he still doesn't know about either. That makes matters all the more difficult. There are so many secrets.

The detectives are going to find out the truth too, one way or another. Abby decides she needs to tell them directly before it's too late. Maybe they'll be sympathetic to her situation when she tells them she was followed. There must be something else going on behind the scenes that she's blinded by.

Really, who could it have been? And what did they want?

Her mind is filled with possibilities, but she's no closer to having any answers. She decides the first step is to go home and tell Kurt everything. Then together they can decide how to tell the detectives. And maybe somehow the four of them can figure out a way to get Chloe back. It's the only hope she has left.

***

At first, Kurt was fuming when Abby left, then he was depressed, and now he feels terrible. Abby won't answer her phone and Kurt has no idea if she's coming back tonight or not. She did say she'd explain everything when she returns, but what does that even mean? Is she going to explain why she's been distant and inconsistent and unreasonable? Is she going to explain why she left the house unprompted with Chloe's backpack on her shoulder? Is she going to explain why she's been so far from her usual self?

Kurt feels lost, abandoned, alone.

Abby must be hiding something. Kurt knows his wife, and he can tell something is up with her, but he doesn't know what. He hates to do it, but since the house is empty and he's out of things to do to keep his mind off Chloe and Abby, Kurt makes the decision that he needs to do some discovery on his own. While he's been downstairs making phone calls and trying to figure out this whole situation with Chloe over the past couple of days, Abby has spent an awful lot of time upstairs. It's like she's been intentionally locking herself in solitary confinement and shutting everyone else in the world out. Especially Kurt. The bedroom has been her personal prison of choice, so that's where Kurt starts.

The first logical place to start is her laptop. He guesses the password on the first attempt. Feeling like an amateur voyeur and hoping he doesn't find anything he doesn't want to see, Kurt scrolls through the contents of the documents stored on the hard drive. He's relieved to find nothing alarming. The web browser's history is empty too. Kurt discovers the browser's settings are set so the history will be deleted upon closing, which bothers him. If Abby has nothing to hide, she wouldn't be making sure her search history is empty. Or maybe it's for another reason completely, but Kurt is having trouble trying to give her the benefit of the doubt. He's not satisfied, but he concedes the laptop to be clean—his limited skills can take him no further. He moves on.

His next stop is Abby's walk-in closet, her dresser, the linen closet, and the medicine cabinet in the bathroom. He doesn't know what he's even looking for, but he finds nothing out of the ordinary in any of those places either. Discouraged, he sits on the edge of the bed and puts his head in his hands, rocking back and forth. Now he feels even worse, not having found anything.

What is he doing? Where has the trust gone?

Abby has been acting strangely, yes, but their daughter has been abducted—how else is she supposed to act? How is anyone supposed to act in a situation like this?

Just as he decides to forgo his search for the unknown and head back downstairs to wait for Abby with his tail between his legs, something stops him. He remembers the one place he forgot to check. A light bulb goes off inside Kurt's head, and it's brighter than the glimmer of hope he now feels.

The nightstand.

Kurt slides off the bed, walks around to the other side, and hovers over Abby's nightstand. His hands are shaking now, beads of sweat starting to form on his forehead. He feels like he's close to something, although he doesn't know what. The top drawer of the nightstand isn't closed fully and isn't making complete contact with the wooden back, which, to Kurt, means Abby's been inside recently.

He opens it.

While everything inside is orderly and easily accessible as usual—the credit cards Abby never uses, her social security card, a half-empty bottle of warming massage oil—something doesn't belong. Protruding from in between two pages of a paperback is the corner of what looks like a torn piece of paper. Abby uses a piece of ribbon as a bookmark, she always has, so it's not as easily explainable as one might think. It's not as simple as her marking her page in the novel.

Kurt ignores the alarm bells ringing in his ears and grabs the book and opens it. His palms are sweaty.

As expected, a narrow ribbon—red, Abby's favorite color—sticks out from the top of the paperback and drapes over the binding like a blanket. Kurt fingers through the faded pages, the smell of fifty years of readers staining his fingertips, until he finds the ones that try to hide the piece of paper that doesn't belong. His hands are a little unsteady, the book rocking as if riding a wave. He squeezes extra tight so he doesn't drop it. With its cracked spine, it looks fragile.

Near the middle of the paperback, Kurt finds the single piece of torn paper with creases and blue lines on the back that caught his attention in the first place. There are some paper shavings still attached to the side of it like someone ripped it out of a notebook, then folded it in half. It's crinkled like it's been hidden deep inside someone's pocket for a while. Kurt picks up the piece of paper, fingers the edges, and stares at the blank page for a while. There's some writing on the other side when he holds it up to the light, but it's inverted and illegible. He holds out as long as he can muster, the rapid drumming in his chest not doing much to help the situation. The knot in his belly tells him what he reads might change his life, so he hesitates. Then he takes a breath, holds it until it hurts, and goes for it.

He flips the paper over.

As Kurt reads the two scribbled words, his heart leaps, and the lump in his throat turns to stone.

CHAPTER TWENTY

The tired headlights of the station wagon do their best to lead Scott back to the cabin. It's a struggle to maneuver through the thick darkness with the moon hidden behind the pines and providing no assistance, and he nearly misses the quick turnoff to the blind drive. The trail is spooky at this time of night, even with the car windows closed. Hooting owls stalk him from the treetops while baby bats flap their wings in front of the windshield. The echo of a hungry beast howls from deep inside the forest. Even the high beams have weakened, surrendering to the night.

Upon approaching the cabin, a single light shines over the front door on the porch, welcoming Scott home. He turns off the lights, kills the engine, and lets the radiator whirl to silence. Scott sits in the quiet of the night for a while, just listening.

He doesn't know what he's going to tell his mother. It's not because he doesn't want to admit what's happened, but because he knows she's going to ask what he's going to do about it. And he doesn't know how to answer that question because that'll mean his plan has failed. After all they've been through to get to this point, she's going to be devastated. He's failed her yet again, and she may not survive the heartache this time.

Still with reservations, Scott reluctantly gets out of the wagon and heads for the cabin. The gravel crunches under his feet as he approaches the porch and breaks up the monotony of the silence, a light breeze at his back pushing him onward. It's quiet inside the cabin, borderline eerie, the only sound is that of the ticking analog clock. It's completely dark.

Moving down the hallway, Scott pops his head into Chloe's bedroom and finds her sound asleep in her bed, sprawled out and with an arm dangling over her head. Benny lies on the floor beside her—his protective Labrador instincts already kicking in—with chew toys scattered all around him. Scott can't help but smile at that, even with the gloom he's experiencing. Benny turns his head to look at Scott when he enters, wags his tail a few times, then turns back over and goes back to sleep. That, Scott can already tell, is a good dog.

Two doors down, Scott finds his mother's bedroom door closed and the room behind it dark. Instead of waking her and spoiling her evening, he goes into his own bedroom where he'll spend the rest of the night formulating a plan to get out of town. But before he closes the door and shuts himself off to the world, leaving just him and his thoughts, a light flicks on from behind his mother's bedroom door and illuminates the doorframe. The door squeaks as it opens, Diane sliding her head out.

"You're home," she says with a whisper.

Scott nods. "And you're awake."

Diane steps further into the hallway and looks past Scott as if she's looking for something. Or someone. "Is Abby with you?"

Scott bites his lip and shakes his head.

Diane frowns. "What happened?"

Scott can already see the disappointment on his mother's face, and it pains him. It's like a scab that refuses to heal, or a fish out of water that refuses to die—Diane's frown simply won't go away, even after all these years. With his eyes, Scott motions inside his bedroom. He walks in, his mother following, and closes the door behind them.

Scott flicks on the light and sits on the edge of his bed, the springs squeaking underneath his heft. The window at his back is covered with a thick curtain, blocking out what little light the stars try to offer, removing any idea of his thoughts of procrastination.

"What happened tonight?" Diane asks empathetically, already sensing it didn't go as planned.

"It's over," Scott says. He drops his head and keeps his gaze away from his mother. He can't bear the thought of seeing her cry again.

But Diane doesn't cry. Instead, she just crosses her arms—not aggressively, but as a way to comfort herself instead—and puts all of her weight on her heels. Keeping her voice quiet, she says, "Tell me what happened."

Still refusing to look at her, Scott tells her. He tells her about the two undercover detectives that had followed Abby and about how she denied knowing anything about it. Scott still can't help but feel she was being genuine about not knowing—the desperation in her voice seemed real—but his mind tells him something else. She deceived him. And the fact she's been working with the police and the media already doesn't help her case either. As much as he wants to believe she didn't know, as much as he wants to think she's the same person he knew so many years ago, he just can't. People really do change.

After Scott tells his mother everything that has happened and has shared his deepest hesitations and disappointments about Abby and how things have turned out, Diane approaches the bed without saying anything. She pats his thigh and sits on the edge of the bed next to him, forcing him to make room. Even in her weakest days, she's still stronger than he could ever be. Scott finally looks at her, tears welling in his eyes.

"I'm sorry," he says. "I'm sorry I couldn't make this all work out. I know how badly you wanted this."

"Please, don't."

"I promised this would all work out. I'm sorry I failed you."

"Scotty, you didn't fail me. You never have. Even with all the mistakes you made when you were younger, I always knew it wasn't really you. I know what kind of person you are deep down. I always have."

Scott wipes his cheek with the back of his hand, the tears drying up. "What am I going to do now?"

"Do what's right for you, Scotty. Do what's right for you and Chloe."

"What about you?"

Diane smiles. "Don't worry about me. Really, I'll be fine. I've only got a year or two left in me anyway," she admits. "You and Chloe have your whole lives ahead of you. I'm just glad I was able to meet her."

"You don't know that. Who knows what could happen? A donor could become available tomorrow. There's just no—"

"Please, Scott. Please don't. I'm in my fifties. I've lived long enough."

"Fifty-four isn't old."

"For me it is. My life up until recently has been hell. Sometimes you just have to say enough is enough."

"Mother—"

"I'm at peace with it. I truly am. If what everyone says is true, then I'll be going to a better place anyway."

"And if they're wrong?"

Diane shrugs. She looks away, her eyes falling to the floor as if pondering. Looking at her, Scott wonders if his mother has ever considered the alternative; what if there is no second chance? What if this is the only life she'll have? What if this is her only chance to get the fulfillment she seeks?

Will he be okay if this is how it ends for her?

After a long pause, Diane looks up and says, "What are you thinking? What's the plan?"

"We have to go, I guess. Nothing else to do. Where, I don't know yet, but I'll figure that out. What about you, though? The police are going to catch on eventually and are going to come here. You know that, don't you?"

"What are they going to do, throw me in jail? Please," Diane jokes. "I've lived in far worse conditions than jail. A nice warm bed and free meals, come on. There are worse ways to live out the rest of my time."

Scott looks away.

If only she knew what it's really like.

Diane puts her hand on Scott's leg, her wrinkled skin smooth, her touch cold. She pushes herself to her feet, her elbows shaking with arthritis. "Will you be here when I get up, or is this goodbye?"

"We'll be here. I have to take care of some stuff first, before we go."

Diane nods. "Okay then. I'll see you in the morning. I'll make you and Chloe a big breakfast, one last time. How would you like that?"

Scott tries to smile. "Okay, Mother."

Diane's lip quivers as she hurries from the room, a hand covering her mouth, the door closing behind her. Scott waits for the sound of the clicking metal before imploding. He throws his face into his pillow and sobs sharp, pained tears. They slice through his eyelids like a scythe.

***

The intercom in the kitchen buzzes just as Melanie pulls a shirt over her head, Hank arriving earlier than she'd been expecting. Bree disappears at the sound, making like a hermit in the bedroom.

Melanie makes her way through the kitchen, her bare feet sticking to the floor like glue, and presses the button to buzz Hank inside the building. While waiting for his arrival, the possibilities of what he's discovered making her anxious, Melanie steps into the bathroom and checks her reflection in the mirror. It's rough, she admits, her hair knotted and falling from its ponytail, her makeup long since wiped clean. She smooths her t-shirt and adjusts the graphic on her chest, making sure what's underneath is fully covered. The mounds of single-serving coconut coffee cups fill the bathtub to her right. She yanks the curtain shut to hide them. She cringes at the thought of Hank discovering the hoard and what his reaction might be, or how badly he might judge her. She closes the bathroom door and steps out, leaving her secret alone in the dark.

Two knocks on the front door come just as she closes the bathroom door. Melanie walks over to it and opens up.

"Hi, Hank," she says as she steps back, allowing Hank to enter into her personal sanctuary. She crosses her arms over her chest for extra guarding.

Without responding, Hank walks in and immediately starts looking around the apartment, nodding his head as he does. As far as Melanie can remember, this is the first time he's actually been inside the place since they've been partners. He's dropped her off many times and has walked with her up to the door before, but he's never been inside until now. Melanie admires his fatherly instincts and hopes he approves.

"Nice place," Hank finally says.

"Thanks," Melanie says, struggling to hide her smile, grateful for the validation.

"Do you have someplace we can sit and talk for a few minutes?"

Melanie wastes no time in leading Hank down the hallway and into the den where a leather sofa welcomes them. Hank sits in the middle, exhausted eyes heavily weighing him down, and thumbs through the coffee table book. Melanie sits in the recliner on the other side of the room, crossing her legs and facing him.

"So, what's up?" Melanie asks. "What was so important that you had to come over here at ten o'clock at night and bother me?"

Hank leans forward on the sofa, his eyes slits. "As I said on the phone, I have some news about Abby Janis. I found something I thought seemed suspicious when going through her files earlier, so I inquired with the state police in Connecticut. I received a fax from them a few hours ago, and they've confirmed my hunch."

"Indulge me, Hank."

Hank reaches into his breast pocket and grabs a sheet of paper, crinkling it as he fights to get it unfolded. "As we know, there's a five-year gap between the time Abby was Abby Weston and Abby Janis."

"Right."

"Well, the Connecticut State Police were able to confirm Abby was indeed still a resident of Connecticut during that gap."

"And how do they know that?"

"State tax returns and voting registrations. They searched for her social security number and found a record under a different name."

"So, it was the same social security number but a different name?"

"That's right. That's why there's a gap. She was going by a different first name too, so no one put it together."

"How does that happen?"

Hank shrugs smugly. "Amateurs in a small town. Combine the two and you get a lack of competence more times than not."

Melanie nods, hoping Hank doesn't feel that way about her, too. "What happened then? Did she legally change her name?"

"They're still working on it. They have a small team dedicated to looking into it. They could be in deep shit with the federal government if it's discovered there was some fraudulent filing that went on."

"You think that's what it was?"

"I have no idea. But that's why they're looking into it. It could have just been a simple oversight at the town office or something. They're cross-referencing all legal name changes with marriage certificates in the town Abby's social security number was last registered in. They seem pretty confident they'll find out what happened. We'll know more in the morning."

Melanie leans back in the recliner and puts her hands over her head. The smooth cotton rubs against her breasts, reminding her how vulnerable the position makes her. She quickly changes her mind and lowers her arms back into her lap. She considers Hank's information and struggles to find a possible connection to their case. Maybe it's just the fact that it's late, but something isn't clicking with her.

"What's the matter, Chase?" Hank asks, recognizing her hesitation.

"I'm just struggling with this. I get there's a pretty large gap in her federal records...but, okay. I mean, yeah, it's a little weird. And her behavior has been a bit unusual, but I'm just not seeing any connection here. What does one thing have to do with the other?"

"I don't know yet," Hank admits, leaning back. "Maybe nothing. But I have a hunch they are somehow related to one another." Hank tosses the sheet of paper on the coffee table and pushes himself to his feet, grunting. "I'll leave this here. Take a look at it, let it soak in. We'll reconvene in the morning. Hopefully then, Connecticut will have some more information for us."

Melanie nods and stands too. "I'll walk you out."

Before they get to the door, Hank says, "I followed her tonight."

"Who?"

"Abby."

"Why?"

"Because I don't trust her. I went to her house and waited for something to happen."

"Did it?"

"More or less. She left the house alone sometime after eight and drove twenty-five miles north."

"Where'd she go?"

"Middle of nowhere. She stayed on route 44 the entire time and got off at a gas station for no apparent reason. She just parked on the side of the building and made a phone call. I was able to see her face where I was, and I could tell she was upset. It only lasted a few minutes and then she left."

"That's odd."

"Damn right it's odd. She drove right past me and went back the way she came. Didn't even fill up her tank or anything."

"Did she see you?"

"I don't really care if she did or not. But no, I don't think she saw me."

Melanie says nothing, opening the front door. She wishes she could say she's surprised by Hank's actions, but she's really not. "There's some weird shit going on."

"And we're going to get to the bottom of it." Hank steps past her and out into the hallway. "Goodnight, Chase."

"Goodnight, Hank."

Just as Melanie is about to close the door, Bree emerges from the hallway, wearing just a long t-shirt and no pants. "Are you not even going to say hi to me?" she says.

Melanie turns and faces Bree, whose arms are crossed. Her lips are puckered, her eyes daring. Melanie recognizes that look, and it makes her cower. Both Bree and Hank have given her that same look one too many times. She pulls the door open further and tries to hide behind it, wanting to stay out of whatever's about to happen between them.

On the other side of the door, Hank clears his throat and says, "Hi, Aubrey."

"Don't call me that, Hank," Bree says.

"Fine. Don't call me Hank. I'm your dad."

Bree scoffs. "I hear there's another missing girl. I see your priorities haven't changed at all either."

Melanie buries herself further behind the door, wishing she could disappear.

"Chase," Hank says.

Melanie hears her name, but ignores it. She really wants to stay out of this.

"Chase, come out from there."

Melanie waits for another second before reluctantly sliding out from behind the door and popping her head out. Refusing to look at Bree, she meets Hank's gaze.

"Not that it matters since you won't be allowed to look at the case while she's around," Hank begins, referring to his daughter, "but in case you wanted to know, the name Abby was using was Courtney Baker." Hank looks back to Bree for a moment, smiles coldly, then he turns and leaves.

Bree scolds Hank under her breath, then disappears into the bedroom. Melanie exhales and closes the door, glad there wasn't bloodshed. She'd do just about anything if Bree and Hank learned to get along; it would certainly make her life a whole lot easier.

Melanie's left alone with the closed door at her back and heat spiraling from where Bree was standing, torn between her mind and her heart. Her mind is telling her to sit down and to try and find a connection between Courtney Baker, Abby Janis, and Chloe Janis. But her heart is telling her if she does, Bree will look at her the same way she looks at her father, and that's the last thing Melanie wants; she sees the seriousness of the disdain Bree has for the man. While he might be deserving of it, Melanie tries to stay out of it.

Melanie decides to do the wise thing for her relationship and follows Bree into to bedroom. Regardless of how things go the rest of the night—whether they finish what they'd started, or if not—Melanie knows her mind will be elsewhere. As much as she doesn't want to admit it, her thoughts will be consumed by another woman for the rest of the night. That woman will be Abby Janis.

CHAPTER TWENTY-ONE

The house is completely dark when Abby pulls into the driveway. Kurt's Mercedes is still in the same spot, so she knows her husband is still home. She doesn't know if that's good or bad. Now she has to face him.

Abby's prepared for a peppering of questions from her husband. He's going to ask her what's going on with her and she's prepared to finally come clean. If it goes to plan, everything will come out in bits and pieces so it doesn't hurt as much. But even still, Abby's worried how Kurt will react. Tonight could end her marriage. The one thing she's committed to standing firm on is the baby—she's not telling him. Not tonight, not like this. It might be an awful thing to do, she admits, but it might be the only way to get her life back once this is all over. Saving the news for another time might be the only way to reconcile her marriage.

With a quick flick of the wrist, Abby turns off the engine and slides out of the safety of her vehicle. The three-quarter crescent moon overhead lights up the path just enough for her to see her way to the front door. She follows it, taking her time while grasshoppers serenade her from the lawn. Before reaching for the door handle, Abby takes a deep breath and prepares herself for the moment she's been dreading for ten years. She turns the handle and lets herself inside.

Once she closes the door behind her, Abby yells out to Kurt. She keeps still in the dark, listening for footsteps either down the hall or upstairs, but she hears nothing. The house feels empty. In the dark still, Abby feels behind her for the light switch and flips it. Light fills up the entrance hallway, staircase, and loft at the next level above, forcing Abby to shield her eyes. She turns around and gasps at what she sees, almost falling to the floor in fear.

Kurt is sitting on the stairs, still wearing his dress slacks, shirt, and loose necktie from earlier. His hair is disheveled and his face is flushed. With his elbows on his knees, he twirls a small piece of paper in between his fingers as if it were a coin. He looks up and meets Abby's eyes with a menacing stare, all emotion lost. Abby is suddenly scared to death of the man with the glassy eyes who she's never seen before.

"Where were you tonight?" Kurt says, his voice deep and resonant. He's not a heavy drinker, but he looks and sounds like he's deep in an advanced state of inebriation.

Abby doesn't know what to say, so she says nothing, her muscles tensing.

"Are you sleeping with someone?" Kurt asks.

"No."

Kurt flicks the rolled paper toward Abby, it unrolling as it descends. It hovers above the stairs for a moment like a bubble about to burst, before eventually floating softly down. It lands a couple of stairs down from the one Kurt is sitting on, the recognizable penmanship becoming clear.

Abby's heart sinks. It was a careless mistake.

The note from Scott.

"It's time, Abby," Kurt says, still sitting. "Tell me what's going on."

Tears well up in Abby's eyes as she looks at her husband. She has no choice but to tell him now. "I don't know what to do," she says. "I think I've made a terrible mistake."

Kurt still doesn't move from the stairs. He just sits and waits for Abby to finally tell him what she's been hiding. He blinks only periodically.

Abby pushes her back up against the door and forces herself to take some deep breaths. Her heart is like a thoroughbred running the Preakness and she can feel herself getting close to hyperventilating. A panic attack is closing in on her, threatening to suffocate. She'd thought it was going to be easier to say this aloud, but it's like her mind is shunning her for keeping it withheld from the world for so long. With labored breathing and a heartbeat pounding loud enough to wake the neighbors, Abby fights to spit out the words.

She says, "I know who has Chloe."

***

On the couch and snuggling up against the warmth of Mindy's bare legs, Jordan feels a little down. His body harmony with Mindy is at an all-time high and he can sense her growing closer to him with each passing day, but it's not about that. Jordan envies her. While she sits next to him with her legs draped across his lap, the smoothness of her skin reflecting off the overhead light, Jordan just watches her. Even when doing the most mundane activity—watching the evening news, for example, as they are now—she has a smile on her face. She's truly enjoying her life.

Something is missing in Jordan's life. He's found the woman of his dreams, and she likes having him around too, so that's more than a lot of people can say. But as the weekend fades and the grim Monday morning sun is just mere hours away, Jordan dreads what's on the horizon. Tomorrow morning, while Mindy heads off to pursue her passion and live out her dream, Jordan will be going to the only place that'll have him. It's his own fault and he knows it, and it's all because of the choices he made when he was younger. He chose smoking dope over studying, and later, he chose to snort cocaine over finding a job. Everything he's done is by his own doing, no one else's, and while he desperately wants to move on and bury his history in the past, he's reminded of his choices every day.

Tomorrow morning, Jordan will walk into the side entrance of the steel factory, he'll wait in line to punch the clock with the others, then he'll suit up and stand in an assembly line for eight hours. He'll put on his earmuffs and protective glasses and safety gloves and wait for the churning and grinding of the gears to start his workday. His primary job will be to feed sheets of steel into a rolling mill—just like he does every other day—until the sheets are completely flat and free of shards. The mill will do most of the work while Jordan monitors the equipment and continuously lubricates the rollers, unjams any stubborn steel, and ensures the conveyor belt is free of debris. Because of his choices as an adolescent and beyond, he lacks any marketable or professional skills, so he knows that's what he'll be doing for the rest of his life. One day the factory will shut down or it'll hire more engineers to make more machines that'll make his job obsolete, and he'll be out of a job then. He's doomed for an inevitable life of misery.

The thought that Mindy even tolerates him for a second blows his mind. He's worthless—he can't cook, he doesn't maintain the house well, and his job has no meaning. His life is monotonous. He might want to have children with Mindy someday—maybe he'll be good at being a father, or maybe he won't—but he's not sure he's worthy of that either. His worst fear is fathering a child who grows up to learn how much of failure his old man is, just like Jordan did with his own father. Jordan is no role model.

He tries to brush away the endless pit of depression that overtakes his mind at the strangest times. He rubs Mindy's legs to let her know he's there. She takes his hand and holds it in her own, rubbing the top of his hand with her forefinger. The gesture means the world to him—it shows she cares, and that's more than enough. As the news anchors share the latest details on the Chloe Janis situation—which there are none—Jordan realizes he hasn't thought about Chloe in hours. He must have been somehow distracted to let it go, but now that it's back in the forefront of his mind, he's no further along than he was before.

He still can't place where he's seen Chloe Janis from.

With a heavy sigh and a quick press of his thumb, Jordan turns off the TV. Mindy doesn't say anything—she's not as wrapped up in the story as he is anyway. A few minutes later, Jordan crawls into bed and lies on his back with his eyes open, exhausted, but knowing he'll be unable to sleep.

Even with the blackness overhead, Jordan can see as if the lights were on—his eyes have adjusted by now. Mindy has been asleep next to him for hours, breathing softly and snoring quietly every once in a while. Jordan does this every Sunday night—he lies awake and wishes for a revelation about what he's going to do with his life. So far, it hasn't come.

Tonight is a little different. While he does lie awake like always, his mind is elsewhere. The image of Chloe Janis's smiling face blinks in his mind like an out of service stoplight—the same image keeps repeating itself over and over and over. And the more it blinks, the further his brain seems to be from recognizing the girl. It's almost as if he doesn't anymore. Maybe it's all in his subconscious.

Jordan's mind quickly shifts to the girl's family. He wonders how they're feeling, what they're doing right now, how frightened they must be. He can't imagine what they're going through, how difficult it must be. Jordan feels sick for them.

He closes his eyes and tries to let himself drift away, but he can't. The clock on the nightstand next to him tells him he only has three hours left, so he's already been through the most difficult stretch of the night—now he's on the back nine. The clubhouse is just up over the hill. It looks like he won't sleep at all tonight. The only comfort he has is that he knows he's probably not the only one.

CHAPTER TWENTY-TWO

After a mostly sleepless night, Hank arrives at the office before 7:00 A.M. He's the first one in. It brings him back to what it was like during the solemn days and insomnia-ridden nights when he was working on the Leanne Corey case. Sometimes he wonders if Aubrey is right about him. After what she said to him last night about his priorities, he's done a lot of thinking—mostly about his personal life and where he's gone wrong.

Aubrey still resents him for all the time he'd spent worrying about Leanne Corey after she disappeared, and now he might be starting to see how it affected his daughter. His then-wife, Mary, had had enough of their marriage just prior to Leanne's disappearance, and instead of him trying to reconcile with her and salvage the relationship, Hank spent more time in isolation. He went into the office early and stayed late almost every night. Mary hadn't yet moved out of the house at the time, so there was still hope for the marriage to be saved. But instead of Hank pushing his pride aside and reconfiguring his life to make it work, he'd shut himself out from everyone. Everyone except for the Corey family. And it cost him the only woman he's ever loved.

Hank senses the pattern starting to repeat itself again with Chloe Janis, but he can't help it. These victims need his help. It's too late for him to change now anyhow, he thinks, since Mary is already gone from his life. He suspects Aubrey would shun him for thinking that way. Aubrey had always been supportive of him and his career up until the time Leanne Corey came into his life, so the idea that she's bitter about him trying to find another missing girl is shortsighted—that's not what she's angry about. Hank suspects she feels abandoned, like he chose Leanne Corey over his own girls, over his own daughter. That was never his intention to make her feel that way, but it's taken him until now to realize what he's done. All he wants is her forgiveness. He knows Aubrey cares about him, despite the front she puts up—she has every right to be angry still. He'll have this conversation with Aubrey someday soon, he decides, and he'll apologize for how he made her feel—that might be all she wants; regretfully, he never did. The last thing he wants is to spend his retirement years without having any contact with his only daughter. She's all he has left. It's about time to reconnect with her.

And he will. After he brings Chloe Janis home.

Hank's email inbox is overflowing with new and unread messages as always, but there's nothing from the Connecticut State Police yet about the Abby Janis and Courtney Baker link. The fax machine is empty too. It's a bitter start to his day—he was told he'd have a detailed report first thing.

The red light on the phone on Hank's desk blinks with a handful of missed calls and unheard messages in his voice mail—hopefully, a lead on Chloe's whereabouts. He scrolls through the list of missed call numbers and doesn't recognize any, then he listens to his messages. There are three different reporters from three different local newspapers asking for a comment on the article in today's paper. He mocks them under his breath for being late to the party and wonders to himself what kind of reporter in this area didn't hear about the press conference yesterday. And to make matters worse, it's not only just one reporter who missed it, but three.

What a bunch of amateurs.

Hank deletes the first two messages. He listens to the third, keeping his finger close to the delete button in case it drags on too long. The voice on the machine mentions today's date along with the article, and Hank pauses. He usually grabs the paper on his way into the office, but it must have skipped his mind today. He listens to the message again to make sure he'd heard correctly.

Hank rushes into the hallway and out onto the front steps of the station where the bank of newspaper bins are, his chest thumping. There's not a soul in sight; in mere hours, this place will be raucous with ringing phones and detectives speaking over one another. For now, Hank basks in the silence. He pops a few quarters into the machine and grabs a paper from the stack. He flips open the spread and flattens the crease of the paper so it doesn't fold in on itself while he tries to read. Above the fold is a dark photograph—a little pixelated, but effective enough—with a bold headline above it: "MISSING GIRLS' MOTHER SEEN CRYING OUT FOR HELP FROM A MYSTERY MAN."

Hank doesn't recognize the photo at first, but once he shades it from the sun with his hand to get a better look, it becomes clear. Hank has to sit on the step to catch his breath—he's shocked.

Could it really be? It's impossible.

The photograph, though grainy, is a solid snapshot of Abby Janis's strained face. She has a phone held up to her ear and her cheeks are wet with tears. The look of despair blankets her face like a bed of snow covering the mountaintops. The angle of the photograph is awfully close to the view Hank had of her last night at the gas station, but he can't understand why. He was alone.

Or maybe he wasn't.

Who else was there?

A sharp leap in his chest forces him to read on. The article is damning. It extends from the front page onto a second and third page inside the paper and provides only details that a detective should know, details only Hank should know. The writer describes Abby's bizarre behavior up to this point in the investigation and describes how she almost seems to be covering something up. Hank is impressed with the accuracy of the details as he reads, while at the same time, he's alarmed that a reporter could be this knowledgeable about the case. Either someone from the inside is feeding the reporter information, which is doubtful, or they're one hell of an investigator.

On the inside flap of the paper is a perfectly clear black and white photo of Abby during the press conference. In the photo, she appears to be staring off into space while the mayor is speaking at the podium. There's a third photo of Abby arriving back home late at night to a completely dark house. The lighting is so poor that it's almost impossible to see any detail. That photo shows her stepping out of her SUV and into the driveway, Hank thinks, with the timestamp as the caption.

Someone else was following Abby too.

Toward the end of the article is one final photo, and as soon as Hank sees it, he grinds his teeth until it hurts. It's a snapshot of his car and a silhouette of him behind the wheel. Worst of all, his name is printed. His cover is completely blown. It reads: "Even the lead investigator on the case, Detective Hank Berger of the Mifflinburg Police Department, was spotted at the scene. It might just be a coincidence, or could it be that there's something more sinister going on? I'll let you be the judge."

To Hank, that doesn't sound like an unbiased report of facts. It sounds more like a reporter with a grudge.

Hank folds the paper in half and slams it to the pavement in rage. His blood boils his hands into fists. Someone was following him too. He gets to his feet and paces on the steps, his shoes scuffing against the concrete. The tie around his neck suddenly tightens, feeling like a noose. He unbuttons his collar and yanks the tie away before it suffocates him. He feels on the verge of exploding.

Then it hits him.

It's obvious. He hovers over the paper and shifts it around with his foot until he can read the byline. Marie Washington's name is written in bold, her inclusion into the investigation as unwanted as a scattering plague, prodding into Hank like a javelin.

Who else would it be?

Hank reaches down and grabs the paper, wanting to tear it half. He screams at it like no one's listening, his voice echoing loud enough to force a flock of giant petrels to scurry from the treetops. He's getting pretty damn tired of Marie Washington already. First it was her hard-hitting questions during the presser yesterday, and now this. He can't help but wonder what else she has up her sleeve, or who she had to sleep with this time in order to get all that confidential information. He can sense his investigation starting to crumble into a million pieces, and he doesn't know what he can do to stop the bleeding.

On his hip, Hank's phone rings. The caller ID tells him it's Mayor Thomas.

Great.

Hank huffs, then grabs the phone and heads toward a bench that's shaded by a sagging pine. He bites his tongue and answers, preparing himself for the mayor's wrath.

***

Chloe is awakened by the vibration of a shaking puppy under her bed. Though soft, she can hear him whimpering. She's unsure of the time, but it feels early. She stretches out her back and leans over the side of the bed to explore. She doesn't see Benny right away, but she smells something funny. It smells like a gutted candle, but it's not in the room. It's the smell of smoke.

The first thing she needs to do is rescue Benny.

Chloe slides off the bed, onto the floor, and drops to her hands and knees. She feels alert and awake and ready to save the furry friend she's longed for. Now's the time to prove she's deserving of him. She finds him hiding deep underneath the bed, nestled in the corner near the leg of the metal bed frame. She speaks softly to him to encourage him to come out from hiding, but he doesn't move. He's shaking violently, practically non-responsive. Chloe pushes herself under the bed with him, barely fitting, and reaches as far as she can until her shoulder hurts, and pulls him to safety. He buries himself into her chest like a baby in need of swaddling.

Benny is her baby.

With shaking hands and cloudy vision from the puddles of water in her eyes, Chloe gets to her feet and heads over to the window at the foot of the bed. She can't see more than a few feet in front of her due to the thick smoke that fills the outside air. There are no flames anywhere she can see. Chloe is confused. On the other side of the room, she stops before reaching for the door. Something her mom told her resonates in her mind, something that she told her one time during a fire drill at home. Chloe surprises herself that she even remembers. She flips her trembling hand over and slowly presses it against the door knob. Her heart is thumping, even faster than Benny's. She's not sure what to expect on the other side of the door.

Am I trapped?

Chloe taps the back of her hand against the knob once, expecting warmth. When it doesn't come, she tries it a second time, then a third. Then she presses it against it. Then she grabs it with her palm and waits for something to happen, waits for the pain. But it doesn't come—no scalding pain or singed skin—so she turns the knob.

The hallway is clear. No flames and no smoke in either direction. But she can hear the snap of a crackling fire coming from somewhere, so she knows what she's experiencing is real.

The cabin is burning down from the outside in. She's going to be torched to death.

Both bedroom doors next to Chloe's room are open, so she pokes her head inside each. Didi's room is furthest away and is neat and orderly with the bed made, but there's no sign of Didi. Scott's room, more alarmingly, is completely empty. All of the furniture has been removed so just the hardwood floor with an area rug is left. Benny must feel the uneasiness too, because he squirms in Chloe's arms and frees himself from her grasp. She tries to catch him while in mid-air, but he slithers away like a snake. His paws slip on the hardwood floor as he runs around the corner and ducks back into Chloe's bedroom, whimpering again. Chloe lets him go. She'll come back for him later.

Something doesn't feel right. A small pit of butterflies start to spread their wings inside of Chloe's belly and rummage around like they're trapped in a cup, desperate to find their way out. Chloe can sympathize with that feeling. The lone window in Scott's bedroom is much like the one in hers—clouded with heavy smoke—so Chloe doesn't even bother looking out. She ducks out of the room.

Back in the hallway, Chloe calls out for Scott and Didi, but gets no response. She tries again a second time, this time louder, but the results are the same. Chloe rushes into the kitchen. Empty.

Where is everybody?

She's getting worried now, scared even. She wants to scream for help. The living room is empty too. Even the shelves of toys Chloe had played with the other day are gone. Benny's bed is missing too. She wonders if she did something wrong to cause this. She hopes it's all one big misunderstanding. Scott and Didi have been nothing but nice to he—it just doesn't make sense that they'd leave her behind.

A big gust of wind blows the smoke outside the window into a funnel and pulls it away from the glass. Chloe walks over to the window, expecting nothing, and peeks outside. Finally, she sees something. Behind the pond and before the beginning of the tree line is a pile of furniture with large, glowing flames crawling over it. Standing next to the pile with her back to the window is Didi—or at least it looks like her from behind. She appears to be alone.

Suddenly filled with a jolt of adrenaline, Chloe bolts back through the living room and into the kitchen, then pushes her way through the unlocked front door. The screen bounces off the wooden frame a few times, reminiscent of a hammer pounding in a nail, as Chloe swings around the corner of the cabin and rushes toward Didi. The dryness of the grass scratches the bottoms of her bare feet, hurting, but she ignores it. The smoke is thick and heavy, and the heat increases in intensity as Chloe nears the pile, but she never slows. The bolt of energy she feels keeps her moving.

Didi turns around as Chloe approaches. She opens her arms just in time to catch her as Chloe throws herself into her chest. Chloe squeezes as if Didi were her mother, feeling relieved to not be alone.

"What's the matter, sweetie?" Didi says, sounding hoarse, as she fights to keep her balance.

Chloe keeps squeezing.

"What's wrong, Chloe?"

Chloe pulls away and looks up at Didi through wet eyes. "I thought you left me."

Didi bites her lip. "Why did you think that?"

Chloe shrugs.

"Were you scared of the fire? The smoke must have woken you. I told Scott it was too early."

Chloe feels better knowing she hasn't done anything wrong to cause this. And she feels better about Benny being stuck inside, too. She looks past Didi and recognizes some of the furniture in the fire pile behind her. A mattress on the bottom looks to be the accelerant—it must be Scott's. The tall shelving unit that held the bins of toys is on the top of the pile, charred on the legs and already turning to ash. The stench of burning plastic tickles Chloe's nose. Sweat, already, trickles down her neck.

"I know you're too young to realize what's going on," Didi offers, bringing Chloe back, "but your...Scott is going to be taking you away for a while."

"I want to go home now. I want to see my mom."

"I don't think that's going to happen, sweetie. Scott will be back soon. You two are going somewhere special."

The way Didi says it—slowly, unconvincingly, and with a touch of sadness—makes Chloe's skin crawl. Somewhere special? It sounds like Scott is taking her again—somewhere away from here, somewhere further away from home. "No," Chloe says. "I'm not going."

"It's okay, Chloe. It'll only be for a little while. We'll all be together again soon."

But Chloe doesn't want that. She doesn't want to be with them anymore. They took her; Scott took her. He manipulated her by lying about knowing her mom, and now he's going to take her even further away.

Unless Chloe does something about it. She has to stop him.

Chloe looks away from Didi and pretends like she's upset, curling her lip and trying to force out tears. But instead, when Didi least expects it, Chloe turns around and runs back toward the cabin. She runs as hard as she can, her legs pumping so fast that her muscles ache. She runs like the wind. Didi calls after her as she does, but she doesn't follow. As Chloe turns the corner, the grass pricking the bottoms of her feet again, she notices the station wagon is missing from the driveway—something she hadn't seen before—which means Scott is gone. But she doesn't know where he is or when he's coming back, so she has to hurry.

Now is the chance Chloe's been waiting for. She's ready to take on the forest.

Inside the cabin and frantic, Chloe finds Benny in the same spot he was earlier under her bed and pulls him out. She knew something didn't feel right when she woke up this morning, and now she knows why. Scott is planning to take her away somewhere, somewhere where she'll never see her mom or dad again.

Chloe slips into her sneakers and finds Benny's leash in the kitchen and attaches it to the loop on his collar. Carrying him as he still trembles, Chloe blasts through the front door again and starts running. She thinks she hears Didi calling out for her again through the crackling of the fire, but she ignores it. Chloe doesn't slow down and she doesn't look back. Didi won't be able to catch her. Together with Benny at her side, Chloe runs like mad away from the cabin. And she's not going to stop until she can run no further.

CHAPTER TWENTY-THREE

Because she knows Hank is going to ask her what she thinks about it when she gets to the office, Melanie wakes up early and reads through the report on Abby Janis. The details are puzzling, she admits, but she doesn't quite know what they mean, even still. Hank seems to be onto something, though, or maybe he's going crazy in his old age. Melanie can sense how desperate he is to not let Chloe Janis become another Leanne Corey. The pain is still too fresh for him. But so far, Melanie doesn't see any connection between Abby Janis's past and her daughter's disappearance, as much as Hank wants there to be.

With jelly-like legs and a still pulsating jaw from a night full of ecstasy—Bree was still in the mood once her father left, after all—Melanie climbs off the couch and heads into the bathroom to get ready. Expecting to hear from Hank shortly—it's a near certainty that he's at the station already—Melanie keeps her phone nearby while she dries her hair. The phone vibrates on her leg just after she begins. It's not even 7:00 A.M. yet.

"Morning, Hank," she says. She has a sudden craving for a hot cup of coffee. She can practically taste the warmth of the tropical paradise lathering her throat.

"Chase, are you up?"

"I'm up."

"Good, I need you down here. We need to do damage control."

"What's going on?" A heap of hope and excitement rise in her voice. "Have there been some developments?"

"Something like that. I don't have time to explain right now."

Melanie knows when to push Hank and when not to. She can tell by the urgency in his voice that now is a time not to. Something must have happened. Her enthusiasm suddenly dissipates. "Okay, Hank," she says. "I'll leave right now."

Before she leaves, Melanie ties up her still wet hair and approaches Bree in the bed. Her breathing is soft and rhythmic, and it mellows Melanie out. She watches Bree for a while, smiling, reminiscing about how they first met.

It was almost two years ago at a local benefit dinner. It was a gathering of the police force, fire department, emergency rescue squads, and some local politicians and their families. Melanie and Hank were there, as were Bree and Mary—Hank's ex-wife—who'd accompanied him to show their support. Melanie remembers how handsome Hank looked that night with his rented tuxedo and black bow tie, his hair slicked. He was proud to be there and it showed.

Melanie knew Hank had a daughter, but she'd only ever seen her in photos. But when Bree walked into the room, time practically stood still. She had on a black dress that sparkled under the chandelier, and her hair was tied up above her head like she was a princess. She wore some kind of strawberry gloss on her lips—which, as Melanie found out later, tasted wonderful—that glistened. Bree was the most beautiful woman Melanie had ever seen. It was infatuation at first sight.

As the months went by and Melanie and Bree became close, their relationship grew to be complicated. Melanie wasn't closeted, but Bree was, so keeping it from Hank at first was a challenge. After secretly and exclusively dating for a while, the holidays came and they decided it was time to tell Hank. It was on Thanksgiving. The look on Hank's face when he opened the front door and found out about the unexpected guest was that of pure shock. Melanie was so embarrassed.

Bree told her parents about the relationship, and while Hank sat quietly, Melanie knew what he was thinking. She could see the disapproval on his face, as if his worst nightmare was coming true; her own father had the same look when she came out to him years earlier. Hank's an old fashioned man with strong Christian values, so accepting his daughter's sexuality was difficult for him. Both Melanie and Bree understood that, so they gave him time and space. Or at least Bree did; Melanie had to see him every day. It took some time for Hank to look at Melanie at the office, but he eventually softened and came around. And although he's still not fully accepting of the situation, he's happy that his daughter is happy. His heart is in the right place most of the time.

The worst part about it, Melanie recognizes as she watches Bree sleep, is the guilt Bree feels. Bree has an underlying feeling that she's part of the reason her parents split up. Bree's sexuality was a major point of tension between Hank and Mary, and it wasn't long after the announcement that they got divorced. Melanie can't get herself to believe that was part of it.

Melanie strokes Bree's hair and lets the silkiness run through her fingers. It's smoother than velvet, even unwashed. Melanie leans down and kisses Bree's forehead, the lotion on her skin still fresh, then she whispers her love for her. Being careful not to make a noise on her way out, Melanie leaves the apartment without waking her.

***

The morning after not having slept the previous evening presents a whole new set of challenges for Jordan. He gets up groggy and irritable and with a cluster headache pounding in his temples. A long day is ahead. His eyes are only slits and are as heavy as a bowling ball. His energy is depleted. Mindy is in bed still, sleeping easy. Jordan is completely jealous of her ability to do it so effortlessly.

The newspaper in the driveway doesn't fool him today—the sun isn't yet up, so the plastic wrap sits idly in the darkness. Jordan goes outside to get it. The morning is brisk and the grass is dewy, looking like it may have rained overnight. But it didn't—Jordan would have heard it. He would have heard the rain pound on the roof like a pattering of snowballs against a brick wall. He loves the rain. It soothes him. Sometimes, even on Sunday nights, the sound of the rain will help him fall sleep. But it didn't rain last night, so Jordan didn't sleep. It's a pity.

Jordan tears off the plastic wrapping and tosses it in the garbage barrel on the porch as he brings the newspaper inside. The crows aren't even awake yet. With a strong pot of coffee brewed and a stale bagel buttered, Jordan opens the newspaper. The photograph underneath the fold catches his attention and sends a shockwave through his body like a jolt of lighting, and he drops the bagel. Melted butter drips from his fingers onto the newspaper when he pulls it closer to his face to get a better look. Even exhausted, his eyes recognize something familiar, but Jordan squints at the photo anyway, just to make sure.

It's not the highest resolution photo he's ever seen—it's almost as if it were taken on a smartphone and enlarged, distorting the original quality—but the woman's face gets clearer the longer he stares at it. He knows who she is.

The engrained image of Chloe Janis from the television flashes inside Jordan's mind. His vision goes blurry as his brain tries to superimpose the images of Chloe and the woman in the picture to see if they're the same. It's definitely a match. Spot on. Jordan remembers that yesterday's paper is still on the coffee table, so he grabs today's and rushes over to it, suddenly awake and excited. He holds them up next to one another, both now streaked with butter. Take away the hair color, and it's practically the same person he's looking at. Chloe is just a younger version of the woman in the newspaper.

That's it!

With a sudden burst of energy like he's been shot out of a cannon, Jordan calls out Mindy's name and rushes toward the bedroom. He has to tell her. She stirs when he enters, but only opens her eyes when he shakes her. She pushes him away at first, grunting, but his persistence wins out. She eventually wakes completely and glares at him like he's just sinned.

"What the hell, Jordan?" Mindy slurs.

"I've got it!" he says. "I know who the girl is?"

"What girl?"

"The abducted girl."

Mindy rubs her eyes, trying to wake herself up further. Jordan shoves today's paper in her face.

"The picture's too blurry," Mindy says as she pushes the paper away. "I can't see a damn thing." She looks like she might fall back asleep.

"It's the girl's mother. She was caught on camera in Montgomery last night."

Mindy sits up. "Our Montgomery? What was she doing up this way?"

"I don't know, the article doesn't say. But I know who she is."

"You do?"

"The little girl is this woman's daughter," Jordan says, pointing to the grainy photograph. "That's why I thought I recognized Chloe. I know her mother."

"Who is she?" Mindy asks, now alert.

"The paper says her name is Abby, Abby Janis."

"How do you know her? I thought you said the family is from Mifflinburg."

"That's what the news said, but they're wrong."

Mindy gives him a look of uncertainty, her eyebrows scrunching. She's not buying it. "Are you sure you're thinking of the right person?"

"Positive. No doubt in my mind. Except, there is this one thing..."

"What is it?"

"When I knew this woman," Jordan says, "her name wasn't Abby Janis. I knew her as Courtney Baker."

CHAPTER TWENTY-FOUR

Kurt's losing his wife—he can feel it. Or worse, he might have already lost her. He wishes he knew where he went wrong. For the first time in his life, Kurt feels used. Abby has lied to him. She's been lying for years. She's been lying forever, for as long as he's known her. He doesn't even know who she is.

Through Abby's inconsolable cries last night, Abby spilled her guts. She confessed, sobbed, and told Kurt her faults. Kurt didn't know whether to console her or scream at her. He did neither. He sat on the stairs, his face in his hands, clammy, and just listened. He was blindsided, shell-shocked, distraught, saddled with disbelief. Even still, so many details are a mystery.

The man who has Chloe, the man who abducted her, is Scott Baker. This man has Kurt's daughter.

The big questions—why and where—remain unclear. Abby's answers were vague at best. From what Kurt can recollect—his mind was in a dense haze at the time, trying to wrap around all that Abby was saying and what she knew—the situation escalated quickly. It had all started with a note in the mailbox, then Chloe's abduction, then the threatening phone calls from Scott Baker afterward. It does explain some of Abby's behavior. Abby didn't really have time to comprehend what was going on—that's what she'd said. She'd thought she could handle it by herself and make it all go away. But once the mayor got involved and a press conference was held, it's all gotten worse. It's all spiraled out of control. And Scott Baker is freaking out because of it.

But Kurt doesn't understand that. Abby's logic is flawed. If it's money Scott's after—which Abby says it is—why wouldn't Abby just come to him? If that's all it'd take to bring Chloe home, she'd already be here. It's impossible to believe Abby's story as currently constituted. There just has to be more to it than that.

But what if that's it? What if Abby is being truthful about what happened? That would mean this is Kurt's fault. Not only was it his responsibility to keep an eye on Chloe at the mall—which he'd miserably failed at—but it was his idea to approach the mayor behind Abby's back. That's why she was so upset about it. While trying to help, Kurt has made everything worse. It's his fault Chloe's still missing.

The realization hits Kurt in the chest with a force strong enough to knock the wind out of him. He gasps for more breath. The pain in his lungs is stabbing. He tosses himself on the couch—the same couch he'd spent the night on—and tries to calm himself down. The reality of the situation is devastating, but he didn't know. If Abby would have told him what was going on at the beginning, he never would have called Wesley. None of this would be happening. It'd be all over by now.

Upstairs, a door creaks, jolting Kurt to attention. He leaps to his feet and listens for more movement. Soft footsteps make their way down the hall and toward the opening of the loft. Kurt's heart is fluttering inside his chest, both out of despair and fear—despair for how he feels, fear for what he's done. He's fearful of the trouble Chloe might be in, and for the possibility he may have caused it. He's fearful Abby may have blown their one opportunity to get Chloe back. And mostly, he's fearful for himself—fearful that if something happens to Chloe because of his actions and carelessness, he might not be able to forgive himself. He might not be able to keep on living.

Kurt walks over to the stairs as his wife approaches the landing.

***

After a restless night, Abby has a lot of clarity. She realizes the only way out of this is to finally come clean. She has to tell Kurt first, then the detectives, and she has to tell them everything this time. Chances are there will be consequences for her having finally confessed to her faults, but she's prepared to deal with that. If she has to spend some time locked away in order to get Chloe back, then so be it. It'll then be up to Kurt to decide what he wants to do. The most important thing is getting Chloe back.

Before leaving the bedroom and heading downstairs to find her husband, Abby pauses in front of the mirror above her dresser and stares into the glass. She doesn't even recognize herself. The woman she sees is a liar, but that's not who she really is. Except it is. She's been lying to everyone she cares about for a decade. And it's been a lot longer than that for others; she's been lying her whole life. But that's not who she wants to be, not anymore. It's time to change her ways. It's time to confess and to start the rehabilitation process. It might take the rest of her life.

Abby pulls open the bedroom door and walks out into the hallway. The morning sun fills up the loft with natural light, but the house is dead silent. If the circumstances were different, it'd be a wondrously beautiful day. Abby's heart is full of gloom. Walking tentatively, she continues down the hallway until she comes to where the edge of the wall meets the railing of the loft. Down at the bottom of the stairs, looking helpless and disheveled, is Kurt. The sorrow on his face is deep enough to drown a fish. He looks like he hasn't slept in a week.

Abby makes her way to the top of the stairs and stops. She and Kurt make eye contact, but neither one says anything. The silence is excruciating. Taking one stair at a time, Abby timidly descends toward her husband, a rush of nervousness showering over her.

"Abby, I—"

"Before you say anything," Abby begins, "I think we should sit down. There's still a lot I need to tell you."

***

"Whatever happened to her?" Mindy asks. She's sitting up fully now on the edge of the bed, attentive and ready to listen. She almost seems interested.

Jordan says, "Not sure. After I got out of jail, I never heard from her again. She'd moved away, apparently."

"How did you know her?"

Jordan closes his eyes and thinks. It was a long time ago. It was when he was living in Pittsburg. Some of the details are foggy—a lot of that has to do with the fact that his drug-laden days were just getting into high gear then—but her face stuck with him through the years. "I lived right next to them. We had a shared wall."

"Who's them?"

"Courtney had a roommate. A guy."

Mindy nods.

"The walls were thin, right, so I could hear everything. They used to talk like they were all alone and no one could hear them."

Mindy shifts her weight around and faces Jordan entirely. "What kind of stuff did they say? Anything good?"

"Tons of stuff. They were cons, scam artists. You wouldn't believe the kind of shit they were pulling. I think they got away with it, too."

"Like what?"

"Crazy stuff. They had a falling out and the guy ended up getting arrested shortly after Courtney left, I guess."

"How do you know that?"

"Because I was the one who tipped off the state about them. One of my old roommates told me the guy was dragged out of his apartment by the cops not long after I was arrested myself. I wish I was there to see it."

Mindy exhales. She, apparently, had been holding her breath. "Why didn't you ever tell me that?"

Jordan shrugs it off. "It never came up. Like I've said before, I'm not proud of the things I did when I was in Pittsburg before I met you."

Mindy nods, seeming to understand.

"But the thing that's strange," Jordan says, "is when I knew Courtney, she was married to the guy she was living with. I'm not sure what happened between them. I've always wondered if she ratted him out to save herself. She seemed like the type of person who would do that, you know?"

"So, the guy she's married to now isn't the same one she was married to when you knew her?"

"Not unless he changed his name too. But I don't think so—the man on the news looks nothing like the guy I knew."

"Do you remember what his name was?"

"I do. His name was Scott Baker."

CHAPTER TWENTY-FIVE

Sticks and fallen branches snap and clusters of moss flatten under Chloe's sneakers as she walks further away from the cabin. It's long gone. Chloe's feet are sore and she can feel a callus starting to form on the back of her heel—it's because she's not wearing any socks. She's not sure how long she's been walking, but it hasn't been long. Her legs hadn't allowed her to run as far as she'd hoped, but she's far enough. Once the adrenaline dried out, Chloe's muscles became weak and very painful, so she was forced to pull up. But it's okay, because she got away. Didi didn't follow her. Now she and Benny have to find their way home.

Except Chloe doesn't know which direction home is. The forest, so far, is winning.

The heat of the sun is draining, so instead of trying to fight it, Chloe stays on the inside of the tree line. A dirt road is on the other side of the trees, but Chloe hasn't seen a car pass by yet. She figures it's only a matter of time. Benny is close by, panting heavily. His tongue is a deep pink and Chloe fears he's becoming dehydrated. She feels like she's dragging him.

Although she had been trying to pay attention to her surroundings when riding in the back of the station wagon after she was abducted by Scott, Chloe doesn't remember much of anything. Nothing around her looks familiar. Part of her thinks she should turn back and walk on the main road, but she won't. Scott might see her then. The forest is the only safe place for her now.

Chloe finds a log to sit on and take a breather. Her belly grumbles, reminding her she didn't eat this morning. She looks over at Benny, who throws himself in a shaded spot under a tree and lies down. He almost looks distressed. Chloe's worried about him.

Chloe thinks of Scott and Didi and how nice they were to her—they fed her well, gave her lots of toys to play with, a warm bed to sleep on. But then she thinks it might have all just an act, just a way to get her to keep quiet. It almost worked. Chloe believed she would see her mom and dad again, believed Scott when he'd said he knew her. But now, as she thinks about it, it was all a lie. If buying her Benny was a way to make her want to stick around, it failed. Even though a puppy is something she's wanted more than anything in the world, Benny won't bring back her old life.

Chloe misses her house. She misses her mom and her dad, her own bed and her own room. She misses the neighborhood and her friends, and she misses school. Summer break has just begun, but it's already been the worst summer ever. And although it's only been two days, she misses everything. If she had to give up Benny in order to get her old life back, she'd do it. It would be hard because she loves him so much already, but she loves her old life a lot, too. Chloe looks at Benny again and wants to cry, but she doesn't. She's strong. But she's only nine-years-old, and she's alone. She wants to go home.

***

New York. That's where Scott has decided he and Chloe will go. He has it all figured out. It's just over a three-hour drive from his mother's cabin to the big city, but it's nearly a straight shot east on I-80. Some people might think going to a heavily populated area while on the run is just asking to be caught, but Scott thinks otherwise. The way he sees it, he and Chloe will blend right into the crowd. No one will even notice them.

There are over eight million people in New York City alone and another eleven million scattered throughout the rest of the state. That's a lot of people. That's a lot of blending. Scott's convinced himself they'll go practically unnoticed surrounded by that many people. They'll be able to fly under the radar and lay low for a while until things cool down. Long term, New York City is probably too close to home to be a permanent stop, but it could do temporarily. In a month or two, he and Chloe can head up north and hide out in the woods, or maybe they can slip into Canada or sail to Denmark. Hell, they could even cut across to Alaska and build a quiet life amongst the icy roads and tanker trucks. The options are plentiful. Financial resources will be limited, but Scott will figure that out. He's confident he can make it all work.

The challenge, of course, will be how to deal with Chloe. She won't understand what's going on, and that'll be the most difficult part. Scott will try to explain it to her and will try to find a way to tell her she won't be seeing her mother again. It'll kill her. That is unless Abby comes around to Scott's way of thinking, and there may just be something that'll make her do that. It'll be just a couple days before the truth comes out.

Behind the wheel of a silver sedan—Scott chose silver at the rental agency so he can blend into the road, just like he will with the people in Times Square—Scott pulls onto the dirt road and treks toward the cabin. The rental seems to grip the road better than the wagon—the maneuverability isn't quite the challenge—which is a nice change. The smoke from the fire he'd started before he left to switch vehicles can be seen from a good distance from the cabin. The smoke has risen above the trees and has filled up the trail like it's an enclosed hallway. Scott flips on the fog lights to help cut through the smoke.

A thick cloud of gray blankets a layer of soot on the windshield as Scott pulls up to the cabin. It gives off the feel of an approaching thunderstorm, one in which Scott has driven right into the heart of. He tightens his grip on the steering wheel in case a twister decides to bite. Flames rise above the height of the roof from the rear of the cabin. The orange darkens as it climbs higher toward the clouds, submerging the cabin with heat. From the driveway, Scott notices that the interior front door on the porch is cracked open, allowing the smoke to seep into the house through the screen door. It feels like a mistake his mother wouldn't make.

Inside, the cabin is deserted. The crackling of the fire in the back echoes through the empty hallway, and that's the only sound. Even the clock seems to have quieted. Scott pops his head in Chloe's room and finds an empty, unmade bed. Her shoes are gone, as is the dog and his collar. Chloe is nowhere to be found. Scott's heart starts to pound, sensing something is off. He hopes Chloe has just taken the dog for a walk.

Back outside and near the pond, Scott finds Diane standing alone, tending to the fire. Most of the wood has turned to ash, and the heat the pile gives off is enough to make Scott sweat. He stands back a few feet to lessen the crisp on his skin. "Mother?" he says.

Diane turns at the sound of his voice and offers a disheartened smile.

"Where's Chloe?"

Diane looks away as she turns a shade of white. Even with the flames near her face, she looks cold. A fast-forming lump in Scott's throat starts to hurt.

"What happened?"

"Nothing, really. She came out and asked when she can see her mother."

"What did you tell her?"

"The truth. I told her I didn't think that was going to happen."

Scott's eyes widen. "Why would you tell her that?"

"I didn't know what else to say," Diane says, looking a little sad. "I didn't want to lie to the girl. She's been through so much."

"What did she do? How'd she react?"

"She ran."

"And you let her!"

Diane only shrugs a guilty shrug. It looks like she's given up. She turns back to the fire and drops her head.

"How long ago did this happen?"

"An hour, maybe," Diane's voice is barely audible behind the crackling flames.

Without saying anything further, Scott turns and runs back toward the driveway like he's being chased. His body temperature has risen so abruptly that he looks at his reflection in the passing window to see if he's on fire. He feels like the flames are suffocating him. Diane yells after him—something Scott doesn't hear—but he presses onward. He's in trouble and he knows it.

Chloe's gone. She could be anywhere by now.

Scott slams the car door and starts the engine. He pushes the pedal to the floor, swinging the back end around, peeling away, the car fishtailing as the rubber struggles to grip the dirt. A sand cloud forms and a cluster of small pebbles spray to the sides as Scott hauls out of the forest. He makes a sharp left and merges onto solid pavement.

A sunken pit of anxiety has formed deep within his gut, as he fears he might be too late. Between Diane's health, Abby's resistance, and now Chloe running off, Scott's starting to feel like his whole life is slipping right through his fingers. He's trying to squeeze his hands to keep everything together, but, like clay, the harder he squeezes, the more it just seeps out through the crevices. His dream is rapidly falling away, and there's nothing he can do to slow it down.

CHAPTER TWENTY-SIX

Coffee in hand, Melanie bursts through the doors of the police station and makes her way toward the cubicles. The anticipation of what Hank is up to is making her mad. She hopes the damage control he spoke about isn't quite as bad as it sounds. She hurries.

When Melanie makes it to the back, Hank is by himself, hunched over his desk, looking defeated. Melanie holds her breath, begging they don't have another Leanne Corey on their hands. A tense, eerie silence fills the empty room. Not long from now it'll be filled with detectives and investigators and uniforms, but until then, the elephant is whatever's bothering Hank. A chill rushes over Melanie like a tsunami as she approaches.

"I'm here Hank," she says. "What's going on?"

Hank grunts but doesn't look up right away. He seems to be trying to wrap his mind around something.

Melanie scans his workspace for the cause of his somberness. There's no fax on the printer, nothing on Hank's desk, no sign of anything out of the ordinary. There's no report from the Connecticut State Police about Abby Janis or Courtney Baker anywhere in sight—that can't be what's bothering Hank. Melanie fears the worst. Out of the corner of her eye, as she continues to scan the workspace for a sign, something under Hank's desk catches her attention. Hank's feet block her vision of whatever it is.

"What's that under your desk?" Melanie asks, suspecting it might be the culprit. Hoping.

Hank rolls his chair back and slides his feet to the side, giving Melanie a clear shot of the hidden item. It's a stack of newspapers, and Melanie cocks her head to the side to scan the headlines. The first and only thought that crosses her mind is Chloe Janis. She fears her body's been found. But when she sees the headline above the fold, Melanie breathes a sigh of relief. It's hard, loud, and catches Hank's attention. He looks at her. The relief only lasts for a short time, though, as Melanie puts it all together.

She crouches down, grabs a paper from the stack, and unfolds the crease. Without hesitation, she reads the entire article, carefully, word for word. All three pages. When finished, Melanie puts the loose pages of the paper back together, refolds it, and tosses it on the top of the stack of the others beneath Hank's desk. There are a lot of them. She flops herself into her own chair and lets what she's just read sink in. She struggles to comprehend what it all means.

"So, you had no idea?" Melanie finally says.

"This is a nightmare," Hank says, his voice weak, desperate. "The mayor called first thing this morning, ripped me a new one."

"What did he say?"

"You know how it goes. I tried to explain to him that Abby Janis is up to something, but he'd have none of it. Wouldn't even let me speak."

"What do we do?"

"Make it go away. That's all we can do."

"And how do you expect to do that?" Melanie says, crossing her arms. "Do you actually think that taking all the papers from out front and hiding them is going to work?"

"No."

"Then why do it?"

"I don't know," Hank admits as he drops his head into his hands. "I don't know what else to do."

Melanie feels badly for Hank. She hasn't seen him this stressed out in a long time. Not since Leanne Corey. She treads lightly. “What can I do? Do you want me to talk to the press? I can easily explain it’s a—”

“Forget that. Screw the press.”

“Then what, Hank? What can I do?”

Hank sits up and leans his back against the worn leather. “We just have to put all of our efforts into finding Chloe Janis. We have to find her today.”

Melanie almost scoffs. “Hank, I want to find her too, but we need to be realistic here. We don’t even have—”

“Today,” Hank says. “It has to happen today.”

“What you’re asking is unreasonable.”

“It’s not me asking!” Hank snaps. “This is coming directly from the mayor.”

“Or what?”

“Then I’m out.”

Melanie pauses, thinks, doesn’t understand. “You’re out? What the hell is that supposed to mean?”

“I’m out. Done. Finished. Everything I’ve worked for, thirty years on the force, gone. He’s going to take everything from me.”

“Your pension?”

Hank nods.

“That’s bullshit!” Melanie is suddenly furious. “He can’t do that.”

Hanks takes a much needed breath and gathers himself. Then he finds and meets Melanie’s eyes with desperation. “Actually, he can. And he did.”

***

Sitting alone on the couch, Kurt has a lot to ponder. Abby has left him alone with his thoughts while she has gone upstairs to feel sorry for herself. Kurt is numb. He knows his wife isn’t being completely honest with him still, and he’s not sure where to go from here. He knows there’s more she’s not telling him.

Everything in his life he thought was pure and honest has turned out to be a sham. He wonders how he could have been so obtuse to not have realized what was happening. He was blinded by love and deception—that’s how. And now, almost a decade later, amidst the most traumatic time of his life, the truth finally comes out. He can't help but wonder what else in his life is a lie too. He can't help but question everything Abby has ever said to him. He feels like a fraud of a man, a moron, like he should have seen it coming. He considers the timeline and thinks back to when it all began.

Kurt and Abby met by chance less than a dozen years ago. Kurt had been working at Mifflinburg Bank and Trust even at that time, although not as a vice president—he had been a personal financial advisor then, a mere stepping stone to his true ambition. Between his natural charisma and superior knowledge of all types of personal investments, clients flocked to him. One even labeled him a guru. His ability to manipulate the peaks and valleys of the market with the best of his peers in his field made him appealing to work with, and he was making money fast. Lots of it. His client base had been growing rapidly and his positive reputation was starting to gain some real traction in financial circles. He was well on his way to stardom in the community.

Then a young Abby Weston came into his life.

Abby was an outsider from Connecticut who had just moved into town and was looking to set up some personal accounts with a local bank in the area. She was a little rough around the edges—her hair was unwashed, her clothes old and faded—but she was friendly. And beautiful. She'd spent over an hour in the bank lobby waiting specifically for Kurt to help her, and when he'd asked her why, Abby had made her intentions very clear: she thought he was handsome. It was an easy way to grabs his attention and break the ice. And it worked. It made Kurt feel like a king.

Kurt and Abby began to date shortly thereafter. Abby's youthful bliss and infectious smile drew him in right away, and he was able to overlook the shortcomings of the first impression; he could see she was much more than a pretty girl without a sense of fashion. She was magnetic. Kurt quickly learned Abby's parents had died tragically in a car wreck in Connecticut in recent months and that she'd inherited a pretty hefty trust fund. She'd moved to Pennsylvania to get away from the memories of her parents back home, and Mifflinburg was simply a town chosen at random. The money she'd invested with Kurt seemed to confirm her story.

Less than a year later, Abby told Kurt she was pregnant. Despite her being barely old enough to drink, Kurt was rapidly approaching thirty and was ready to settle down. He was ecstatic. This was his chance, he'd thought, a sign from above that it was meant to be, so he decided to take the plunge. He never thought she'd go for it, with her being so young, but she said yes and they were married when she was seven months pregnant. With Kurt's career on the fast track to management and having enough money between his personal savings and investments and Abby's new trust fund, they put a down payment on a big house in the suburbs and moved in when baby Chloe was three months old.

Everything was perfect.

Abby stayed home with the baby while Kurt continued to grow his career, and everything was great. The arrangement had stayed the same for nine years, made easier by Kurt's promotion to bank manager and then eventually to vice president. Kurt had everything he'd ever wanted in life—a career he loved, a loving family, and the home of his dreams—and he couldn't have been happier.

Until two days ago, when everything changed.

Fast forward back to the present and Kurt can't figure out where things have gone wrong. He'd been genuinely happy and thought Abby was too. She'd told him as much. She insists she still is, but Kurt doesn't know what to believe anymore. He feels betrayed. He feels like an idiot for having rushed into marriage with a woman he barely knew.

But it's not that, he realizes. He's grown to learn everything about Abby, or so he thought, and he loves her even more because of it. They've fallen deeper into love over the years instead of going the other way after years of marriage; Kurt had thought that meant something.

Apparently, he was wrong. He'd thought the life they'd built together was beautiful. Storybook.

But he now suspects it's all been a lie.

***

Abby has lied to her husband again. She doesn't know why and it hadn't been her plan going into it, but the look on his face was heartbreaking. She couldn't go through with it.

Abby is curled up on the bed with her back facing the door, clutching onto a pillow. Its feathers resting against her belly help to soothe her and shield the growing baby from the mess of a life she's made. She doesn't know why she continues to make it worse, but she does. She's ashamed of herself. Her eyes are filled with tears of sorrow and regret because of it.

For some reason unbeknownst to even her, Abby never felt it would come down to this. While the last ten years of her life have been covered up and made to look like a fairy tale, she never actually thought she'd be exposed. Maybe she even convinced herself that by trying to forget about it and not talking about her past, it would just go away and disappear forever. For a long time, it did. Maybe she just hoped Scott would forget everything and let her live her life in peace. Now, looking back on the last ten years, Abby realizes how ignorant that sounds, how naïve. Scott had no choice but to do what he did; she gave him no other option.

Now what? Now that Abby has lied even more to her husband about the truth, she'll never be able to dig herself out of her predicament with her family intact. She'd told Kurt that Scott Baker is an ex-boyfriend who abducted Chloe as a way to get back at her.

That's a lie.

She'd admitted that Scott was the one who wrote her the note that Kurt found in her nightstand, but her reason for why he did it was a lie. She'd told Kurt that Scott used to hit her and that she ran out on him when her parents died so he wouldn't take the money from the trust fund she'd inherited. Kurt bought it. Kurt thinks this is about the money. Ransom.

All of that is a lie.

She'd told Kurt her reason for bringing Chloe's backpack with her when she left last night was to have a change of clothes in case she was able to convince Scott to let Chloe go. She and Scott had agreed to meet up to talk and reconcile their differences, after which he was to give back Chloe.

That, too, is a lie. Or at the very least, it's a major exaggeration.

After digging herself deeper and deeper into a labyrinth of interconnected lies, Abby left Kurt downstairs to soak it all in. Even now, as she digs the tips of her fingers into the pillow, feeling the soft feathers sink deeper into her belly, she knows it's only going to get worse from here. Not only has she still not told Kurt he's going to be a father, but she still hasn't told him that other thing, either. Aside from the fact it might kill him and completely shatter his life into a million pieces, Abby knows it might be unforgivable. If she were in his shoes, she's not sure she could forgive herself. She can't even now, from the other side of it. She wouldn't blame him if he just up and left and never came back. She wouldn't blame him if he hated her. And to think there's still more to come—Kurt knows very little about the first twenty-one years of her life before they got together, and much of that isn't factual either.

Abby's darkest secret of all might just be the final straw that makes him leave for good. Or maybe he's already going to—she doesn't know. Abby doesn't know what he's thinking. She doesn't dare even ask. The truth, whenever it's revealed, will twist the knife even deeper and make the wounds bleed just a little bit more than they already are. The pain will be unrelenting.

***

Downstairs, Kurt's phone buzzes on the glass top of the coffee table, breaking his concentration. He sits up on the sofa and welcomes the distraction—anything to get his mind off the stranger upstairs. He recognizes the face of the caller right away—his smile wide and bright, his hair combed and slicked, his necktie tight and evenly centered with the split in his collar. Kurt picks up the phone.

"Hey, Wesley."

"Kurt," Mayor Thomas says, "have you seen the newspaper this morning? Please tell me you have an explanation."

"Things have been a little busy around here, Wesley. I haven't had time to read the paper."

"Well, you damn well better find the time. Your wife is on the front page snooping around thirty miles north of here. What the hell is going on?"

Kurt pulls the phone away from his face and scratches his head, hard, with his fingernails. Things are going from bad to worse. "I think I know what that's about."

"Good, I'll be over in an hour so we can talk about it. We have to kill this, Kurt. This could be devastating."

"No, you can't come over. I'm sorry."

"Why not?" Mayor Thomas is taken aback, maybe a little hurt, the spike in his voice expressing that.

Kurt pauses for a long while before finding the courage to admit the truth. "Wesley, something happened last night between me and Abby."

"Is everything okay?"

"Can I talk to you—as a friend? I need you to take off your politician's hat for a minute. Can you do that?"

"What happened?"

Kurt takes a deep breath, holds it for a few seconds, and pushes it out with a loud burst. Then he proceeds to tell his friend everything Abby has told him—all the lies. He starts where he thinks the beginning is.

CHAPTER TWENTY-SEVEN

Before Jordan knows it, the alarm on the production floor sounds, the conveyors stop, the machines power down, and the roughnecks clear the shop. Lunch time. Jordan joins the line at the punch clock, then at the sink. The men take turns scrubbing their hands and forearms, then cut through the side door to retrieve their lunchboxes and brown paper bags from the kitchen. Some men are thrilled with the leftovers their wives have packed them, while others mumble obscenities under their breath. A few poke fun at their neighbors.

The whole scene is very routine. Long tables line the exterior wall, parallel to one another. Each clique of workers occupies their usual tables while a separate group blows cigarette smoke into one another's faces just outside the door. Most of the conversation is hushed and isn't much more than a murmur. In many ways, the lunch room reminds Jordan a lot of prison. Aside from the lack of a serving assembly line and the plastic trays, it's all very familiar.

By the time his turn comes up to retrieve his lunch from the back of the refrigerator, Jordan finally feels the hunger beginning to form in his stomach. He's been distracted all day, thinking about Abby Janis and who she's become. He fingers through the moldy containers and pushes a carton of spoiled milk to the side. He quickly learns he forgot his lunch. It must have been the revelation he had this morning that distracted him.

The guy behind him in line grunts a bit at the amount of time Jordan is taking, so Jordan steps to the side and lets him pass. The oversized clock hanging above the doorway tells Jordan he has twenty-five minutes left of his thirty minute block for lunch. Without traffic, Jordan can make it back to the trailer in eight minutes, or twelve with traffic. If he hurries and leaves now, he should be able to go home, put together something quick to eat, and scoff it down on the ride back. He heads for the truck.

Jordan has to hurry. Despite being permitted to leave for lunch and being paid more than a nickel an hour, the regime in the blue-collar sweatshop is just as authoritarian as it was in prison. If someone punches in even a single minute past the scheduled time or if their lunch is more than the thirty minutes, people are written up. Three strikes and you're out; it's pretty simple.

Jordan cracks the windows and lets the gusts of fresh air fill the cabin of the truck. The stuffiness of the heat on the production floor suffocates him during the day, so the freshness is welcome. His back sticks to the torn cloth of the seat, so he removes his work shirt to allow himself some relief. The armpits of the white t-shirt underneath are stained with sweat, and there are holes covering where the neckline used to be.

Jordan hasn't stopped thinking about Abby Janis all day. He's trying to figure out what this all means—her missing daughter and if there's any link to her previous life. He's not sure of Scott Baker's status—whether he's still in prison or if he's been released but the thought of this being revenge for Abby ratting him out does cross Jordan's mind. It seems like a plausible explanation.

How about the girl? How about Chloe? What a nightmare this is for her. She's just the victim of being in the wrong place at the wrong time. She's being used as leverage for whatever game Abby's up to this time. What a disgrace. The biggest problem Chloe has is that she was born to the wrong mother, that's all. None of this is her fault. Jordan hopes she knows that.

But Jordan knows none of this to be factual—it's merely speculation on his part. Maybe it's shortsighted, or maybe it's unfair to Scott Baker. Maybe Scott has nothing to do with this at all—that's a real possibility too. In spite of everything, and as much as it pains Jordan to think it, he can't help but feel like Abby got what she deserved in the end. As far as Jordan knows, she never went to prison for all he'd heard her confess to through that wall, while Scott did. That just doesn't seem fair. And while Chloe has been unfairly thrown into her mother's web of deception and lies, it's really Abby—or Courtney, Jordan's struggling to decide what he should call her who deserves this. Karma, after all, spares no one.

In his rearview mirror, something catches Jordan's attention. His first instinct is that it's an animal. When he takes a second look, he sees nothing. No animal. But then he hears something. It's only faint, but it sounds like someone screaming. A kid maybe. With no one on the road but himself, Jordan slowly taps the brakes until the thinning pads bring the truck to a stop in the middle of the road, the rust clunking underneath. He listens for the sound of the scream again once the squealing from the brakes dies down. It takes a moment, but the sound does eventually return. It's definitely a kid screaming, he concludes, but he can't make out what they're saying. The voice doesn't sound distressed.

With no one behind him, Jordan jams the ignition into gear and reverses his direction back down the street. Another minute ticks away on the clock, bringing him that much closer to receiving his second strike—the first came when he was late after he couldn't find the building on his first day. He stops the truck again and listens.

He waits.

Another minute passes. The voice doesn't return. Jordan shrugs. Realizing his little detour might be the difference between being down in the count and still having two strikes to spare, Jordan continues back toward home. He doesn't get very far before he's interrupted again. In the woods on the side of the road, he sees some shuffling of branches. There's not a lick of wind, which tells him something looms behind the trees. Expecting a wolf or a coyote or the like, he grips the steering wheel extra tightly in case he has to floor it. A healthy wild animal shouldn't be wandering the streets at this time of day.

The shuffling worsens and Jordan's adrenaline heightens. The anticipation is a thrill, not knowing what might be on the other side. Maybe it's a Sasquatch. Then, just like a Jack-in-the-box popping out in surprise when least expected, something emerges from behind the trees. Jordan freezes. It's not a wolf or a coyote and any other disease-ridden wild animal.

It's a person. A child. A girl. And she's holding something in her arms.

When she looks up and meets Jordan's eyes, he can see the fear. It takes him just a moment to recognize her face, and when he does, he becomes short of breath. His head spins and all he can see is stars. He can't believe who it is. It doesn't even seem possible. He has better odds of winning the Powerball.

***

Chloe is rapidly approaching defeat. Without a watch or a cell phone to tell her the time, she doesn't have any idea how long she's been in the woods. She's starting to get restless.

A single car sped by where Chloe and Benny sit maybe an hour ago, but besides that, she's seen no one. It was moving much too fast for her to slow it down. Chloe wants to keep moving through the woods with the hope of stumbling upon a gas station or an idle vehicle, but something in her heart tells her not to. It seems crazy—to not keep moving—but maybe it's the hope telling her somebody might come by and rescue her. Or maybe it's the lack of hope telling her she's on the deadest road in the history of mankind and that there's zero chance of someone driving by. She wonders if her own thoughts are trying to sabotage her.

Benny serves as a calming device. Just as the tears of frustration start to well up in Chloe's eyes, she turns to Benny for comfort. Not being bothered by the elements and not understanding the circumstances, Benny is fast asleep at Chloe's feet. He seems to have recovered from his earlier distress, which Chloe is thankful for. His little paws are crossed to keep his chin from lying in the dirt, his tongue just barely contained in his mouth. His golden coat moves with the rhythm of his gentle breathing. Chloe can feel his tranquility as he snoozes, and it motivates her. Benny's going to be alright, and she will be too.

She doesn't want to wake Benny, but she has to do something. They have to start moving again. They have to find help before dark. A distant hum somewhere out past the trees grabs Chloe's attention. Something flutters in her belly, and she suspects it might be that hope thing again. She gets to her feet, loosely holding the leash in her hand, and puts her ear to the sky. It sounds like a swarm of a thousand bees buzzing as one. The sound is getting closer. And louder. Then she recognizes it.

It's the sound of tires on gravel; someone is coming.

Chloe starts to freak out. In a hurry, she stumbles around, trying to find her footing and a clearing to the road. The leash is ripped from her hand as she gets stuck in between a couple of oversized tree limbs, and she reaches back for it. Benny doesn't even stir at the commotion. She lets it go and pushes toward the road. Large tree limbs threaten to trip her. A smaller one whacks her in the face while a prickly bush claws at her ankles. She pushes the stinging pain aside and moves forward. She has to stop the vehicle.

A red truck screams past just as she finally reaches the dirt of the road, her breath heavy. The thorn stuck in her flesh aches, but she ignores it. The only thing she can think to do to capture the truck's attention is to yell out after it. So she does, as loud as she can. So loud that her larynx burns and her voice cracks. But it works.

The truck slows and eventually stops.

A heap of joy heals her wounds, and she jumps up and down, waving her arms above her head. She continues to yell out toward the truck so it doesn't leave. In doing so, the brake lights illuminate and the truck starts moving back toward her. Chloe acts quickly. She gathers the sense to rush back into the woods to scoop up Benny. She hates to wake him, but it's now or never. Before the truck goes away.

Benny grunts a little and tries to roll over onto his back to expose his belly, but Chloe doesn't have time to wait for the cuteness to pass. She can see the outline of the truck through the trees—it's right there waiting for her. She bends down, picks Benny up in both arms, the end of the leash, and shields his face as she scurries back out of the woods. Her heart is thumping in her chest as she crawls underneath the branch that whacked her before. She's scared to death that the truck is going to leave and she'll be stuck in these woods forever if she doesn't hurry. The handle of the leash drags behind her and tugs on some branches, but it doesn't provide enough resistance to stop her momentum. With a final thrust through the brush, Chloe pops out of the woods, Benny still secured in her arms, and stares right into the face of the man with the red truck.

The man has a look of astonishment on his face, his mouth open, his eyes wide. Chloe can see how tightly the man is gripping the steering wheel, and the look bothers her. She fears he may just take off and leave her alone again. Or worse. The look doesn't disappear from his face, either. It's like he's staring directly into the eyes of a ghost. Chloe is that ghost, she realizes, except she's very much alive.

***

It's her. It's the girl from TV, the girl that drove Jordan mad for two days as he tried to figure out where he knew her from. It's Abby's daughter. It's Chloe Janis. She's standing just feet from him, her eyes locked on his through the open window, looking terrified.

"Hi," Jordan says, a little awestruck. "Are you okay?"

Chloe doesn't respond right away. She just stares back at Jordan, dumfounded. Jordan is struck by how beautiful she is in person. Despite the obvious signs of stress and exhaustion on her face—the streak of dirt on her forehead, the grass stain on her cheek, the sleepiness in her eyes—Jordan can see the natural beauty she has. He sees a miniature version of Abby. Minus the difference in hair color—blonde for Abby and brunette for Chloe—they're carbon copies of one another. Except Chloe is twenty years younger and two feet shorter.

"Are you hurt?" Jordan tries.

Chloe shakes her head.

Sweat starts to saturate Jordan's pores. He wipes his brow with his wrist to eliminate the wetness and to give himself time to think. "Are you lost?"

Chloe pauses for a second, then she shakes her head again.

"What's your name?" he says, trying to get her to actually say something.

"Chloe," she mumbles.

Jordan nods. The confirmation makes his heart beat even faster, although he already knew it was her. He leans across the seat and wraps his fingers around the passenger side door handle and pulls. The door slides open, and Jordan looks back to Chloe. She hasn't moved at all.

***

Chloe stares at the strange man as he leans across the seat and opens the door to the rusted truck. The rust is so bad that she almost expects the door to fall right onto the ground as it opens. It doesn't. The man looks at Chloe and offers a gentle smile through the now open door. Chloe can't tell if he's trying to be nice or if he's just another one of those creeps who's looking for his next victim.

"I've seen you on the news," the man confesses. "Your parents are really worried about you."

Chloe's mouth drops open. She had no idea she'd been in the news. It's like she's a celebrity. A burst of joy rushes through her body, and she can almost feel the warmth of her dad's strong arms wrapped around her. The whiff of her mom's exotic perfume tickles her nose, flooding her eyes with water. She's going to be home soon, she just knows it.

"My name's Jordan," the man says. "I'm not going to hurt you."

Jordan seems genuine and harmless, although Chloe is still a little unsure if she should trust him or not. The memories from what happened at the mall are still fresh. Really fresh. Although she does have a sliver of doubt about Jordan's intentions, the thought of Scott coming back and forcing her to go back with him sends a chill down her spine. He'd take her away and she'd never see her parents again. If she goes with Jordan, maybe she has a chance.

"Can you bring me home?" Chloe asks. "I'm not sure where I am."

"I can bring you to the police station," Jordan says. "It's not far from here. I'm not sure about the rules on what I'm supposed to do, so I think it'll be better if the police handle it. They'll call your parents. Will that be okay?"

Chloe hesitates for a second, just to make sure. Then, without responding, she nods and walks toward the partially open door, opens it all the way, and climbs inside the truck. A waft of sweaty baseball hat hits her nose, causing her to gag. Benny starts to stir as he reacts to the sound of Chloe closing the door.

***

Scott has been driving around all morning. He's driven up and down the same dirt roads with wooden fences, the same strips of pavement that are shaded by overhanging trees, and the same sections of grassy neighborhoods. He hasn't seen Chloe or the dog. This will be his last pass through. He's long past discouraged. Hope is all but lost.

Adjacent to the two-lane highway that would lead Scott into town and back toward Mifflinburg is a semi-private dirt road. The road has no street lights and doesn't have the infrastructure to support dump trucks or tractor trailers. It tends to get washed out with regularity during the rainy spring months and it's one of the last roads to get plowed during snowstorms. There's not much over there besides a couple of trailer parks at the end and an abandoned pizza joint that at one time used to be the hottest place in town. It's been closed for four or five years now.

Scott has never been on that road before. Diane had told him about it when he was first released from prison and she was driving him around town, showing him all of the places he'd need, but she never brought him over there. Unless you live in one of the trailer parks, she'd said, there's no need to ever go over there. It's the one place Scott hasn't checked. He heads in that direction, hoping for a miracle.

Potholes cover the dirt like someone's been digging for buried treasure. Despite it not having rained in over a week, the road is still all washed out. Scott now understands why no one comes over this way if they don't have to—it's just not worth the effort to put their car through it. He does his best to follow the tire tracks that weave through both sides of the street, but they're so faint at times that he has to make up his own route. He'd always thought the road leading to his mother's cabin was bad with the exposed tree roots and branches laying everywhere, but this is worse. Way worse.

A good distance up ahead of him, Scott spots a truck. The brick red color stands out amongst the mostly dull browns and tans that cover the ground and surrounding trees. As Scott approaches, he notices the truck is stopped and the passenger side door is open. He wonders if it's broken down. But then he sees a child who appears to be standing next to it. Scott pulls off to the side of the road and watches for a moment. He has a bad feeling about this; something about the scene doesn't smell right. Missing his binoculars that are still in his mother's station wagon, Scott squints to try to get a better look, but it doesn't help. He sits back and waits to see what happens.

Scott can only speculate about what's going on up ahead of him, but the combination of the appearance of that truck—old, decrepit, and predatorily idling—and being so close to the trailer parks gives him an uneasy feeling.

What if that's Chloe up there? What if it's not?

He quickly realizes, though, that he can't do anything about it either way. If it is Chloe up there, he can't approach the truck and rescue her because she'll never go with him. Worse, she'll probably tell the other guy that he'd abducted her and he'll call the cops. On the other hand, if it's not Chloe, it's almost worse. What is he going to do, call the police and tell them he's witnessed an abduction? So, what, the cops can knock on everyone's door in the area and ask if they've seen something? His mother's cabin is only a mile and a half from here, of course they'll knock. Then what? That's too many law enforcement officers too close to home. There's no way this can't end badly for Scott.

Scott can't help but feel like a hypocrite. The blood in his veins is starting to warm as he can feel himself getting angry. It's just another innocent girl becoming prey to a grown man who can't control his urges. It's sickening. The irony, of course, is that Scott has done the same thing. His motives are very different from this guy's, mind you, but he's still taken a girl. He's no better than the men he hates so much—the ones who poach on innocent children. Sadly, this is the first time he realizes that. A sharp pain suddenly forms in his stomach.

The little girl up ahead gets into the man's truck. Scott clenches his teeth together, grinding them, wanting to help. But for fear of being caught, he can do nothing. He feels helpless. Then something unexpected happens. The truck's reverse lights shine and it makes a three-point turn in the street. Frantic, Scott looks around the rental for a distraction while the truck makes its way directly toward him, picking up speed. Inside the glove box, he finds the paperwork from the rental agency, so he grabs that and holds it up to his face, pretending to read through it. The thought is that he'll look like a lost tourist with a map and the out of state plates. That'll enable him plenty of time to take a quick peek inside the cab of the truck as it passes by.

As the truck approaches, Scott's hands tremble, struggling to steady the paperwork. He looks up as the truck passes, its engine clunking, its suspension grinding. Time seems to move in slow motion as Scott shifts his eyes from the papers to the truck. He meets the eyes of the driver briefly, not recognizing the man, then he switches his attention to the passenger. It's a girl. She doesn't look over at him, but the long dark hair and feminine features makes it obvious.

Then he sees it.

The driver of the truck shifts forward slightly, leaving a gap between his back and the cloth seat of the cab. Through the gap, Scott sees the same t-shirt Chloe's been wearing for the last couple of days, the same graphic, the same shade of purple. He recognizes it immediately. Scott grips the steering wheel angrily, smacking the top of it until his hand hurts. To make matters worse, as the truck pulls further away, the barking of a puppy echoes through the air. Scott shakes his head in angst, recognizing it as Benny's.

She's gone.

The anger quickly changes to trepidation. Scott takes a minute to consider his options. The truck turning around probably means the driver is bringing Chloe back into town to get some help. That's good, of course, considering what Scott had thought the motive to be. But this also means Chloe is going to tell the police everything that's happened and will give a full description of Scott. He drops his head.

It's official now, he's failed. It's over.

But Scott's not about to give up that easily. He sees a way out of this. The likelihood it'll work is slim at best, but what it might do is create enough confusion to buy him some time to get out of town. They'll eventually put it all together and come after him and his mother, so this is the only thing he can do. He grabs his mother's phone from the center console, dials the number, and puts it up to his ear.

A woman picks up before the first ring even finishes. "911," she says, "what's your emergency?"

"Hi," Scott says, trying to sound authentic. "I've just spotted the missing girl from TV."

"You mean the missing girl? Chloe Janis?"

"That's right."

There's some shuffling on the other end of the phone. The emergency dispatcher is almost giddy. "Where are you?"

Scott gives his location, a fake name, a description of the red truck with the partial license plate number he was able to grab, and a brief description of what he saw of the driver. Then he hangs up and removes the battery from the phone before the police have a chance to trace where the call came from. He turns the car around and speeds toward the cabin.

CHAPTER TWENTY-EIGHT

The morning comes and goes without a hitch. Other detectives, police officers, and investigators pile into the office and get busy with their cases, files, and reports. Hank sits uncomfortably in the back corner, his skin itching, just waiting for someone to give him a smug look of disapproval. No one does. No one says anything to him. The stack of newspapers is still under his desk and taking up his foot space. Him taking them all must have worked—maybe no one saw the article. He pushes them as far back as he can with his foot and tries to relax.

The fax Hank has been expecting from the Connecticut State Police still hasn't arrived. That worries him. It could just be a matter of the information being compiled together, or maybe they got caught up in something else. But still, he was told a team would be working on Abby Janis's case through the night, so that part does make him curious. There must be something big that's making it take so long.

In the cubical next to him, Melanie works vigilantly to handle the press. The phone has been ringing almost non-stop since she arrived at the office, with reporters wanting a comment on the article in today's paper. Hank has only been partially listening to her responses, but he's been satisfied with how she's handling it so far. He can see her growing right in front of his eyes. He's proud of her for stepping up. Although it's difficult to tell for certain, he's pretty sure she's hung up on at least two or three different callers so far. He loves that about her. She gives the aura of being soft-spoken, understanding, and sympathetic to the victims, but she can be a bulldog when she has to. She must have sensed Hank's urgency and desperation this morning because she's handling the situation exactly the way she should. She's showing Hank what kind of professional she is and making it a lot easier for Hank to recommend her for lead detective once he retires, which she doesn't know about yet.

The phone calls finally start winding down shortly before noon. Melanie looks exhausted. Bags of stress are starting to show under her eyes and the back of her neck is covered with a greasy perspiration, which is leaving streaks on the leather chair. She doesn't smoke, but she looks like she could really use a cigarette right about now. She pushes her back into the chair and exhales.

"You did good, Chase," Hank says, looking at her.

Melanie offers a half-nod and smirks. "Not done yet," she says. "We still have to find Chloe."

Hank nods. "You're right, but you took care of that for me when you could have told me to screw off. It was my mess, so thank you for that."

"Partners, right? You'd do the same for me."

Hank nods again and looks back down to his work. She's right, he would.

"What about you?" Melanie continues. "What have you found out so far today?"

Hank sighs and looks back up and faces Melanie. "Not much of anything. Kurt Janis is as clean as a whistle."

"That's good, though, right?"

"I guess so. Doesn't really help us right now, though."

"What about Connecticut?"

"Still waiting."

"Still?"

Hank nods.

"Any other leads?" Melanie asks.

"Not one. The only people who've called this office are those reporters. Not a damn soul has seen or heard anything since Saturday. It's like she vanished." Hank suddenly has a flashback to the Corey case and the similarities of how he felt then to how he feels now. The same sense of failure and loss of hope is rapidly entering his mind. His throat is suddenly parched.

Melanie says nothing.

A few minutes later, after a drought of silence between them, the fax machine rings. Hank's eyes widen with anticipation and he pops up from his seat like a spring. Melanie, too, is awakened from a trance. Hank is hopeful this will give them, at least, an avenue to pursue, even if his suspicion about Abby isn't quite what it seems. At the end of the day, it's not about Abby, it's about Chloe. And if the information from Connecticut helps them bring Chloe home, it'll all be worth it. He hopes for the best but prepares for the worst as he rushes over to the fax machine.

The header for the Connecticut State Police comes out first, followed by a page and a half of tiny text and a couple of grainy graphics. Hank feels like an excited kid, anxiously awaiting the results. He scans the details quickly, then he rereads certain sections with concentrated precision. When finished, he looks up to Melanie and grins.

"And?" Melanie says.

"I think we need to get Abby Janis on the phone and get her down here," Hank says. "We need to find out what she knows about where her daughter is."

***

Jordan's truck rumbles down route 44, the engine sputtering, the metal vibrating. The combination of having the missing girl from TV sitting beside him and having the dog she's holding barking at him has gotten Jordan's heart thumping. Everything has happened so fast. And the fact that Chloe is Abby's daughter makes it even wilder. It is a small world, after all.

To try to ease in and make the dog feel comfortable and unthreatened, Jordan slowly offers his hand to it, keeping it below its head. With his palm up, he offers encouragement to the dog and lets it approach at its own pace. It's timid at first, but it does eventually stop barking long enough to take a whiff of Jordan's hand, its wet nose tickling Jordan's skin. It doesn't take long for it to lick his hand, then nibble on his fingers playfully. Jordan breathes a sigh of relief when the tension drifts out the still open windows and the barking vanishes for good. Chloe sits motionless.

"What's her name?" Jordan asks, now smiling, one hand on the wheel, the other being saturated with saliva.

"He," Chloe says.

"Oh, sorry. What's his name?"

"Benny."

Jordan nods, keeping his eyes on the road. "That's a nice name. Did you name him?"

Chloe doesn't answer.

Silence fills the cabin.

Jordan clears his throat. It doesn't feel like the best timing, but he wants to lighten the mood. He doesn't want Chloe to be frightened of him. "I know this might sound strange," he says, partly chuckling, "but I know your mother, you know. We used to be neighbors many years ago. Long before you were born."

Chloe's eyes widen like she's seen a ghost. Her grip tightens on Benny's collar and she pushes herself further away from Jordan. Her back is practically against the door.

Jordan looks ahead. He's not sure what he's said that's caused this reaction out of Chloe, but he decides he needs to keep his mouth shut. If he's not careful, she might try to run. She could open the door and run into the woods at the next stoplight, or she could try to signal another driver that she's in danger. Jordan is walking a fine line here. He needs to get her to the police station, give his statement, and call his parole officer. The last thing he wants to do is break the terms of his probation while trying to do the right thing.

Just as the worst-case scenarios run through his mind, police sirens sound from somewhere behind the truck. Jordan peeks in the rearview mirror but sees nothing—just open road. He brushes it off. But then the sirens get closer as if approaching from the rear. Switching his eyes between the road in front of him and the mirror to see what's approaching from behind, a single police car finally comes into view. Jordan pulls off to the side of the road, watches in the mirror, and waits for the car to pass.

Except it doesn't pass.

It pulls right up behind him and stops. Just moments later, a second squad car appears from the front, then another. They all leave their sirens on, their reds and blues swirling, the sound deafening. The three cars box him in—the fourth side being the woods on his right. He tightens his grip around the steering wheel and flexes the muscles in his arms. He's trapped, and he's not sure why.

His first instinct is fear. Why is he being boxed in? What has he done wrong? These officers must have the wrong impression. Jordan's second instinct is joy, relief. He doesn't carry a cell phone, so he's been unable to call someone and tell them he's found the missing girl. And now that the police have found him, he can tell them what happened. Jordan actually smiles—he's relieved the police can take Chloe off his hands and bring her back to her parents. Now, without a doubt, Chloe will be safe. Jordan looks over to Chloe to gauge her reaction—she's frozen, trembling, squeezing onto that dog's collar like her life depends on it.

Through a megaphone, a deep and intimidating voice demands Jordan to get out of the vehicle with his hands up, so he does. Benny's barking is drowned out by the sirens and the commotion of the police hollering and preparing their weapons from behind opened car doors. The sight of the guns sends a chill down Jordan's spine, forcing goosebumps out of his skin.

What's happening?

Continuing to follow instructions, Jordan places his hands above his head, slowly drops to his knees, and waits for his wrists to be twisted into cuffs. It doesn't take long, and neither does it for his chest and face to get slammed into the ground. Not expecting it, he gets a mouthful of sandy soil, his front teeth jamming into a small rock. A jolt of pain rushes through his mouth as if on fire, and he screams. The more he screams and writhes in pain, the harder the pressure is on his back. It takes until the pain passes and Jordan relaxes that he realizes he's being sat on, with a knee being the cause of the pressure on his back.

"We got the scumbag," one of the officers says. "And the girl is with him. Appears to be unharmed."

Jordan is pulled up to his feet by his wrists and finally gets a chance to spit out the dirt. The pebbles stick to his tongue and fall into the pits of his blackened teeth like daggers. It's like he's chewing on a wedge of chalk. From the backseat of one of the cruisers, he watches as Chloe and Benny are quickly ushered toward a different vehicle, the transporting officer staying low and covering his head. Jordan looks up, expecting a helicopter, but doesn't see one. Only clouds accompany the sun in the sky.

Once Chloe and Benny are secured in a different cruiser, the group of cops gather in a circle and shake hands, peeking in Jordan's direction periodically. The way their eyes stare at him like he's a monster makes him uneasy. They seem to seethe at the sight of him.

And then, for the first time, the realization of the entire situation finally hits him. How did they even know he had Chloe? And why have they been treating him this way? What if they think he was the one who abducted her? Jordan can't help but assume someone saw him pick her up and got the wrong idea—maybe it was that lost tourist he passed on the way out. It must have been, he decides, since he saw no one else.

A combination of anxiety and terror fill up Jordan's belly. He needs to tell these officers what happened before they draw the wrong conclusion about the situation. He yells out to the group of officers, banging his forehead on the glass, hoping one of them will pay attention to him. But none of them do. They all ignore him.

Jordan's throat fills up with bile and his vision blurs. Everything starts to spin. He thinks he might pass out.

He can't believe this is happening. As the cops break their huddle and head over to Jordan's truck, he knows something bad is happening. While this situation began as a coincidence—a miraculous one, at that—it's quickly turned into something a whole lot more serious. It's gotten out of hand. And Jordan knows, as the officers begin to tear through his truck like he has something to hide, that if he doesn't get the chance to tell his side of the story soon, it might be too late.

CHAPTER TWENTY-NINE

Kurt feels better for having confided in someone about what he's going through, although he's not sure he has any more answers about where to go from here. Although supportive and understanding of the situation as a friend, Wesley had made it clear that Kurt needs to bury this. If the press gets ahold of this information, their campaign is over. Nobody will vote for someone who's married to a liar.

But Kurt doesn't care about the campaign. His one and only aspiration is to get his daughter back—it always has been. Sometimes Wesley can be so insensitive and selfish, and quite frankly, Kurt is tired of it. Abby was right—Wesley is not Kurt's friend; this just proves it. But Kurt brushes it aside for now. He has more pressing matters to deal with. His insides are twisting in knots just thinking about it.

Kurt heads upstairs to find his wife. He hasn't heard a peep from her all morning since their second talk—this one had provided him with more details than the one last night, but he feels no better about things—and he wonders if she's up to no good again. He can't help but wonder if she's reached out to Scott Baker. Kurt suspects she's still hiding something. He can tell her heart aches when she talks about him. She shouldn't have reacted the way she did when talking about an ex-boyfriend from fifteen years ago—all the tears, all the angst, all the pain in her voice. And why Scott would go after Chloe makes no sense, even with Abby's half-hearted way of shrugging it off. Kurt has a deep suspicion something more sinister is going on. He wonders if Abby's still in love with the guy.

Kurt stops outside the bedroom door and places his ear to the cold wood. He hears nothing, just silence. He holds his position for a second, holds his breath, and wraps his fingers around the door handle, pushing into the bedroom. Now it's his turn to get some answers, on his terms.

Abby is asleep on top of the bed. A hand is covering her belly and the other is under her head, making a pillow. She's fully dressed. Kurt walks around the bed and next to her, keeping his eyes locked on her. Her breaths are shallow but smooth, and the rhythm of her soft exhales is real.

She looks so peaceful, so free, like a burden has been lifted off her shoulders. And maybe it has. As much as Kurt's head is in a whirlwind, he tries to put himself in Abby's shoes for a moment. She's been hiding everything from him for so long, and she probably felt like she couldn't say anything. She probably felt threatened that Scott might do something to harm her. Kurt tries to be sympathetic, but it's difficult. It's because of Abby that Chloe is still missing—he realizes that now—and that's not something he can look past very easily. But he decides, as he watches her sleep, they'll get through this together—him and her, as husband and wife, mother and father. After they bring Chloe home and get everything sorted out, then they can have an honest discussion about where to go from here. Kurt's not sure he can ever trust her again.

Abby's body stiffens as she jerks awake unexpectedly. Either a nightmare has filled her dreams or she's startled by the presence of her husband. Kurt puts a hand on her shoulder and massages it with his thumb, not wanting her to be frightened.

"Hey," Kurt says in the gentlest tone he can. He tries to smile, but he's not sure it happens.

Abby says nothing. She scoots toward the headboard and pushes herself up, breathing heavily. Her eyes are sunken and swollen, and it's clear she'd cried herself to sleep.

"I've been thinking," Kurt says, "and I'm prepared to move everything between us to the side until after we find Chloe. Together. When she comes home, she's going to expect to see both her mom and dad."

Abby swallows like her throat aches, then she nods. "Okay," is all she says.

Before Kurt can ask what the next steps are, the landline rings. The phone on his nightstand illuminates like an alarm going off, and he scoots off the bed and grabs it. He answers the phone and mostly listens and nods his head, saying only that he understands a few times when prompted. The call disconnects after only a minute, and Kurt sinks deeper down the sinkhole he's already in. Abby curious eyes are on him when he turns back to her.

"Who was that?" she asks.

"Detective Chase."

Abby's eyes light up with excitement. "Do they have some news?"

Kurt shakes his head. "No, but they need us to come down to the station immediately."

"Why?"

"She didn't give specifics. Just that they've found out some stuff about you and they need to talk to you right away."

Abby's face turns whiter than an albino. Her expression is of guilt and onus, and Kurt immediately knows there's more she hasn't told him. He shakes his head at her and wonders if it's ever going to end.

"What the hell is going on, Abby?" Kurt says, now pissed again. "What have you gotten us into?"

***

The fire behind the cabin has died out completely. Smoke still remains, but the flames have dissipated. Scott pulls up to the cabin and parks where his mother's station wagon usually would, the outside heat penetrating the rental. He sits in the quiet for a while. The smell of smoke seeps in through the air vents.

It's obvious now—Chloe is really gone. Permanently. By default, that means Abby is gone too, which means Scott has failed. Everything he's ever wanted, the only hope that got him through his time behind bars, is gone.

He spends some time reminiscing. He thinks back to how he and Abby first met, what they grew to become, the bond they had, how perfect of partners they were. Then he remembers when he first got locked up and all the visits she'd made early on, and how she eventually stopped coming. Then the letters stopped too. But he never thought she'd fall so far. He never thought she'd actually fall for him—for Kurt. That had never been part of the plan, nor did it cross his mind that it could actually happen. Despite all of it, he still doesn't think Abby wanted it to happen the way it did. He refuses to accept it.

Maybe Scott is just trying to give Abby the benefit of the doubt, or maybe he doesn't want to admit she may have played him. The more he thinks about it and considers all that's happened, the idea of her having set him up just doesn't seem plausible. No, something else must have happened along the way that made her change her mind. Scott should be pissed about it—he thinks even Abby would agree with that—but he's not. For some reason, he thinks he understands. Ten years gone is a long time. Combine that with the new life she's been given, and it'd be nearly impossible for someone to want to go back to how things were before. He wonders what he would've done if the situation had been reversed. He'll never know for sure, but now he's convinced he would have done the same thing. Maybe Abby deserves some slack.

Scott has an epiphany. He knows exactly what he has to do. Abby has made her choice. What he did to her and the way he scared Chloe was unfair. Although he and Diane did try to treat her like the princess she is, what he did was wrong. He shouldn't have taken her like that. There was another way; there had to have been. For the first time, he realizes that. He wishes he could tell Chloe how sorry he is.

There's only one thing he can do to give himself some closure. It's time to consider what Abby wants—or doesn't want. It's time for Scott to let her go. When you love someone, sometimes you have to let them go—this is one of those times. What's best for her and Chloe is to stay where they are and continue to live their lives away from Scott. Kurt Janis has built them a good life—a better life than Scott could have ever provided, admittedly. He knows that now. He'll learn to cope with that reality in time. Their unhappiness isn't worth his own fulfillment. He just hopes his mother will understand.

Satisfied with his newfound mindset, Scott finally steps out of the car. The smell of smoke is still heavy, but it's thinned out over the past few hours. The birds overhead don't seem to mind, as they fly in circles right through the haze. Scott makes his way toward the cabin and climbs up the stairs, which shift under his feet.

Inside, he finds his mother swaying slowly in the rocking chair in her bedroom. Her eyes are closed, but Scott can tell she's still awake by the way she continues to rock. He knocks on the doorframe with his knuckle to grab her attention without startling her. She opens her eyes and looks to him, then smiles. It's a smile, but it's weak. Sickly. Her skin is pale and her lips are dull and washed out. She looks alarmingly ill.

Scott doesn't say anything when he enters the room. He walks over to her and sits on the edge of the bed, keeping his eyes on hers as he does. He fears the heartbreak might literally kill her. But it has to be done, so he does it. He looks deep into his mother's eyes, past the pain, and tells her. "She's gone," he says. "Chloe's gone."

Diane nods. "I assumed that to be the case by now."

"But there's something else too." Scott waits for a reaction from his mother, but he gets none. "I'm going to surrender."

Diane closes her eyes and turns away. She puts a hand to her chest and makes a noise like she wants to say something, but no words come out. She can only muster up the energy to place a weak hand on Scott's knee and pat it twice.

She doesn't have to say anything—Scott knows. The gentle touch of his mother's hand—the same hand that fed him and raised him all those years ago—tells him all he needs to know. It tells him she'll be there for him no matter what and that she'll always support him. He can't help but wonder how much longer that'll actually be, though. She seems to worsen every day. But finally, and most importantly, Diane's gentle touch tells Scott that she knows he's doing the right thing. And that's all he needs to be completely at peace with his decision.

Scott takes his mother's hand and squeezes it. He feels like everything is about to come to an end. He makes the decision at this moment that he's not going to let go of her hand until the police physically pry it from his grip. He's made the choice to let Abby go, but he won't do the same for his mother. She's been there for him through thick and thin, through the good times and the bad. She's never wavered, not even once, and Scott knows he can never repay her for all she's done for him. All he can do is show her his appreciation.

Diane starts to cry, so Scott does too. Her cries sound painful and her tears look dry as they stick to her cheeks, and Scott can't imagine what she's going through. She leans her head toward him and rests it on his shoulder. Scott lays his head down on top of his mother's and they just sit there, their hands locked, for a long while. Her wrinkled skin feels like a prune, and that's a reminder of how deeply her heart has failed her. It's a reminder of how much her disease is controlling her life.

Scott closes his eyes and lets the tears stream down his face. He and Diane cry together for what he knows deep down will be the last time. He won't waste another moment away from her until he's dragged away in handcuffs.

CHAPTER THIRTY

Melanie hangs up with Kurt Janis and leans back in her chair for a breather. It's been a long and exhausting day already, and it's not even lunchtime. Something tells her that it's just beginning.

"How'd he take it?" Hank asks, referring to Kurt on the phone.

"Surprised, shocked, saddened. Pick a word," Melanie says.

"So, you don't think he has any idea? You think she hid this from him too?"

"Oh yeah. He sounded hurt, like he could have never expected it. I feel bad for the guy."

"I wouldn't go that far, Chase. It could just be an act. He might be just as bad as she is."

"Yeah, well, we'll see," Melanie concedes. Hank is right more than he's wrong, but she thinks he's wrong this time. There was something in Kurt's voice, a hint of despair maybe, that makes her feel the way she does. First his daughter and now his wife—the guy just can't seem to catch a break.

Melanie finally gets some quiet time while waiting for the Janis's to come into the station. Her coffee has gotten ice cold and the marshmallows have all but disintegrated, and she's in desperate need of a refill. In the breakroom, she pops in a new coconut flavored cup and waits for the brew to complete. When complete, she returns to her desk and drops some marshmallows in the fresh cup. Her mouth salivates as the steam of the coconut starts to melt the white cylinders of sugar that float on the surface like buoys. The aroma hits her nose like a freshly baked pie in her mother's kitchen during the holidays. She licks her lips, lifts the cup to her mouth, brings it toward her tongue, and is interrupted by a ringing phone before she can indulge. She stares at the phone, disgusted. "Really?" she says aloud, wanting to take two seconds to herself to satisfy her desires.

"What is it?" Hank asks from his desk.

"This goddamn phone just won't stop today," Melanie says. She doesn't recognize the number on the caller ID, so she assumes it's yet another reporter.

"Want me to get it?" Hank offers.

Melanie waves him off and answers the phone. "What?" she says, then she just listens while the man on the other end tells her what's going on. Her mouth quickly dries out and a stampede of emotions begins inside of her chest. The thrill of the chase never gets old, but the satisfaction of the capture is even better. She thanks the man on the phone and finally lets out a breath.

"Who was it?" Hank asks without looking up.

"That was the Montgomery Police Department."

"Who the hell is that?"

"They're about twenty-five miles north of here, close to the Tiadaghton State Forest."

"What do they want?"

"Two deputies are on their way here now."

Hank looks up. "We don't need their help. We've got this under control. Call them back and tell them to turn around."

"That was my reaction at first. Then they said why."

"And that is?"

Melanie pauses and tries to find the right words without smiling too widely. "They have Chloe and her captor, and they're bringing them both to us."

***

Jordan sits in the back of the police car and just listens. The sweat under his arms is heavy in the pits of his t-shirt, and he can feel the shirt weighing him down. The officer in the front radios into dispatch and tells them he's going to personally drive the perpetrator to Mifflinburg. It makes Jordan wince. Perpetrator? How can he be a perpetrator? He's done nothing wrong. If only they gave him a chance to tell his side of the story, they'd realize they're making a terrible mistake. Jordan's palms suddenly moisten behind his back. And of course, since he can't address it, his entire body begins to itch.

The officer drives toward Mifflinburg without making a peep. He doesn't even peer in his mirror and acknowledge Jordan when he asks a question. It's like Jordan's alone in the car. He feels isolated, quarantined, and he doesn't understand what's happening.

Everything is a blur. Throughout the chaos of stumbling across Chloe and being accused of being her kidnapper, Jordan had completely forgotten why he's even here in the first place. If only he hadn't forgotten his lunch this morning, none of this would be happening. Chloe might still be in the woods, lost and afraid and hoping someone might come along and rescue her. Visions of Chloe and Abby Janis and Scott Baker run through his mind in a flash. He still doesn't know how all the pieces fit together, if they even do at all. And the way things are going, he may never get the answers he seeks. The crawlers underneath his skin worsen with the stress.

Like a bolt of lightning coming out of nowhere during a dry thunderstorm, Jordan is suddenly hit with a realization. Not only does he have to find a way to get out of this mess without going back to prison, but his new life as he knows it might be over. With him being late back from lunch now, he's up to two strikes at the factory. Add an automatic third strike for not calling and not showing up at all, and he's out. Fired. Everything he's worked so hard to maintain—even though he despises the work like no other—is gone. Mindy will never be able to afford the double-wide on her income alone, so that'll be taken by the bank before long too. And there's no telling what might happen to their relationship because of it all.

Jordan drops his head. The frustration he feels has surpassed all other emotions now, and it's by a wide margin. After all the hard work he's put in to get his life back in order and pay his dues to society for his wrongdoings, it might all be ruined by a simple act of kindness. He could have just left the girl there. And now, as he sees how it's ruining his own life, he thinks maybe he should have.

CHAPTER THIRTY-ONE

Melanie is with Hank, standing by the entrance to the police station, both with their arms crossed, waiting for the arrival of Chloe Janis and their mystery man. Hank has a scowl on his face as a way to get himself in the mood for an intense interrogation. Melanie, on the other hand, is trying to calm her nerves so she can get into the mind of a nine-year-old girl. Their roles are clearly defined.

Melanie is anxious. She can't place the root cause of her anxiety, but her intuition tells her this might be her big chance to shine. She's always taken a backseat to Hank, maybe rightfully so, considering how badly he trumps her in experience. But he's coming to the end of the line in terms of his career. Admittedly, she hasn't thought too much about it until now. Six months is not a long time in the police world, and that'll go by in an instant. She'll have a new partner before she has time to blink. Although she and Hank don't always see eye to eye, she loves him to pieces. She sees him as a second father. And while she doesn't know what her own future has in store for her, she does know it just won't be the same without Hank around.

Melanie looks over to Hank, admires his concentration as he gets into the zone, and smiles at him. He doesn't seem to notice. She loves that about him. But it depresses her a bit too. It won't be much longer now before he's gone and everything's different. That's just yet another reason why she has to keep encouraging Bree to reach out to him.

"Chase, what are you doing?" Hank says, interrupting Melanie's thoughts.

Melanie shakes away her daydream. "What?"

"You're out in left field over there. Time to put your game face on. Here they come." Hank scrunches his face and straightens his posture.

Melanie smiles, half expecting him to start saluting. Then she looks out into the parking lot and the smile falls from her face. A uniformed police officer escorts a disheveled man toward her and Hank. Melanie takes a deep breath and follows Hank's advice. She puts her game face on and prepares herself for what's about to unfold.

***

Jordan keeps his head turned downward and his eyes concentrated on his feet as he walks toward the Mifflinburg police station. The same cop that had driven him in silence leads the way, his fingers penetrating deep into the flesh on Jordan's bicep. Jordan refuses to look anywhere else besides the ground until he has to, too ashamed to meet the eye of a passerby. He does finally peek up once he's forced to a stop and the transporting officer engages in conversation with some unfamiliar voices at the top of a set of concrete stairs.

Waiting at the entrance to the police station are two more officers, one man and one woman, although they're not dressed in police uniforms. Jordan places them to be detectives. Simultaneously, they scan him up and down as if they're trying to determine if he's capable of doing what he's been accused of. Jordan can't help but wonder what they're thinking.

The group stays stationary for a bit while the older male detective asks a lot of questions and the woman stays mute. Jordan can feel the back of his neck being warmed by the rays of the sun without any clouds or trees to block it. He's suddenly sweaty all over, his back still itching with invisible crawlers.

Another moment passes before the transporting officer finally releases Jordan's arm. The older male detective looks Jordan in the eye and asks him if he's going to be cool. When Jordan nods his head in confirmation, the handcuffs click and slide off his wrists. The blood flows evenly down his arm again, warming his fingers. He finally gets a chance to tend to those itches. The male detective, placing a loose hand on Jordan's arm, leads Jordan into the station while the woman stays behind. Jordan was dazed and hadn't been listening to the conversation outside, so he doesn't pick up why.

Jordan is led through the lobby of the police station and all eyes lock in on him. Some of the women shake their heads at him while some of the men seethe with jealousy that they aren't the one transporting him. Jordan tries not to look at anyone in the eye or stare at any one thing for too long. He doesn't want people to judge him even more than they already have without hearing his side of the story. They'll all be sorry when he walks out of here with his freedom intact and his head held high. He'll look them all directly in their faces then.

The interrogation room is narrow and dark and hot. The air is stale and smells likes it's been vacant for years. Musty wooden panels cover three of the four walls and a rickety table with a couple of old chairs wait in the middle of the room for daring occupants. The fourth wall is made of a bulletproof window that looks like it's made of fiberglass. Jordan recognizes it right away as being a one-way mirror. Every police station he's ever been in has one, and this one looks no different than all the others. Jordan finds the red light of the recording camera in the far corner of the room, mounted up toward the ceiling tiles, and positions himself in the chair so he can avoid looking straight into the lens. The detective sits across from him.

"Can I get you anything, Mr. Huff?" the detective asks. "A soda or a water or anything? Maybe a little snack?"

Jordan is taken aback that the detective knows his name already, as he doesn't even remember giving it to the police in Montgomery. His entire memory of the whole event is pretty blurry. "If you could give me a job making twelve bucks an hour, that'd be great," he tries. "It'll replace the one I'm going to get fired from for being here today."

The detective squints a little and flexes his jaw, unimpressed. "Cute."

Jordan sinks into the chair. His attempt at humor has fallen flat.

"As mentioned outside, I'm Detective Berger," the detective says. "I'm going to assume the officers read you your rights earlier, yes?"

Jordan can't remember. He shrugs. Just in case, the detective keeps his eyes locked on Jordan's, and without blinking, recites him his Miranda rights. When finished, Jordan says, "What's your first name?"

"Excuse me?"

"You said your name was Detective Berger. I was just wondering what your first name is."

"My first name doesn't matter. Not to you. Only my friends call me by my first name, and we're not friends. You can address me as Detective Berger, you got it?"

Jordan nods.

"Good. So, why don't you tell me what happened?" the detective says. "Let's hear your side of the story."

Jordan straightens his back and sits up in his chair, feeling energized. He puffs his chest out and loosens his throat so his voice will project confidence. He's been waiting for this exact moment since he was stopped by the police in Montgomery. He's been wondering when he was going to get a chance to speak. The detective offers him a sickened glare as if reading his mind. Realizing the floor is his and that this is his chance, maybe his one and only chance, Jordan says, "Let me start by saying this is all one big misunderstanding."

***

Once Hank and the captured abductor head into the station for Hank to start interrogating him, Melanie turns her attention to the parking lot. Two more Montgomery police officers escort Chloe Janis and a little golden puppy toward her. Melanie can see the stress on Chloe's face even from a distance, and she can't help but wonder if she'll be scarred for life for all she's been through in the past few days. Melanie scans the parking lot for a press truck and is pleased when she doesn't find one. Not even Chloe's parents know about her safe return yet, so it'd be awful if the press got film of this first.

"Hi, Chloe," Melanie says as Chloe and the two officers approach. "Are you okay?"

Chloe says nothing.

"Whose dog?" Melanie directs to the two officers.

They both shrug. One of them says, "It was on her lap when we picked her up. I'm not sure where it came from and she won't talk to us."

Melanie nods once. "Alright. Well, thank you, gentleman. Good work. I'll take it from here. We'll be sure to give your department credit for bringing her back."

The officers nod, turn back, and head for their car. Melanie places a gentle hand on Chloe's shoulder and leads her through the front doors of the police station. Both Chloe and the puppy are timid, their muscles visibly tense and trembling. Melanie holds her chin up high for everyone to see. She wants to bask in this moment.

***

Thirty minutes after first sitting Jordan Huff down and giving him the invitation to tell his side of the story, Jordan finally stops talking. Hank crosses his arms, leans back in the chair, and tries to process what he's just heard. One of the legs of the chair slides slightly, so Hank drops all of the legs back to the floor and tosses his hands on the table in front of him where it's safer. "That's a nice tale," Hank says. "Have you ever thought about writing fiction?"

Jordan frowns. "It's all true. Every word."

"It's a nice story, it really is. A vigilante admirer of the case just happens to stumble across the missing girl while on his way home to get his lunch. That's quite a coincidence, don't you think? You just happened to forget your lunch on today of all days?"

"I'm telling you the truth," Jordan pleads. "You can check with my work. I was there and accounted for this morning."

Hank rises from the chair and heads for the door. "Yeah, well, we'll see about that." He leaves the room without waiting for a response.

Melanie is waiting for him on the other side of the door. Hank is surprised to see her—he thought she'd still be with Chloe.

"Been there long?" Hank asks as he unbuttons his collar. The interrogation room doesn't have any ventilation—natural or manufactured—so it's hotter than a desert in the middle of summer in there.

"Just for a few minutes," Melanie says. "What did you find out?"

"Take a wild guess. He says he didn't do it."

"And you don't believe him?"

"Hell no. He's lying through his teeth."

Melanie nods apprehensively.

"What about you?" Hank says. "Did you get anything out of the girl?"

"Almost nothing. She's spooked, won't say much. Asked for her mom a couple times, though. She came in with a dog too—she said it's hers. Do you know anything about a dog?"

"A dog? Didn't Kurt tell us they had an argument over him not letting her get a dog?"

"I thought so."

Hank ponders it for a moment, shakes it off, then says, "She must have found it in the woods. Must be a stray."

Melanie shrugs. "It has a collar."

Hank says nothing.

Melanie quickly changes the subject back to Hank's conversation with Jordan Huff. "Anyway," she says, "I heard what he said about the lunch break. Do you want me to check it out?"

"Might as well, just to make sure."

Melanie accepts the assignment and heads off to make a phone call. Hank is left standing alone in the corridor, overheating. He thinks about Mayor Thomas and about how much he's looking forward to throwing this in his face. He can take his threats and shove them up his ass. Hank's pension has been saved.

Hank's mind quickly switches to the Janis's and the shock and joy they're going to experience when they arrive and discover Chloe has been found. Hank's looking forward to seeing it firsthand. But that'll just be the beginning, as Hank and Abby have some unfinished business that needs to be addressed. He's been wanting her alone in a room since the second he met her. Hank still has so many questions, and only she can provide the answers. The report from Connecticut only scratches the surface.

Hank thinks of Leanne Corey. The memories of how much he'd failed her and her family and what her eventual destiny was still haunts him. He'll never get over it, he knows that, but now that Chloe is safe and her destiny has turned out much more favorably. He hopes at last the healing process can begin.

CHAPTER THIRTY-TWO

"So, two years in prison for drug possession," Hank says as he reenters the interrogation room after compiling and reviewing Jordan Huff's records. "Repeat offender. You tried to escape from rehab. You almost died of a drug overdose not once, but twice." Hank tosses the manila folder containing Jordan's records on the table and directly at Jordan. The folder almost slips off the table and falls right into his lap. "That pretty much describes you in a nutshell, wouldn't you say?"

Jordan slides the folder to the side and tries to brush it off. "That was a long time ago. I'm a different guy now."

"Thirteen months isn't that long ago," Hank challenges. He walks over to the table, his collar still loose, and sits across from Jordan, staring at him. He snags the folder and slides it under his elbow. "Why don't you tell me what's really going on?"

"Everything I told you was the truth. Honest."

"Can I tell you what I think?"

Jordan says nothing.

Hank says, "I think you've gotten yourself into some trouble and you're trying to cover your tracks. I think you still have a drug addiction. I see your forearms, I see the marks."

"Those are old scars," Jordan says as he tries to cover his bare arms with his hands. His self-consciousness is clear.

Hank holds up his hand to stop Jordan from saying any more. "I think you know far too much about this case to be just an innocent bystander. There's no way in hell you just came across her in the woods like you said. I'm not buying that. I've been around too long to fall for that. I think you abducted that innocent little girl so you could use her to feed your habit." Hank crosses his arms and takes a breath. He watches Jordan carefully for any sign of distress.

"You're wrong."

Hank slams the table with two open palms and gets to his feet. He leans over the table and gets right into Jordan's face, breathing heavily, the saltiness of his own sweat on his tongue. He can smell Jordan's fear. "You took her for the money, didn't you?"

"What are you talking about? What money?"

"The reward money, don't give me that! You knew the family was wealthy and you knew they'd offer up a reward for information. You just sat and waited around until they did so you could collect. It was simple—you knew who Abby had become, so you tracked her down and picked up the girl when you saw the opportunity. Then you waited around for the family to get desperate. You knew they'd make a public plea. I'm right, aren't I?" Hanks says, his blood boiling. "You think you're so damn smart. Well, guess what? I'm on to you. I don't know how you pulled it off, but I'll find out. I'm going to bury your ass."

"You're crazy. Why would I do that? My relationship, if you can even call it that, with Abby was finished long ago. I haven't thought of her in years. Not until I recognized her face in the paper."

Hank scoffs. He hates to admit it, but Jordan's motive is a little weak. There are far easier ways to get money for drugs than kidnapping an old neighbor's daughter. But stranger things have happened. Jordan looks away. Hank can't tell if he's about to confess or break down in tears.

"You know what I think?" Jordan says. "I think I want a lawyer now."

Hank pulls back. He slowly backs away from Jordan and rests on his heels. He knows once a suspect asks for a lawyer he can legally go no further. He's made plenty of mistakes in his career, but never about this. He knows denying someone their right to counsel is grounds for having the case completely thrown out. He's seen it a hundred times. He's seen murderers walk free because the detectives pushed it too far. This is a case he cannot afford to lose, so he stops. He just stares into Jordan's eyes and nods his head. "Fine," he says. "You're a criminal—do you have someone in mind already?"

Jordan shakes his head. "No money. A public defender is fine."

"Sit tight. I'll go make a call." Hank grabs the folder from the table and leaves the room. He slams the door on the way out for effect.

***

Abby drags her feet. Although she and Kurt have been summoned to head down to the station with urgency, she's in no rush. She wants to delay the inevitable as long as she can. Abby has fallen back to her old tricks—not talking and refusing to answer any of Kurt's questions. Kurt's at his wits end; Abby can tell. She doesn't know why she continues to lie to him.

After showering, Abby towels off in the bathroom, the steam thick. She wipes the condensation from the mirror and looks at her reflection. The stress of the last few days has begun to take a toll on her once lively features—her blonde locks have lost a bit of their shine over the past few days. The once vibrant color has turned to a dull, almost faded look. Or maybe it's a compilation of the last ten years that have finally caught up with her. It looks like she's aged fifty years overnight.

Although she's scared to death of what might happen to her, she's relieved she's finally going to be forced to toss the burden of secrets off her chest. The monkey that's been on her back for all these years has gotten too heavy and she can no longer handle the bulk. It's finally time to get rid of it. By doing so, by telling the truth about everything, she's hopes it'll give the detectives what they need to track down Chloe. Scott hasn't called back like Abby had expected, so she's officially worried now. They could be anywhere.

Abby gets dressed in the loneliness of the bedroom she once passionately shared with her husband. The memories of all the steamy nights they had together while Chloe slept down the hall flood her mind. So much of it was real; that's what hurts the most. Kurt may never understand that, and she's not sure she'll be able to explain it to him, but she's going to try. She doesn't want to lose him. She can't lose him. She needs him. And hell, she loves him, too. But still, she can't help but think everything's going to end bitterly between them.

Outside, Abby joins Kurt in the car. She looks at him and wants to tell him how much she loves him, but she can't. The pained look on his face makes her heart ache and she does all she can just to stop the tears from flowing and smudging her makeup.

Kurt backs the Mercedes out of the driveway without as much as even looking at his wife. His coldness shreds Abby to pieces, but she can't blame him. She'd be upset too if she were in his shoes. Based on his reaction, Abby concedes that this might be it between them. Once Kurt finds out what she's done—all of it—he may never speak to her again.

Abby stares out the window as Kurt pulls away from their house. All the memories. All the love. All the deception. All the blatant lies. It has all somehow finally reared its ugly head. She truly thought she'd get away with it. Abby closes her eyes and lets the memories of her once perfect life disappear into the abyss of the darkness of her mind.

CHAPTER THIRTY-THREE

The melting chocolate and drizzly caramel sticks to the roof of Chloe's mouth, sending her into another world momentarily. The sweetness of the delicious treat satisfies her sweet tooth, and it helps to satisfy some of her hunger too. The nice policewoman had offered to buy her something from the vending machine to ease her growling belly, which Chloe had accepted. She's still really hungry, though, not having eaten all morning. Benny's warm breaths add an unwanted humidity to the already compact room, but Chloe promised him she wouldn't go anywhere. But nature is calling and Benny needs some water—his panting is strong and his tongue is too pink—so she has to break her promise.

The door squeaks when Chloe opens it, cooler air rushing in, knocking her back on her heels. She slips into the hallway, closing the door behind her, and looks in both directions. The corridor is empty. Mumbled voices sound from the other side of the wall, not to be understood. Chloe's not sure which way to go. She drags her feet down the carpeted hallway, crinkling the candy wrapper in her hand, and searches for a bathroom, the callus on the back of her heel stinging with each step. She heads down the corridor toward where the L-shaped walls form an intersection and lead back to where she had originally entered the building with the policewoman.

The last couple of hours have been chaotic. It's taken Chloe this long to finally wrap her mind around what's happened to her today. For some reason, the anxiety of the day has made her mute. She's starting to feel better, though. The policewoman—Chloe only remembers her first name as being Melanie—was gentle and calming and really nice. Chloe likes her. But when she'd asked Chloe what happened and who the man was that she was with, Chloe couldn't tell her. As much as she'd wanted to, it was like her tongue was nailed to the bottom of her mouth, not letting her speak. While Benny sat in her lap, exhausted and panting, Chloe just stared, dumbfounded, while the policewoman pounded her with questions. Chloe could sense the frustration starting to build just before Melanie excused herself from the room. It took until then for Chloe to finally address the hunger pains. Benny watched, of course, and begged. But Chloe remembers from reading a book on dogs that they aren't supposed to have chocolate, so she'd refused to give in to him. It takes discipline, she's learning, to care for a puppy. She bets her parents would be proud.

Chloe makes her way through the intersection of walls and turns the corner. She nearly runs right into the two people standing and chatting on the other side, and it makes her leap backwards. It's Melanie and some other guy Chloe's never seen before. He's dressed similarly and is significantly older than Melanie. A tie around his neck is loose.

"Chloe, what are you doing out here?" Melanie says in a genuinely surprised tone, her voice high.

Being put on the spot unexpectedly, Chloe forgets her purpose. "Benny's thirsty."

The older man turns to Melanie and makes a face. "Who's Benny?"

"The dog, Hank," Melanie says. "Why don't you go back into the room, okay, sweetie? I'll be back in a few minutes and we can keep talking, okay? I'll bring some water for Benny."

Chloe nods, still forgetting about the real reason why she emerged from the room in the first place, and heads back the way she came. When she disappears around the corner and out of sight, the older man with the receding hairline—Hank, as Melanie called him—speaks out again.

"Well, well. What do we have here?" he says with a spike in his voice.

Chloe stops and listens. There's some commotion further down the corridor.

"Nice of you to show up," Hank says. "Check it out, Chase, we got a family reunion."

A family reunion? Chloe is confused. It seems like a strange thing to say to someone. Then she hears a woman's voice, and it's not Melanie's. It's a familiar voice too, one that she's heard before. The hairs on her arms stand up on end. Her eyes widen. The muscles in her legs tense up so tightly that she fears they may spasm.

Could it be?

The woman speaks again, this time her voice closer, and Chloe starts to lose it. She knows that voice. She's heard it a thousand times: all those bedtime stories, all those Sunday morning breakfast conversations around the kitchen table, all those car rides to school in the mornings.

It's her mom.

Chloe lets the tears pour out of her as she turns and runs around the corner like she's being chased. She brushes past Melanie and Hank and catches the eyes of her mom, who's slowly making her way from the opposite direction. They both stop in their tracks and stare at one another. Chloe's entire body is quivering.

***

Abby drops to her knees and wails at the sight of her daughter. The speed of her heart beating causes weakness in her other muscles, and it's a struggle to stay upright—even on her knees—as the joy she's experiencing is far greater than she ever thought possible. The wind is sucked out of her like a vacuum. Vertigo comes and Abby's head spins. She thinks she might tip over.

The two hearts inside of her patter—one small and rapid, the other struggling to keep up. Abby's ears are ringing. She's afraid she might drown in her own tears as they pour down her face like an open faucet, passing over her nose and lips. The bitterness of the salt teases the tip of her tongue. With her arms spread out wide, Abby trembles in anticipation of wrapping herself around Chloe. Chloe sprints toward her, a high-pitched noise coming from her that Abby's never heard before.

Chloe leaps off the ground and directly into her mother's arms. They embrace like they're meeting for the first time after spending years looking for one another, squeezing and twisting each other's torso. It feels that way to Abby—like she hasn't felt Chloe's warmth in forever. It's been the longest two days of her life. But it's over. Chloe is alive, safe, and back home where she belongs. Abby may never let her go again.

"I'm so sorry, Chloe," Abby whispers into Chloe's ear during a break in her sobs. "I'm so sorry."

Chloe says nothing. She just squeezes tighter.

Abby can't help but wonder how this happened, how Chloe got away. Did she escape from Scott, or did he decide to surrender? Did he treat her right, or was he a monster? She doesn't know him anymore, doesn't know what he's capable of. There are so many questions she needs to ask Chloe. And so much she has to tell her.

For the first time since making eye contact with Chloe, Abby feels Kurt's presence behind her, and it takes her mind away from Scott. Kurt's hand is on her shoulder, the tips of his fingers digging into the meat around her collarbone. Abby's numb to the pain. Still holding Chloe close, Abby looks over her shoulder. Like her, streaks of tears roll down Kurt's cheeks. Abby had forgotten what he looks like when he's glowing with joy.

Once the reality sets in that Chloe is back and their nightmare is over, Abby starts to reconsider what she's about to do. Chloe appears to be unharmed and no worse for wear—besides the unwashed and frizzed hair, dirt on her face, and a faint scent of smoke that comes from her clothes—so maybe everything can just be swept under the rug and forgotten about. Maybe there's a way Abby can get out of this without telling the secrets of her past after all.

Or maybe not.

Detective Berger, who's overseeing the scene from a distance with Detective Chase, takes a few steps forward and clears his throat. "I hate to be the one to ruin this heartwarming family moment," he says coldly, "but I must."

Abby releases Chloe—much to Chloe's dismay—and stands up to face the detective. He's only a few feet away now and standing with his arms crossed.

"I think we need to go in the back and discuss some things," Detective Berger says.

Abby nods once but doesn't allow her eyes to meet with his. She fears he'll be able to see right through her and expose her true, fraudulent self. Kurt takes a step forward too, as if to follow, but Detective Berger stops him.

"Alone," the detective insists. "I think it's best if she speaks with Detective Chase and me alone."

Kurt stops in his tracks, unsure what to say.

"It's okay," Abby says, turning to face him. "Stay here with Chloe."

Abby tells Chloe to stay with her dad, who she must not have noticed was standing there, because they embrace for the first time. It breaks Abby's heart to walk away from Chloe so soon, but she's given no choice. She follows both detectives around the corner and into one of the empty interrogation rooms, her heart feeling whole again.

There are no pleasantries between the three of them as they sit in the broken plastic and metal chairs. Detective Chase folds her hands and places them on the top of the table, looking to Detective Berger to take the lead.

"We know you're not who you claim to be," Detective Berger says, his demeanor steady. He retrieves two sheets of paper from his breast pocket and tosses them on the table. Abby refuses to look at them. "Tell me, who's Courtney Baker?"

Abby is suddenly short of breath. She hasn't been called that in more than ten years. All of the memories that were hidden so deep reemerge to the front of her mind. She's numb with fear of the truth.

"Before you lie," Detective Berger says, "I want you to think long and hard about that question. I have someone being detained down the hallway who seems to know a hell of a lot about that exact subject. And these papers here," he taps on the two in front of her, "fill in the rest."

Scott. He must have surrendered and brought Chloe in. And now he's told the detectives everything. It's all out in the open. Part of Abby feels relieved. Maybe now she doesn't have to shock everyone. Maybe they already know everything. Abby takes a deep breath and doesn't try to fight the tears from pooling in her eyes. Avoiding eye contact with the detectives, she finds a crack in the table where the wood has faded and a split has formed. She locks in on that. Then, as much as she dreads it, she prepares herself to answer the detectives' questions, beginning with the one about who Courtney Baker is.

CHAPTER THIRTY-FOUR

After intently listening to Abby's personal account of the last fifteen years of her life over the past hour, Hank and Melanie excuse themselves from the interrogation. They need some time to let it all sink in, so they go their separate ways to internalize.

Hank finds the bubbler in the lobby and quickly downs three of the cone cups worth of water. The thin paper cup can't handle it, though, and it breaks apart at the seam when Hank squeezes too hard. He flicks the beads of spring water off his fingers and finds a place to sit and process what he's just heard. If there's something going on around him, he doesn't know it.

It's a lot worse that even he'd been expecting. Based on the documentation he'd received earlier from the Connecticut State Police about Abby's bizarre past, Hank knew he was on to something, but he never thought he was going to strike gold. At worst, he thought he'd uncovered a case of mistaken identity. But as it turns out, Abby Janis is a stone-cold criminal, and she's even gone as far as confessing to all she's done. Whether or not she's holding something back is a mystery, and it'll probably stay that way. Hank is struggling with deciding on what to do with the newly acquired information and where exactly to go from here. A direction will come in time, he realizes, but he has Abby in the building now, and this might be a chance he doesn't get again.

A moment of clarity comes sooner than expected. The answer on what to do with the information from Abby is still buried somewhere deep inside of his overloaded mind, but the first step in all of this is clear. Sometimes when a man is wrong he has to put his pride aside and admit it; if only he'd done the same thing with Mary, maybe his relationship with Bree wouldn't in such turmoil. Hank had made a mistake earlier, he was wrong about his judgment, so he has to correct that. By doing so and going after the real criminals, Hank hopes it'll lead him to the right answers.

***

An anxious Jordan paces the tiny, humid, enclosed space that he's been confined to for the last hour or so. The wooden panels sweat from the heat and Jordan fears they might give way and collapse in on him. He never knew he was claustrophobic, but being stuck in the same room that's not much bigger than the bathroom in the trailer he and Mindy share for this long has made him feel that way. Every subtle creak or unexpected shifting of the panels makes him jump. He's desperate for air.

Just when he's about to lose it—whether that be his hope or his sanity—the door on the opposite end of the room finally opens. A small dose of new air makes its way into the room and Jordan inhales it like he's been submerged in water without an oxygen tank. His pores suck in the freshness as if they were dehydrated cells in need of replenishment.

Detective Berger walks in.

"You're not a lawyer," Jordan says, disappointed.

"No, I'm not," the detective admits.

"Then I don't want to talk to you. I'm not saying another word without a lawyer present."

"You're free to go."

Jordan falls back on his heels. "What?"

"You were right, I was wrong," the detective says. "Your alibi checked out, and so does your story. Abby Janis has confirmed herself what you'd told us about her."

Jordan sits in one of the chairs and puts his hand to his chest in relief. A weight lifts off him that he hadn't realized was there.

"I'm sorry about all this. You were a general match to the description of the man we've been looking for, but it's clear now you're not him. One of the officers will give you a ride to pick up your truck from impound." The detective says it in one breath, then he turns to leave.

"Wait," Jordan says, stopping him. "What about the girl? Chloe Janis. Is she going to be okay?"

The detective pauses for a moment, as if to choose his words carefully. "She'll be fine," he says. "She's with her parents now, thanks to you." Then he leaves.

Jordan lays his head down on the table and exhales. He doesn't know what he's happier about—that Chloe is going to be alright, or that he, himself, has just seen justice served. A sense of pride rushes over him as he thinks about what this all means. Abby Janis, it sounds like, has finally admitted and owned up to her mistakes from all those years ago. Now both she and Scott Baker will pay their debts to society properly, earning everything they've so rightfully been awarded. And most importantly, an innocent girl who's done nothing wrong has been reunited with her family—that's the best part. And the strange thing is, the part that makes life so unpredictable sometimes, is that Jordan—who, admittedly, is a flawed man in his own right—is solely responsible for all three justices being served. He has officially turned his life around, and he's never been prouder of himself. And he can't wait to tell Mindy all about it when he gets home.

***

Hours have passed and Scott still hasn't been so much as contacted by anybody. He's shocked—he'd thought he'd already be apprehended by now. Surely, Abby must have called the police after their failed meeting last night—that's a given. The thing is, Scott's tired of hiding already. He's ready to face his fate and is just waiting for someone to come and find him. Even the front door to the cabin is unlocked, practically inviting them inside.

Diane continues to deteriorate. Scott has never seen anyone die before, but the complete emptiness in his mother's eyes makes him wonder if that'll change soon.

It's amazing how quickly things can change. As recently as yesterday morning, Diane had been feeling well enough to go into town, and now, less than thirty-six hours later, she's on her deathbed. Scott can't help but wonder if all the smoke inhalation from the fire in the back had some negative effect on her. He should have known better than to ask her to watch over it. Between that and his botched promises, he continues to fail her more than he thought possible.

Scott warms up some tea on the stovetop for his mother. He looks out at the windless sky through the window, seeing a flock of birds flying in a figure eight above the trees. Scott envies their freedom. The teapot quickly comes to a boil and whistles at him, bringing him back, reminding him to finish the job. With the silence that fills the cabin and the lack of furniture left to absorb the noise, the whistle sounds like a freight train is screaming through the kitchen. Scott wishes there was—he'd jump right in front of it and get it over with. He pours the scalding water in the cup with the teabag hanging over the rim and lets the steam warm up his face. It reminds him of the sensation he gets when he opens a dishwasher that's just finished its cycle—when the mist pours out of the open door and is almost too hot to even touch. It's the little things he'll miss.

As he makes his way back down the hall and toward his mother's bedroom with the cup in hand, the floorboards start to rumble under his feet, and he stops. Earthquakes aren't something that's even on the radar in this part of the country, so the thunderous feeling that runs up his legs causes him some worry. A nervous jolt of energy sends a trickle of panic through his body.

In an instant, the ground stops rumbling and the framed photos hanging up in the hallway stop rattling. Silence returns. Scott is relieved, but confused. He calls out for his mother to ask if she felt it too, but gets no response. He's not surprised. She probably fell asleep. Scott steadies the tea in his hand and starts back toward the bedroom.

A knock comes from the front door. It's subtle and a muffled voice says something from the other side, but Scott can't understand what it is. Although he's been preparing for this moment all day, his body still starts to tremble uncontrollably at the thought of what's about to happen. People around here don't just stop by for a visit. Hell, most people don't even know the cabin exists—it's not even shown on some of the older town maps.

Halfway between his mother's bedroom and the kitchen, Scott decides to abandon the tea run and answer the door. There's no point in delaying the inevitable any longer, he decides. They've finally come for him. "Mother!" he calls out. "Mother, wake up!" He slides the full cup of tea onto the counter in the kitchen and takes another peek out the window.

Whirling lights of red and blue almost blind him. There are two squad cars in his line of sight and another unidentified boxy black truck behind them. Scott takes a few steps closer until it comes into view and he recognizes the lettering on the side of the truck—and the likely source of the rumbling floorboards from a moment ago. His eyes bulge and his muscles stiffen. He freezes where he stands.

The sound that follows is louder than a gunshot. It's more like a cannon going off on a battlefield, an explosion. The cabin, as it turns out, is the battlefield. And Scott is the target. Scott instinctively drops to his knees and plugs his ears with his forefingers.

The front door blasts open with a boom and is torn off its hinges with the force of the blow. A line of men—all dressed entirely in black with face masks and bulletproof body shields and with machine guns drawn—thrash through the opening of the doorway like an infantry invading Normandy.

Except they're not soldiers. They're SWAT.

Before he even has time to process what's going on, Scott is trampled by a trio of SWAT men and handcuffed faster than the blink of an eye. Glass shatters behind him, booted footsteps clank against the hardwood in the hallway, and men scream in his direction. His ears are ringing from all of the noise and the shock of the surprise entrance into the cabin, so Scott struggles to comprehend what's being said. Then he remembers where he is and what he's doing, and he fights back.

Mother!

His mother's desperate cries overshadow the sounds of everything else that's going on—that's all Scott can hear. Everything else is just static.

"Mother!" Scott screams out as the men on his back apply pressure and force him even further against the tile. The pressure on his ribcage makes it hurt to speak, but he pushes onward. "Please stop! Don't hurt her, she's sick! She has nothing to do with this!"

Scott is pulled to his feet by two men—both of whom had been sitting on his back just seconds before—and is slowly pulled away from the scene. He kicks and howls like a toddler throwing a tantrum, so the two men simply lift him up by placing a forearm under each of his armpits and carry him out the open doorway. He feels nothing. Scott only catches a quick glimpse of the damage caused by the brute force used by the men as he's thrown into the back of the black truck. From what he can tell, the cabin has turned into Hiroshima, and the still raiding men inside are the active atomic bomb wrecking everything in their wake. And all for what reason, Scott wonders. Chloe is already gone.

***

Diane is startled awake by the crash of something from the kitchen, her eyes opening with fear. She sits up in the bed and listens, her heart leaping, and thinks she hears Scott yelling for her. She tosses the blankets aside and swings her legs over the edge of the bed, but is stopped when her bedroom door is blasted open. She screams as men in black uniforms terrorize her, pointing machine guns in her face. Two men quickly approach the bed and drag her to her feet, treating her like a ragdoll. She barely has time to think.

The two men wrap their hands around Diane's frail arms so hard that she fears her bones might snap in half.

The men shout in her face and force her to walk with them down the hallway. She tries to obey, but she struggles. Her breath is short, her muscles weak. The men are intolerant and in a hurry, and Diane simply can't keep up. Her knees give out and she falls with a thump down to the hardwood, pain sweeping through her body. The men scream some more and keep moving forward. The top of Diane's feet drag on the hardwood as her muscles fail to give her any strength, the pain too great. She feels humiliated.

The kitchen is a mess: a broken coffee cup is shattered on the floor, a dark liquid—tea, perhaps—covers the tile and is starting to seep underneath the stove, and the front door is lying face down on the ground. Diane witnesses Scott being thrown into the back of a big SWAT truck out in the driveway, so she calls out for him. Her voice is weak and pained and barely audible, so he probably doesn't hear. Diane is forced out through the hole in the wall where the front door used to be and is dragged down the front steps that lead to the graveled driveway, the skin on the tops of her feet being torn away and bloodied.

Something isn't right. Her heart is working overtime and the palpitations are increasing in intensity with each subtle movement. That all too familiar feeling is returning—she can sense it. Her breath is becoming shortened and her airways are starting to close up. She feels like she has a paper bag over her head. Getting air is difficult. This is not like the others, she recognizes. She knows something far worse is going on inside of her than anything she's ever experienced in the past.

A sharp pain in her neck starts to pulsate. It makes her muscles spasm and it quickly spreads to her back and abdomen. Before long, her entire upper torso muscles spasm simultaneously and she can hardly breathe at all. Her chest is tight and she can feel the oxygen being sucked right out of her, her world spinning. It's like she's drowning. Or suffocating. The back of her neck is drenched with sweat and her consciousness is quickly fading away.

She grabs one of the men's hands and yanks on it until he looks down at her. She stares into his eyes and pleads, hoping he'll recognize her terror. She opens her mouth to try to speak to him, but nothing comes out. With every ounce of fight she has left in her, she gasps for more air, tries to talk again and manages a weak, "Help." Then she clutches at the stabbing pain in her chest and blacks out before she can say anything else.

CHAPTER THIRTY-FIVE

"SWAT, huh?" Scott says to the detective who sits across from him as he wriggles in his chair. His hands in front of him are still cuffed. His ribs are a little sore from being jammed against the kitchen floor back in the cabin, but other than that, he's physically okay. He hasn't heard anything from his mother—not that he would, being locked in here—and he's worried about her. He never did see what those men did to her. "Why didn't you just shoot me? It would've cost less."

The detective crosses his arms. His face is tired and the top button of his collar is undone—both signs that he's been agonizing over this.

The detective reaches for a glass of water and takes a long swig. He fills up his cheeks and lets the wetness moisten his palate. He looks right into Scott's eyes as he does it, knowing he must be dying for some water of his own. Scott's throat had dried out quite a while ago now.

"Refreshing," the detective says after he swallows.

Scott stares back at him like a deer stuck in a set of headlights on a busy freeway, holding his ground. The detective's stalling is puzzling. "Don't you think SWAT was a bit of an overkill? The girl was already in custody."

"The girl?" the detective says. "What, you can't say her name? Is this so impersonal for you that you just refuse to even say her name?"

"No."

"Then say it."

Scott stares the detective down. He has no idea what Chloe means to him.

"Say it, you son of a bitch!"

"Chloe."

The detective scoffs. He almost seems intoxicated. "That's what I thought. You coward."

Scott crosses his arms the best he can, the cuffs a nuisance. He hasn't asked for an attorney yet, and he doesn't plan to. There's no need to waste the man's time since Scott is going to plead guilty anyway. "Are you going to answer my question?"

"What question?"

"SWAT—why send them in?"

"Simple. Because I could. I wanted you to experience what Chloe went through. I wanted you to suffer. Do you realize she's only nine-years-old? Do you not realize you've probably traumatized her for the rest of her life?"

With that, Scott puts his head down. It's one thing to be hard on yourself, but when someone else calls you out on it, the hurt is far more severe. The knife in his heart twists a little bit deeper. He wishes he could go back in time and fix all of this.

"What, cat got your tongue?" the detective says.

Scott stays silent for another moment before looking back up to the detective, tears threatening. "Can I tell you what happened?"

"No need. Her mother already told us what happened. You tracked them, followed them to the mall, and swooped in and grabbed Chloe in the middle of the day. You know, trying to hide at your mother's cabin wasn't very intelligent. It was too easy at first, so we almost didn't even try it—we thought there was no way you could be that dumb. But we were wrong, obviously, because here you are. Once Abby told us your mother's name we were able to look up her legal address and have the SWAT team there faster than you could blink. Quite frankly, it's idiots like you that have made my job so damn easy sometimes through the years."

Scott looks away again, frustrated. It's clear to him the detective is still so much in the dark about the truth. He wonders what Abby actually did tell the detective.

"Tell me," the detective continues, "why didn't you run? I've got to know."

Scott looks back up and says, "My mother."

The detective is taken aback a bit. His head actually cocks a little. "Pardon?"

"My mother. She's sick. She has congestive heart failure. The doctors have said she has less than a year to live unless she gets a new heart. I couldn't bear the thought of her dying alone."

"So, you do have a soul?"

Scott says nothing to that. There's nothing to say.

"You were willing to risk your own freedom and your own life to save your mother?"

"She's my mother."

The detective almost looks sympathetic, like he knows what Scott's going through. And considering his age—the man has to be approaching seventy, his remaining hair beyond gray, the skin loose under his chin—his parents are probably long gone, so maybe he does.

"I've answered all of your questions," Scott says. "When is it my turn?"

The detective leans back in his chair and crosses his arms. A pinch of white chest hair bursts out the top of his opened collar. "Fine. Ask away."

"There's just one thing," Scott says. "I just need to ask you a favor."

"No promises."

"Please," Scott says, stammering, with a crack in his voice, "please don't press charges against my mother. She had nothing to do with this. I'll tell you everything you need to know, but please let her go. She needs to see a doctor."

The detective sighs. "Like I said before, no promises. But I'll see what I can do. She's in the hospital as we speak."

Scott nods his head a few times, satisfied with the response. This is the first status update he's received since being detained. He's thankful for the detective's subtle courtesy.

"Is there anything else I can do for you?" the detective says, mockingly. "Do you want a room with a view? How about room service directly to your cell? I've got it, how about a get out of jail free card so you can watch over your ill mother? Any of those things sound good?"

"Well, there is one more thing, actually," Scott says with complete seriousness, his face as straight as an arrow.

The detective chuckles to himself and looks over to the one-way mirror on the wall. There must be someone watching on the other side—his partner, maybe. "Please enlighten me. I can't wait to hear this."

Scott takes a moment to suck a big gasp of warm air into his lungs. He holds it until his chest is heavy, then he slowly exhales through his nose. The whole process completely relaxes him. "I want you to let Abby go too."

The detective swallows hard and uncrosses his arms. He shoots a quick glance to the one-way mirror again, which shows Scott the man's intrigued. Scott recognizes he has the detective's full attention.

"I don't know what else she told you," Scott says, "but I bet she left some things out. If you just give me the chance, I'll tell you everything. I'll sign an affidavit. I'll do it on video. I'll give my confession to the court. I'll do whatever you want. Please just let my mother and Abby go."

The detective takes another sip of his water. It's like he's trying to hide behind the glass. "Why?"

"Because I love them." Saying it aloud hits Scott like a sack full of sand, crushing him. An unexpected lump starts to grow in his throat. It's either the fastest growing esophageal tumor in the history of mankind, or it's something else. Scott tightens his jaw so the tears will stay away. He loves them both so much. "And because I know how much Abby means to Chloe. I could see it in Chloe's face. The way she asked about her and the look on her face when I told her she may not see her, it just tore me up. Chloe needs her mother. Please don't penalize Abby for the mistakes I've made."

The detective fingers the top of the mostly empty glass, running a tip across the rim. "And what if I don't?"

Scott takes a peek at the one-way mirror on the wall. For some reason, he suspects Abby is listening on the other side. He wishes he knew what she was thinking right now. He looks back to the detective, and without hesitation, says, "Then I'm done talking. You won't get another word out of me. I'll plead not guilty and you'll never know what really happened."

The detective doesn't react at all. He just stares back at Scott with a face as solid as stone. Scott's seen the newspapers; he's seen how little evidence the police have. The footage of him taking Chloe from the mall is practically worthless. He knows how much they'll need his confession in court to get a conviction. Scott highly doubts any good lawyer would want to put the nine-year-old Chloe on the stand to relive what happened to her. With a good defense attorney behind it, this case could be thrown out in a second—there's too much doubt. It is still innocent until proven guilty, after all. Until Chloe tells her side of things, if she ever does, Scott holds all the cards.

"Fine," the detective says, sighing. "But I'm not promising anything. Based on the information you provide, we'll see where to go from there."

Scott nods in acceptance. "I understand. Thank you."

The detective guzzles down the last of the water and slams the empty glass onto the table, startling Scott. "You've got what you wanted," he says. "The floor is yours."

Scott takes one more peek over to the glassed mirror before beginning. He wants Abby to know this isn't personal. "Okay," he begins, "it all started seventeen years ago."

***

Abby places her open palms against the one-way mirror and takes in all Scott is saying. She's been watching him since the conversation began with Detective Berger. Her cheeks are already drenched with tears and her palms leave moist handprints all over the glass. Her heart weeps. This is the first time she's seen Scott in years, and so many memories—both positive and negative—flood her mind. Despite him having aged quite a bit since their last meeting, Abby had forgotten how handsome he is. A touch of gray penetrates his dark, thick locks. His eyes are sunken and the skin on his face is blemished with fine wrinkles. He looks exhausted.

Although she can feel Detective Chase's presence a few feet behind her, the smell of coconut strong, Abby's whole world is locked in on Scott. Everything else is just noise. The words coming out of his mouth are the only things that interest her. The thought of Diane suffering almost makes her want to rethink everything. For all Diane has done for her, it's not fair she has to deal with this. Her heart must be too big, that's why it's failing. Abby lets the memories of her past take over her mind as Scott says it all out loud to Detective Berger.

Seventeen years ago, Abby met Scott Baker for the first time. She was sixteen and still in high school. He was eighteen, but they were both sophomores. There was a regional holiday basketball tournament held in New York City for some of the top high school teams in the northeastern United States. Both Abby's school from Connecticut and Scott's school from Pennsylvania were in attendance.

Abby first spotted Scott in the crowd. Their eyes had locked unintentionally and the connection was electric almost immediately. Without having spoken a word to one another, sparks flew. Abby's pretty sure the temperature in the gym had been turned up, but looking back on it now, she wonders if it was just the flames from her heart that made it seem that way. Either way, her skin was on fire.

They eventually got introduced, hooked up, and became close. They stayed in touch over the phone twice a day for the next three months and tried to have a relationship. But with the distance between them, it was difficult, especially for hormonal adolescents. Then tragedy happened and everything changed. Everything suddenly became even more complicated overnight.

Abby remembers it like it was yesterday. It was the first Saturday in March. Snow was still on the ground but the forecast for the day was for clear skies. Spring was coming. Abby's parents had left early in the morning to bring her sister, Courtney, to visit the University of Connecticut. Courtney was a senior in high school and had just been accepted to the state university. They were on their way for a campus tour for accepted students. She was going to study English.

The three of them never made it.

One of the tires on Abby's dad's SUV exploded on I-84 on the way to campus. Eyewitnesses had said it was sudden and unexpected with no warning signs of trouble beforehand. The SUV was in the right-hand lane when it happened. The driver's side front tire blew out completely down to the rim and the rubber was torn away like meat from a bone. Abby's dad immediately lost control and the SUV whipped across both lanes and was sent airborne over the guard rail on the left side. Opinions varied—some witnesses had said they flipped twice while others had claimed it to be three times—but the end result was the same. The vehicle caught on fire and exploded before help could arrive. All three of them died on the scene.

The news was devastating for Abby. She went to bed on Friday night a daughter and a sister, and by the time she awoke on Saturday, she was an orphan and her sister was gone. It was a whirlwind. Her parents had a good amount of life insurance that covered all their debts and expenses, so Abby received a check for just under five thousand dollars far less than the trust fund she had later told Kurt she received—as the sole remaining beneficiary.

Even now, as Abby listens to Scott tell the story to Detective Berger, it pains her to hear him say it aloud. Out of all the things she's done in her life, what she did back then might have been the worst of all. She can't even bear to look into the interrogation room while Scott continues, so she turns away. The shame is just too strong. Even after all these years have passed, she still feels like a scoundrel.

What happened next was Scott's idea. It doesn't make it any less racketeer or let Abby off the hook by any means, she realizes, but the facts are the facts. Abby had been hesitant when Scott proposed it to her—resistant, really—but then he brought up a valid point. With Abby being sixteen and still legally considered a minor, she'd either be forced to go live with an aunt in Kentucky who'd said she'd take her in, or she'd be placed in a foster home. Neither option was viable for her. So, Abby took Scott's advice and moved to Pittsburg to live with him, his mother, and his younger brother.

That's how Courtney Baker was fabricated.

Courtney Weston—Weston was Abby's maiden name—was eighteen. Abby was not. Courtney was dead. Abby was not. They had similar appearances—the same wavy blonde hair, pointed chin, and soft blue eyes that, when crying, would look like they were holding a glass of water. After Scott put it in the context he did, it was a no-brainer. Abby Weston took her sister's first name, claimed to be her, and moved to Pennsylvania to marry Scott.

Problem solved.

Scott was of legal age already and didn't need his mother's consent to get married, but she'd hated the idea. She'd made it clear from the start. What made it easier for Diane to accept was the $5,000 that Abby had received from the life insurance. Five grand was enough to pay for more than six months' worth of rent, and the help was desperately needed. So, Abby moved in, agreed to find a job to help out, and Scott stayed in school—those were the terms of the agreement.

It was less than two weeks later that the eighteen-year-old Courtney Weston was able to provide all of the documentation needed to marry the eighteen-year-old Scott Baker at the courthouse downtown. On paper, both were consenting adults, so no one questioned it. Just like that, Abby Weston became Courtney Baker. And then all hell broke loose.

***

Scott takes a break and lets his mouth regenerate the saliva he's lost from his long-winded filibuster-like tirade. He massages his palate with his tongue. The sandpapery texture makes him wince. He wonders how Abby feels as she, in all likelihood, listens to it all being said out loud for maybe the first time. He can only imagine how painful the memories are of her family's death, especially under these circumstances. If he could find a way to get the story out without putting her entire past on the chopping block, he would. None of this is because he's trying to get revenge for her not wanting to be with him; it's the complete opposite. By doing what he's doing—telling the story of himself and Abby and how they've got to where they are today—he hopes he can save her. He knows the detective has refused to make any promises, but the hope that she'll be able to walk free and raise Chloe is all Scott has left. That, and the faith that his mother will somehow get the help she needs to finally get the chance to enjoy life.

The detective is getting restless. "This is all really great," he says, "this story about how you two met, but it's nothing I haven't heard already. You're telling me nothing new here. All you're doing is piling up the felonies. I've got two so far."

"Two?" Scott says.

"That's right. The first was statutory rape. It doesn't matter if Abby had consented or not—you were eighteen and she was sixteen. That's rape. The second is fraud. I don't think I have to explain that one to you, do I?"

Scott shakes his head.

"Are you sure you want to keep going?" the detective asks. "You can invoke your sixth amendment right at any time, you know. I would consider it if I were you."

"I don't need a lawyer, I told you that," Scott says. "Please, just let me continue."

The detective sighs and crosses his arms. "Fine," he says. "It's your grave."

"As I was saying," Scott begins, "we were married and she was living in the apartment with me and Tommy and Mom, and we were happy. School was going okay and Mom was pleased with Abby helping out around the house. Everything was great. But then a few months later, Abby's hours started getting cut back at work, and then she was down to only one shift a week for a while. Five thousand dollars only goes so far, especially with three kids now in the house, so Mom was getting irritable. Not that I could blame her. I could tell she was getting stressed out again—I'd seen it so many times through the years—and I couldn't stand seeing her like that again." Scott pauses and looks over his shoulder at the glass on the wall. Although he knows he'll never be able to see what's on the other side, he wants Abby to know he still cares. He knows she's watching.

***

The memories of how difficult those times were in Diane's two-bedroom apartment are still fresh in Abby's mind. Tommy had one room while Scott and Abby shared the other. Diane would sleep on the couch. That couch was repulsive. Abby still feels that way about it, even now.

The apartment they'd lived in was previously furnished—everything but the mattresses were left behind and some of it was in rough shape. The couch might have been the worst of it. It had the constant smell of cat urine and feces, and there were cigarette burns covering the cushions and the arms. It was a faded gray and had gum and some unknown sticky substance stuck to the legs. The worst thing about it, Abby remembers, was the rat. Every so often, the couch would squeak in the middle of the night and a trail of droppings would be found the next morning. No one ever saw the rat, but it was always assumed to be a nest. The closest anyone got to catching it was when its outline was seen scurrying down the back and disappearing into the stuffing underneath, leaving crumbs of bread on the floor. Diane slept on that couch every night for a year while she let Scott and Abby sleep in her bed. The woman's heart was made of gold.

After Abby had basically lost her job—one five-hour shift a week was hardly even worth the effort—she became depressed. Her new lifestyle was starting to take a toll on her and she was still grieving over the loss of her parents and sister. She hadn't heard a peep from her aunt in Kentucky, which led her to believe that she never really wanted to take her in in the first place, so Abby was feeling isolated on top of that. She was spending days completely by herself while Scott and Tommy were at school and Diane was at work. She couldn't re-enroll in school either, considering how she was living in Pennsylvania under a fraudulent identity. It would have been too easy for the state to void her marriage to Scott and send her back to Connecticut—probably to an orphanage, as Scott continuously reminded her—and that was the best-case scenario. She was alone, miserable, and bored. It was a recipe for disaster.

They couldn't afford cable in the apartment and Abby didn't have any money to do anything, so she had to find something to do to keep her mind occupied. The fear of dying of boredom, if there was such a thing, was becoming a reality. She began watching people. There was another apartment complex across the street. Abby would pull up one of the non-matching chairs from the kitchen to the window and would sit and watch the neighbors. She would find patterns in people's behaviors and had a running list—all in her head, of course, since there was never any paper around the apartment to write on—of who would leave and when they'd return.

A few weeks of watching, Abby came up with a plan.

She brought it to Scott's attention one night after he got home from school and before Diane had returned home from work. He was hesitant at first—much like she was when he'd suggested she use her sister's identity and move to Pennsylvania—but he'd admitted he thought it might actually work. So, they tried it, just to see what would happen. And it worked. And it was so easy.

Like the apartment that Diane rented, the complex across the street was section eight. Some people left for work for short periods of time, but some didn't. Some people didn't work at all. That made Abby's recognition of patterns difficult initially, but it also made it easier at times too. Through her diligent spying, Abby was able to determine there were a handful of vacant apartments. The bank of mailboxes in the lobby was unsecured and Abby could see right in through the window from the apartment. She would wait for the postman to arrive and fill the various boxes with envelopes and flyers. There were three boxes that were never filled. Ever.

Abby finally got the courage one day to go over to the other side of the street and confirm this for herself. Those same three mailboxes that were never filled were also the only three boxes that didn't have a label on them. And the corresponding door buzzers on the wall were also free of name labels, which meant one thing: Abby was in business.

It was a new low. For all she'd done in the previous year, what she was considering was taking it even further. She'd already put one foot over the invisible line in the sand, and doing this would put both feet firmly over. She'd be in deep. But she saw no other option, so she leapt.

And all it took was a simple paper application.

Using her dead sister's identity again—she couldn't use her own still, since she was a minor—she filed for welfare assistance using one of the vacant apartments across the street as her residence. The application had only asked for basic demographic information that was easily verifiable and required little proof of her identity. Without having received as much as a phone call from the state, the first check arrived ten days later and the rest was history.

Abby would simply walk across the street, pick the lock to the mailbox, and grab her check on the second Tuesday of each month. No one ever questioned it, the postman included. It went on that way for months and Abby's check arrived on time and in full each time. It was pure thievery.

Scott graduated from high school a few months later in December, and he and Abby moved out of Diane's apartment soon thereafter. They stayed in Pittsburg so they could walk to the vacant apartment and keep up the scam. And they were doubling up now too—the original scam was at the vacant apartment under Courtney Baker, and the second one was under their new legitimate address under Scott Baker.

But it didn't end there.

They got greedy.

Abby and Scott had gotten used to sitting around all day, doing nothing, not working, and collecting checks from the state, but they wanted more. So they pushed it even further. Abby changed her legal name from Courtney Baker to Abby Baker, but never changed the paperwork with the welfare department. Scott's brother, Tommy, was now sixteen, so he was next. After another simple paper application, Tommy Baker was now living with Scott, according to the state welfare department. Abby and Scott were collecting for four people: Abby Baker, Scott Baker, and Tommy Baker in one apartment, and Courtney Weston in the other. The problem was, Tommy didn't live with them, and the state eventually found out.

What made it all work was Diane's pride. To her credit—or maybe it was her stubbornness—she'd always refused to ask for help. She worked full time and was still well under the poverty line, but she never received a cent of public assistance. Because of that, Scott and Abby were able to use Tommy to get the extra funds, and Diane wouldn't be affected by it. But there was one thing they forgot to consider, and it ended everything.

The scam ended once tax time came around. Diane hadn't known Scott was claiming Tommy lived with him and also claiming him as a dependent, so when she tried to claim him on her own state tax return, the inconsistencies were finally recognized and the state stepped in to investigate. Apparently, someone had tipped off the state that something was wrong, but Abby never found out who the tipster was. It seemed impossible that anyone would have even known.

Although Diane had been in the dark about their scam, she covered for Scott like any mother would do. She testified to the fraud committee that Tommy did, in fact, live with Scott and Abby at times during the year—although he hadn't—and it was all boiled down to a simple mistake in the paperwork. The committee ended up putting a stop to the checks paid out to Scott, but they didn't move forward with pressing any criminal charges against him. Out of fear of being watched and found out about too, Abby—or Courtney, as the state saw it—stopped filing for welfare assistance. Just like that, the two of them went from receiving monthly checks to support four people to zero.

It was over. And they were broke.

Tommy went along with it and testified as his brother and mother asked, but he never forgave Scott for putting him in that situation in the first place. He eventually reconciled with Diane when he realized she was only doing what she had to do to save her son, but he hasn't spoken to Scott since.

Abby remembers the way Scott used to talk about it years later. He used to think Tommy had thought he was better than everyone else because he went to college and neither Scott nor Diane did, but Abby always felt differently. Scott felt that Tommy abandoned him and their mother for bigger and better things, but Abby always thought it was because he was ashamed of what he'd done—he'd lied to the investigative committee, making him partially liable too. Even to this day, Abby still feels the same way about it. And she accepts she'll never be able to get Scott to agree with her, because that's just the way he is.

***

Hank is up and pacing. His shirt is choking him again. His mind is racing, trying to sort through the details of Scott Baker's statement. It will take a lot of fact checking to confirm everything, but it seems straightforward enough. If what Scott has said is accurate, then Abby deserves to be in prison for this. Something has to give.

Conveniently, Abby had failed to mention any of these fraudulent activities earlier, which now solidifies that everything she says is pure garbage. Going forward, Hank decides to make a conscious decision to either completely disregard everything Abby says or to take it with a huge grain of salt. He knew his intuition was right about her from the get-go: Abby is liar and a con.

The amount of fraud Scott and Abby have committed is astounding, and the scary part is that they were only kids during it all. Some of the laws and eligibility requirements and procedures have improved since then, Hank knows, but the fact that no one caught on to what they were doing is troubling. If these two relatively uneducated people were able to pull something like that off, there's no telling how many others have done the same thing. The idea of Hank's hard-earned tax dollars going to people like Abby and Scott makes him cringe. He's worked far too hard in his life to be okay with giving handouts.

"Okay," Hank begins, "I think I'm following you so far. We're going to have to go back and review the audio to find out how many felonies you should be charged with since I've completely lost count."

No response from Scott.

"So, what are we up to now," Hank says, "four, five years in?"

Scott nods. "Sounds about right."

"Okay, that still leaves us with more than a dozen years of crap to sift through. Please tell me it wasn't all like that."

"Actually, I'd rather not get into details, if you don't mind. I've already served a lot of time for what happened over the next few years. I've paid my debt back to society. It's all in my file."

On the corner of the table is that file. It's thick. There's enough data in there to write a full-length true crime book, and there'd still be enough content left to write a supplemental novella afterward. Scott Baker is a terrible criminal.

Hank grabs the file and fingers through the first handful of pages. Aloud, he reads, "Wire fraud, mail fraud, check fraud, bank fraud, insurance fraud, welfare fraud." Hank stops and turns his attention to Scott. "Welfare fraud? I thought you said you just got a slap on the wrist?"

"I did, for a while. Once I got busted for all those other things, the state came back after me," Scott says.

Hank closes the folder and tosses it back on the edge of the table. His head hurts. "If the state came back after you, how come Abby got away with it?"

"Time. Too much time had passed. They started investigating her, but the process all took too long."

Hank nods. "Statute of limitations."

"Only two years in Pennsylvania for fraud."

Hank fumes. Shit like that pisses him off. Everyone knows that Abby is a criminal: she does, Scott does, Hank does, the state of Pennsylvania does. But because the overworked and underpaid case workers didn't have the time to look into each claim with a fine-toothed comb, Abby slipped right through the cracks. And because she couldn't be charged with anything, her record is clean. People who take full advantage of scenarios like that are the worst kind in Hank's eyes, and he hopes Abby gets everything she has coming to her. She deserves every last bit of it. Everything about her is duplicitous.

Once he cools, Hank refocuses himself on the task at hand. The questions that have been bothering him the most have still yet to be answered—the ones that stem from the documentation received from the Connecticut State Police, the ones that'll explain how Kurt Janis got involved. Hank still doesn't know how Chloe fits into all of this, either. He pushes onward. "Why do it all?" he asks.

"We were broke."

"You could have gotten a job."

Scott shrugs.

Hank shakes his head in disgust. "I think we can now establish you're the worst type of person. Can we agree on that?"

"I've served my time."

"But, you haven't changed. Once a crook, always a crook. Anyway, I've said my peace. Let's get back to it. Sometime in between your arrest and Abby's marriage to her current husband, something happened between the two of you. What was it?"

Scott looks over his shoulder at the one-way mirror and sighs. "There were no problems between us. It was just another one of our scams. As it turns out, it was the stupidest one we ever came up with. I lost her forever because of it."

"So, you're telling me her marriage to Kurt Janis was just another one of your games?"

"That's right. It was a terrible idea. The worst."

"Before you go any further, I want to bring her in here."

Scott visually tenses. He stiffens like a board, his eyes widen, the hairs on his arms stand on end. It's as if Hank has said the worst possible thing he could say to someone.

Hank walks over to the mirror on the wall and looks right into it like he can see right through to the other side. "Chase," he says, "bring Abby in here, will you? And grab Kurt, too. I want this all out in the open. And stay with Chloe, please. I don't want her to hear this."

Hank walks back over to the table and crosses his arms. He leans against the wall and closes his eyes for a moment while Scott nearly hyperventilates in the chair across from him. Hank can smell the fear, and he's thoroughly enjoying it. It's about time these two get their feet held to the fire. He opens his eyes and offers a phony smile to Scott. "Hang tight," he says. "It'll be just a minute."

CHAPTER THIRTY-SIX

Abby looks anywhere but straight ahead. After all these years, after all he's done, she refuses to look into Scott's eyes. The man is gutless, weak, not worthy of her time. He's a complete coward for doing what he did to Chloe. She'd spit in his face in a second if her mouth wasn't so dry.

Detective Berger pulls out a couple of chairs at the table across from Scott and motions for Abby to sit. She does, reluctantly, and is joined by Kurt a moment later. She watches Kurt burn his eyes into Scott's, and she can feel the heat. Her skin is suddenly sizzling. Kurt doesn't even look at her.

Detective Berger puts his hands on his hips and surveys the trio. Abby can only imagine what he's thinking. "I don't think introductions are necessary here," he says with a grin on his face. "Do you?"

No one answers. Abby is disgusted that the detective seems to be enjoying this. This is and has been her worst nightmare for years.

"Well, good. Mr. Baker was just about to tell me the story of how you met your husband, Abby. I thought it might be nice to have our lovebirds all here at the same time to hear this."

Abby feels ill.

"Mr. Baker," Detective Berger says, "please proceed."

Abby's eyes meet Scott's for the first time. The hatred she feels is like a tsunami, powerful enough to drown an entire coastal city. Scott quickly shifts his eyes away from the storm and searches elsewhere for a life preserver. Abby hopes he drowns.

Scott says, “As I said, we were broke. Most of the scams had already run their course and we had nothing left. We were desperate.”

Kurt looks puzzled, his eyes scrunched. Abby wonders how much he’s been informed of already, if at all.

“So, one day I came across this financial trading magazine while waiting at the doctor’s office,” Scott continues. “And there was an article on the first page about some local guy who was starting to become a hotshot in the personal finance industry. His clients were averaging like twenty percent returns or something.”

“Impressive,” Detective Berger says.

“I know, right? Crazy. That was unheard of,” Scott says. “Anyway, so I did some research and found out the guy was single and approaching thirty. So, I figured a rich guy like that must be looking for someone to share all that wealth with, you know?”

“Was he?” Detective Berger asks.

Scott motions to Kurt but refuses to look in his direction. “Turns out, he was.”

Abby drops her head.

“I see,” Detective Berger says, scissoring through the tension like a hot knife through butter. “What happened next? Abby seduced Kurt and convinced him to marry her? Just like that?”

“Something like that,” Scott says.

“Something like that, or was it that?”

“That was basically what happened. She’s a beautiful woman, as you know, so it wasn’t very difficult. It would have happened to you too, I bet.”

Detective Berger scoffs.

“But things were taking too long,” Scott admits. “As it turns out, Kurt is a gentleman. We weren’t expecting that. Abby had practically thrown herself at him, but he didn’t bite like we’d thought. Did they have sex? Sure they did, after the first date even, I think. But he wouldn’t go further than that. Abby was giving him clues left and right."

"Clues?" Detective Berger says.

"Yeah, clues. She was giving him hints—some subtle, some not so much—and was trying to get him to ask her to move in. That was the first part of a three-step plan. After that, she'd get him to marry her—that was step two."

"What was part three?" Detective Berger asks.

"Please," Kurt interjects with a hint of fury in his voice. "Do tell. I'd love to know."

Abby's heartrate picks up a tick. A dampness forms under her armpits and she can feel the walls starting to close in on her. She can sense she's about to be ganged up on.

"Part three," Scott pauses and looks to Abby. She quickly looks away and finds some more chipped wood on the edge of the table to stare at. "Part three was the exit strategy."

Detective Berger had been pacing. He stops now and puts a hand to his face, rubbing his stubble. "Is that supposed to mean something?"

Abby refuses to unlock her gaze from the table, sensing Scott is staring at her again.

"Divorce."

The word lands hard in the center of the room. Everyone is quiet. Everything stops. Even the hands on the clock are at a standstill. It feels like a bomb is about to go off, tearing through everyone in its wake. Abby looks up just enough to catch of glimpse of Kurt in her peripheral vision—his head is buried in his hands; he seems to have taken the news the hardest. She thinks she can hear him sigh.

"Why go through all that?" Detective Berger asks, breaking the silence. "Why the urgency to get married just to get divorced so quickly? What's the point of all of this?"

"Let me take a step back here," Scott says. "We were trying to clean our lives up, okay? Before Abby even approached Kurt, she and I got divorced."

"Divorced?" Kurt says, suddenly alert. He turns to Abby. "You were married to this asshole?"

"You mean you and Courtney got divorced?" Detective Berger says to Scott.

"Well, yes, technically. Courtney's identity. But it was still Abby to me."

"Who the hell is Courtney?" Kurt asks.

"Abby's sister," Detective Berger says.

"Abby has a sister? Abby, you have a sister?"

"No, she doesn't have a sister," Detective Berger says. "At least not anymore. Her sister passed away almost twenty years ago."

"Then who was this guy married to?" Kurt says, referring to Scott. He looks like he might spontaneously combust.

"I'll explain it all later," Detective Berger says.

"No, I want answers!"

"Mr. Janis," Detective Berger says, "if you're going to be disruptive then I'm going to have to ask you to step outside until we're done here."

Kurt sinks in the chair and pulls at his hair. Abby wants to reach over and offer her sympathy, but she doesn't dare. It's her fault why he feels the way does after all, so she doesn't think anything she might do could help. She doesn't want to make it worse.

"Mr. Baker," Detective Berger says, "please continue."

"As I was saying, Abby and I got divorced before she and Kurt even got introduced. Even though she changed her legal name back to Abby and she wasn't using her sister's identity anymore, we wanted to make sure everything was completely legal. No mistakes. We figured Kurt would have the money for some good lawyers, so we didn't want to get exposed. Like I said, we were trying to clean up our lives, so we wanted everything done right."

"Can we get on with this, please?" Detective Berger says, getting frustrated. "You're telling me nothing. What happened? What was the purpose of all of this?"

"If you'd just let me talk—"

"What do you think I've been doing! We're going around in fucking circles here. What is the goddamn point to all of this?"

"Fine," Scott says. "Here's the quick version. Abby was going to marry the guy, then divorce him and take half of his money, okay? Then she and I were going to get back together and use his money to get straight. But when she stopped reaching out to me over the years when I was in prison, I wasn't sure if she was still on board with that. So, I kidnapped Chloe, brought her to my mother's cabin, and waited for Abby to join us. We were going to disappear forever and live as one big happy family, just like we always wanted. It was the only way I could get her attention." Scott gasps for air, having said all that in a single breath. "Is that what you wanted to hear?"

Kurt just sighs.

Detective Berger turns to Kurt. "You didn't have a prenuptial agreement in place? If she was worth nothing and you were in the position you were, why wouldn't you? It's the only way to protect yourself."

"I see that now," Kurt admits. "But I never thought I'd need it. It didn't even cross my mind, to be honest. We were in love. Besides, it's not like she had nothing."

"Excuse me?" Detective Berger says.

"She had a trust fund."

"What trust fund?"

Abby bites her tongue. There's that, too.

"The trust fund from the death of her parents," Kurt says, his voice cracking, almost like he's surprised no one else knows. "What, are you going to tell me next that her parents aren't really dead?"

"No, they're dead," Detective Berger says. "But there was no trust fund."

Kurt looks to Abby, then back at the detective. He fidgets in his chair. "She invested twelve thousand dollars with me. We used that money to help buy our home."

All three men turn and stare at Abby. None of them say anything, but they don't have to. She feels it. She feels the three sets of eyes burning into her skin like lasers. Abby just wants to disappear. She'd rather be anywhere else but here. She'd rather die. With a heavy heart filled with some of everything, she finally looks up from her daze and into each of the six eyes, a pair at a time. None of them are welcoming. "What?" she says.

Detective Berger says, "I think I can speak for all of us when I say this: That twelve thousand dollars—where'd it come from? According to Mr. Baker, you gave the five thousand dollars that was remaining from your parents' life insurance to his mother."

"That's right, I did," Abby says.

"Okay, then where did that twelve thousand dollars come from?"

Kurt and Scott stare in silence. Only she knows the answer to this one.

"I had to protect myself too," Abby says, breaking down. "I was all by myself. Scott had his mother and his brother. I had no one." As if they even went away in the first place, more tears start to pour from Abby's eyes than she'd thought were possible. "What if it didn't work out between us? What if Diane kicked me out? I had to protect myself."

"Mrs. Janis," Detective Berger says, speaking with his hands. "Abby. If you've never told the truth about anything in your entire life, this has to be the first time. I need you to tell me what you've done. Where did that money come from?"

Abby throws her face in her hands and bawls, her core muscles contracting. This is all too much for her; the tension is going to be what kills her. She places a hand on her belly underneath the table to try and relax the stressed baby. The tension in the room is thicker than concrete. "I was home by myself every single day," Abby says when she lifts her head back up. "I don't think you understand what that kind of isolation does to somebody. All I had was my thoughts and the worst case scenarios to consider. I had to make sure I was protected."

"Abby, please," Detective Berger says, almost sounding desperate. "Please just tell me how you got that money."

"My sister."

There's a brief silence.

"You got the money from your dead sister?" the detective asks, not sure what to make of that.

"I was her, she was me. I'd been using her identity. I knew she had a savings account with some money set aside, so I did what I had to do."

"How'd your sister get that kind of money? She was only eighteen."

"College. She was already accepted at the University of Connecticut before she died. I just filled out the acceptance letter and sent it back."

"I'm not following."

Abby sighs. "At the time, all you needed to request a student loan was a copy of the acceptance letter from the school and some basic personal information. I had access to all that. So, all I had to do was send it all in with the financial aid package from the university, and they sent a check to the house to cover the rest of the semester. Courtney had some money in her savings account already—not much, but some—so I deposited the money into her account and left it there. And after a while, it started earning interest and getting bigger."

"So, you were using her identity even before Scott suggested it to you then?" Detective Berger says.

"I didn't want to. But I felt I had to."

"You're sick, Abby," Kurt adds. "You're really sick."

Abby drops her head. Her husband is completely right. She's beyond humiliated.

"How'd you get it?"

"There was a branch of the bank just around the corner from Diane's apartment. I had all the necessary identification. I withdrew all the money and went to a different bank and opened up a new account under my real name. I signed the check over to myself and just left it there in case I needed to access it later on."

"How could you?" Scott says, sounding truly hurt. "We could have used that money. Don't you remember what it was like living there? We went days without eating sometimes."

“I had to protect myself.”

“Did you ever plan on coming back to me at all?” Scott asks. “Ever?”

“Yes,” Abby says without hesitation. “At first.”

“What made you change your mind?”

Abby turns and faces Kurt, but his attention is elsewhere. “Love. I fell in love. I never thought it would happen, but it did. I fell in love with you, Kurt. I’m in love with you.”

When Kurt doesn’t react, Abby looks away and covers her face. She can’t stand having these men judging her any longer. They don’t understand what it was like for her, being sixteen and losing everyone. She had to do what she did to survive.

Nobody says anything for a while. There’s not much left to be said.

Then, out of nowhere, Kurt says, “Abby? Abby, look at me.”

She doesn’t.

“Abby, please look at me.”

Sensing Kurt’s despair, she gives in. She can hardly look into those eyes of his, the pain is just too much.

“I need to know,” he says. “Is Chloe mine?”

Abby’s heart leaps. She’s been wondering the same thing for ten years. She’s surprised it took this long for the question to be asked. “Kurt, it was never supposed to happen that way, I swear,” Abby pleads. “The pregnancy was never part of the plan. It just happened. You have to believe me.”

Kurt holds up one hand to stop her. He stares into her eyes and grits his teeth like he’s ready to go off. His hands curl into fists. “Abby, please!” He slams both fists onto the table, making everyone jump. “Is Chloe mine?”

Abby wants to look away, but she can’t ignore the anguish and pain on Kurt’s face. She never meant to hurt him like this. He doesn’t deserve it. But at the same time, this is the exact moment she’s been dreading for nearly a decade. And for the first time through all of this, she has to be honest. She can't hold anything back. "I don't know," she says. And it's the complete truth.

CHAPTER THIRTY-SEVEN

Wednesday. Two days later.

After a long two days of information dumping with the mayor and the county district attorney, Hank has taken some time off. Melanie too. Their work is done for now. Everyone involved in this mess of a case is in the hands of the courts now. Hank will try to put it out of his mind until the trial. Chloe Janis being alive and well reminds him that there is life after Leanne Corey, and he's going to start living it while he still can.

Mayor Thomas pulled Hank aside just before he left to go home and apologized for everything—for the threats he'd made, for his attitude about the whole thing, for his shenanigans at the press conference—and Hank forgave him. With only six months left until retirement, Hank saw no point in burning bridges with the man. He suspects the rest of his time will go smoothly now, and his pension will be just fine. But he's still not going to vote for him come the fall.

Aubrey's apartment complex is less than ten miles from his own, although it seems like a thousand. Hank's is in a quiet area with patches of green grass and open spaces and a water fountain, while Aubrey's is on the corner of a busy road with lots of traffic and mostly on-street parking. Hank finds an open spot a block past the complex and parallel parks for the first time in years. The rear wheel thumps when it scrapes against the sidewalk, but Hank is satisfied enough with the first effort to leave it. Not bad for it having been so long, he thinks.

Hank looks for Aubrey's car on the street before he enters the complex, but he doesn't find it. That doesn't necessarily mean she's not home, though, as he recalls there being a private lot in the rear of the building for some of the tenants to park in. He probably should have called first, he admits, but this is something he feels he needs to do in person. She probably wouldn't have taken his call anyway.

In the entranceway to the complex, Hank pushes his index finger into the sliver of a button on the intercom panel, pressing the one that lists his own last name on the sticker. Hank is looking forward to seeing his daughter, and he really hopes she's home. He's a little nervous about it too, though, unsure how she might react to him showing up unannounced.

Aubrey's voice greets him through the speaker just a moment later. "Hello?"

"Aubrey?" Hank says, smiling at the sound of the familiar voice. "It's Dad."

It takes a long few seconds of silence before Aubrey finally says, "What do you want? What are you doing here?"

"I want to see you."

"Well, I'm busy."

"I just need a minute," Hank says. "Can I come up?"

Aubrey sighs into the microphone.

"It'll just be for a minute. I promise."

Aubrey sighs again, but the buzzer sounds. Hank grabs the door before it closes.

On the third floor, Hank finds Aubrey's apartment in the middle of the hallway. He remembers well the nightmare it was to move all of her furniture up three flights of stairs when she'd moved in. It had been the hottest day of the year that day. Hank knocks on the door twice with his knuckles. An anxious chill rushes through him while he waits. There's some shuffling behind the door, followed by a squeaking hinge, then it opens. Aubrey slides out into the hallway and closes the door behind her.

Hank smiles. "Hi."

"Hi."

"Can I come in?"

"It's kind of a mess right now, actually."

Hank nods once. He won't push. "Okay, no problem. I can do it right here."

Aubrey's expression changes from defensiveness to worrisome. "Is everything alright?"

"Everything is great," Hank says, then he smiles again. "I'm sure you've heard the news about Chloe Janis by now?"

"I have. Congratulations."

"Thank you. But that's not what I'm here for."

"It's not?"

"No. Listen, I've been doing a lot of thinking about what's happened between us, and I want to fix it."

Aubrey crosses her arms, just like Hank always does. "And?"

"And I think I can finally see where you were coming from."

Aubrey keeps her arms crossed, but the expression on her faces changes again, softens. She obviously hadn't been expecting that.

"I realize I wasn't there for you the way I should have been," Hank continues. "And I'm sorry for that. I never meant to leave you feeling abandoned."

Aubrey shifts her weight and bites her lip as if to tell Hank she needs more than that.

"And I love you, and I miss you, and I want to try and rebuild what we used to have between us." Hank waits for a reaction but gets only a stone face in return. "I know it's going to take some time, but if we both put in the work—"

The muscles in Aubrey's face tighten, disapproving.

"Mostly me."

The stone starts to soften around Aubrey's lips, and Hank can see a hint of a smile starting to form. He's slowly chiseling his way through to her.

"I'd like that," Aubrey says. Her arms are still crossed, but a smile has now completely broken through.

Hank hasn't seen her smile in a long time, and it makes his heart melt. "Saturday," he says, "are you free for dinner? I'd like to cook some steaks on the grill."

"You have a grill?"

"First floor, baby," Hank says, then he grins.

Aubrey can't hold it in anymore. She laughs, spitting a little on Hank when she does. Hank laughs too. They laugh together. The façade, her emotional shield, breaks. It splits right down the middle like a pane of glass. The pieces of stone crumble in midair and disappear before they hit the floor.

"I'd love to," Aubrey says, then she leans in and gives her dad a hug.

Hank accepts it and wraps his hands around his daughter for the first time in what feels like years. She squeezes tight. The smell of the ocean in her hair reminds him how much he's missed her. And it reminds him how much he needs her in his life.

"Can I bring Melanie with me too?" Aubrey asks as she pushes away from her father. She looks into his eyes with complete seriousness, as if to test him.

Without hesitation, Hank smiles and says, "I'd like that." Then he heads back down the empty corridor and toward the street to enjoy the sunshine. He might float away and join the clouds up in the sky.

***

Hiding behind the closed door of Bree's apartment, her muscles tensed, Melanie listens in to the long overdue conversation between Bree and Hank. It's an intimate moment she doesn't feel right listening to, but there's nowhere else to go. She can't help but eavesdrop. Her face hurts from smiling.

The door closes once Hank's voice disappears down the hallway, sending Melanie scampering. Bree steps back into the apartment, pushes her back against the door, and exhales. She doesn't say anything at first, which Melanie recognizes as a sign of what's about to come.

Bree faces her, her lip quivering and her eyes narrowing. The outline of her jaw protrudes from her skin as if she's clenching her teeth, trying not to cry. Melanie takes a step toward her, invites Bree into her chest, and wraps her arms around her. Bree finally lets it go—the anger, the resentment, the jealousy. Puddles and puddles of tears soak Melanie's blouse and chill her skin as the recipient of the wave of emotion, but she doesn't care. A shirt can be changed. Hank has finally stepped up.

When Bree pulls away, wipes her tears, and looks into Melanie's eyes, the animosity is gone. All the pain has been replaced with happiness and bliss. Melanie hasn't seen that in Bree's eyes in far too long, and seeing it now warms her heart.

Bree throws herself into Melanie again and rocks with her. "Thank you," she whispers.

"For what?" Melanie whispers back.

"For believing in me. For believing in my father."

Melanie chokes away her own tears and sways with Bree to the imaginary music. She closes her eyes and listens hard, and eventually, she hears a violin start to play. The vibration of the strings tickles her insides, making her hum to the rhythm. She squeezes Bree and buries her nose into her neck, smelling her soul, and her own tears finally come. In this moment, as she continues to dance with the woman she loves without wiping the water from her cheeks, Melanie knows everything will be alright. Everybody, she knows, will be just fine.

***

Once Scott Baker was formally arrested and transferred to one of the state prisons, Kurt and Abby spent four or five good hours with the detectives. Abby filled in the rest of the missing details while Kurt listened, numb from the betrayal. The initial plan Abby and Scott came up with was exactly how Scott had described it—Abby would seduce, marry, and eventually divorce Kurt and take half or more of his money—and she and Scott would be set for years. Maybe forever. Between the splitting of the assets and the anticipated alimony payments she'd receive, she may never have to work again.

But something changed along the way, and she swore it to be the truth. It didn't take long—mere months, according to Abby—for her to fall for Kurt. Aside from the career he'd built and the money he'd been making, he was a good man. He'd been gentlemanly, compassionate, and genuinely loving—Abby's words. They shared the same desires and Abby quickly started to envision a life with him.

When she got pregnant with Chloe, she was ecstatic. But she'd still been seeing Scott at the same time too, so she didn't know which one of them had actually gotten her pregnant. Scott had been thrilled about the news—not so much that he was excited about the baby, but more so that it would help to speed up the process of their plan. It was at that moment, realizing that Scott was truly only in it for the financial reward, that Abby decided to stop wasting her energy on him.

Kurt wanted to believe Abby's story, but it was hard to.

Abby confessed that she'd visited Scott in prison before and after Chloe was born, and Chloe even met him once too. She was just a baby, though, so she'll never remember, Abby had argued. Not that it made it hurt any less for Kurt; his heart ached just thinking about it. But, at the time, Scott's attorneys were still going through the appeals process with some of his fraud cases, so Abby had to see those through. With Scott having taken the blame for everything that'd happened, Abby was still a free woman—free to be with Kurt and free to raise Chloe. But if Scott knew Abby had never intended to see him again, Abby feared Scott would tell the police all she'd done and have her arrested too. Abby went to Scott's final appeal hearing to keep up the act in case he was freed—which he wasn't—and she never saw him again after. She'd never intended to.

Then nine years later, an envelope showed up in the mailbox, and the rest is history.

Equipped with all the information he needed to know about Abby and her past, Kurt took a couple of days to decide what he wanted to do.

***

After a long and difficult night filled with only sporadic sleep and wounded feelings, Kurt finally stirs. Two days in isolation has worn his mind to nothingness, and he's ready to start moving forward again. Even before he slides out of bed, the heaviness of his head overpowers him. Sleep deprivation, stress, and uncertainty have all played a part in that. He hopes his neck is strong enough to hold up the extra weight.

Last night, Kurt had a long chat with the mayor. The detectives had debriefed Wesley on all that'd happened during a closed-door meeting after the police station settled on Monday, so he knew the details already. Kurt wouldn't have even known where to begin if he hadn't. The discussion Kurt had with Wesley was blunt. There has been so much deception surrounding Kurt's life, and he couldn't take it from the mayor too. Kurt told him off. He'd told him to forget about their arrangement and to find a new running mate. Wesley fumed initially, but he'd sounded tired and confused too, so that quickly faded. Kurt told him that he needs to separate himself from the public for a while and worry about dealing with his personal challenges. And most importantly, Kurt told the mayor to screw off. Wesley had been trying to use Chloe's abduction as a way to help boost their campaign, and Kurt had found that to be disgraceful. Wesley had stayed quiet on the phone once challenged on that, and he didn't make an effort to defend himself. He had to have known Kurt was right—there was no denying it.

"Kurt, I'm...I'm sorry," was all Wesley was able to say.

Kurt didn't forgive him. They disconnected after a moment of awkward silence afterward. While Abby has been wrong about so many things in her life, she was right about one thing: Wesley Thomas was not Kurt's friend. It was merely a business relationship, nothing more. And while Kurt had expressed his gratitude for Wesley expediting Chloe's case through the system, Kurt doesn't plan to speak to the man again. Chloe will not be used as a political pawn.

Kurt has made a decision about his future. To him, it feels like the right thing to do, the only thing to do. He heads downstairs to tell Abby what he's feeling. He finds her in the kitchen. Her hair is tied up and frizzy, looking unwashed. She's sitting in a chair, staring at something on the kitchen table. When she doesn't react to Kurt entering the room, he walks around the table until he's in front of her. She still doesn't acknowledge him, so Kurt looks down. On the table is an unsealed manila folder large enough to hold a short stack of standard printer paper. Abby stares at it like it's a foreign object that's never before been seen. It's like she's discovered a new species and is having a difficult time processing the breakthrough.

"Abby?" Kurt says, breaking Abby's concentration.

When she looks up, her eyes are slits. "What?"

"I've been doing some thinking."

"Okay."

"Before I begin, I just want you to know that I still love you, okay? I always will."

Abby only nods. She looks too tired to cry.

"We've been through a lot in the last few days, and it's changed everything."

Abby says nothing. She puts her head down and shows Kurt the top of it. Her part shows off her blonde roots.

"I don't even know who you are," Kurt continues, "and what you've done might be unforgivable. But even still, I'm willing to try. I'm not sure I'll ever be able to trust you again, but Chloe's been through hell. She doesn't deserve to have her parents broken up over this. For her, I think we have to try to make it work. It'll be like starting over. And I want to warn you, I'm not sure I like what I see so far. You're going to have to earn my trust again, if you want it."

Abby takes a deep breath and looks back up to Kurt. Ignoring everything Kurt has say, she says, "So, apparently Scott took a DNA test to see if he's Chloe's father or not."

Kurt's heart sinks, and his momentum goes with it.

"The results were delivered this morning," Abby says as she points at the folder. She pushes it toward Kurt. "Are you sure you don't want to look at this before you say anything else?"

Kurt looks down at the folder. The tip of a single white page sticks out from the top of it, tempting him. The laboratory's logo and business address is in the header, bright with color. He recognizes the town as being somewhere in Canada, but the organization doesn't mean anything to him. As much as he wants to know what the results are, he can't muster up the courage to go through with it. What if the results aren't what he wants? Will it even matter? He pushes the folder back toward Abby.

"That's the thing," he says, "I don't want to know what the results are. That's what I've been thinking about. The bond Chloe and I have will never be taken away from us, so whether or not we share the same DNA doesn't matter to me. That's what I've realized. It doesn't matter what you and I have gone through, she deserves a father in her life. And I need her in mine. Nothing will change that."

"I think you should read the results."

Kurt sighs and grabs the folder. He slips the edge of the white paper out further, pinching it between his fingers. But he stops before pulling it all the way out, his hand shaking. He can't do it. Just like he told Abby, the results don't matter. He's raised Chloe as his own, so to him, she's his daughter. That's good enough for him. Kurt carries the folder over to the sink and jams it into the trash bin in the cabinet, his anxiety over the contents going with it. When he turns around, Abby is standing in front of him, face level. He leaps, not having heard her get up.

"Kurt," she says with an earnest tone. "Are you sure about this? What I've done to you, what I've done to Chloe, is—"

"I know. I don't need you to remind me."

Abby sinks.

"Listen, this is going to be difficult. I know that. We're going to need some serious therapy, and even that might not work. I'm not making any promises here, Abby, but—"

"I'm not asking you to. What you're offering is more than I ever expected from you. You're a far better person than I am. And you're a far better parent than I am too."

"Don't say that."

"No, it's okay," Abby says, almost smiling. "It's the truth. But I recognize it, right? That's the most difficult part. You're right—we need to work on us, and we will. But I need to learn how to be a mother first. And I have seven months to figure that out."

"Chloe loves you to—" Kurt stops himself. He thinks about what Abby has just said for a second. It hits him. "What did you say? Seven months until what?"

Tears well up in Abby's eyes. Even through her darkness, a light shines through her that Kurt hasn't seen in a while. She looks how she did nine years ago when she was pregnant with Chloe. Abby forces a smile as she puts a hand on her belly.

Kurt's breath is taken away. He falls back on his heels. He looks at the loose blouse that covers Abby's stomach and wonders how he missed it.

"Surprise," Abby says, half-joking, half not.

Kurt's not sure how to react. He's in shock. "Is it...?"

"It's yours," Abby says. "It's definitely yours."

A tornado of emotions rushes over him. He's happy and thrilled about the news, but he can't help but think, why now? Why tell him now, after all that's happened? There are surprises around every corner, it seems.

Kurt reaches forward with an open hand and moves it toward Abby's belly. He stops when he gets close and looks up to her, feeling timid. Touching her feels so wrong, so wildly inappropriate; he doesn't even know her anymore. Abby offers a weak nod in return, along with that glow. With an unsteady, trembling hand, Kurt goes for it. He pushes his insecurities aside and places his palm on her belly and leaves it there for a second, feeling for movement, even though he knows it's too soon. If Abby's timeline is right, the baby isn't big enough yet. Kurt speaks to the baby in his mind, hoping it'll understand his thoughts. Regardless of what happens, Kurt thinks, he'll always be there. He'll never abandon it, no matter what.

Kurt straightens his back and looks at Abby. His mind is in a haze. "Wow," he says, "a baby." Then he walks out, adding that to his list of things to consider.

When he turns the corner to head up the stairs to try and make sense of all this, he walks into something, almost stumbling. When he catches his balance and looks down, Chloe is chest-high, the puppy in her arms, with tears streaming down her face. She, apparently, had been listening.

"Dad?" Chloe says, sniffling.

Kurt crouches down to Chloe's level until their faces are parallel. She wipes her nose with her wrist and looks at Kurt like he's the most important person in the world. Just looking at her makes Kurt forget about everything that's wrong in his life. "Yeah?"

Chloe wraps her arms around his neck, pulling him toward her, and embraces him. The puppy squirms between them, trying to avoid being crushed, but Kurt hardly notices. He squeezes Chloe back with all the love he has to give, trying to assure her it'll never waver. "I'm glad you're home," he says.

"Me too," Chloe says. "And I don't care what the results are either."

***

There are two things Abby has to do before she can officially shut the door on her past. She's still young enough that she has time to rebuild her life from the inside out and can try to make amends for all she's done wrong. She knows she'll never be able to repay what she's stolen from her sister or take back the damage she's caused to Chloe, Kurt, or Scott. But with time, she hopes she'll allow herself to move past it. Forgiving herself might be the most difficult part.

Abby hits the road to clear her mind. Equipped with the information she needs, she heads north on route 44. Redemption, for her, begins in Montgomery.

For the first time since her parents and sister were still alive, Abby feels a genuine sense of relief. This is still far from over, she realizes, with Scott's trial looming and possibly her own too, but she's never felt better. Nothing can compare to the guilt she's held onto for so long, and being free of that burden is liberating. It feels so good to be truthful. What happens in the coming months with the legal system is out of her control—she hasn't been charged with anything yet while the investigation is still ongoing, but that could change in the coming weeks and months. If she is eventually charged, she'll deal with it as it comes.

She does a lot of thinking. She reminisces about the good times she and Courtney shared growing up, and about their loving and supportive parents and the family trips. She thinks about the accident—what it must have been like, how they must have felt as the vehicle was spinning out of control—and realizes she could have just as easily been in the car that day as opposed to not. She thinks about Scott and Diane and Tommy and how much she still cares for them all and always will. What they did for her—taking her in when her parents died and treated her like part of their family—is something she'll never forget. She thinks about Diane's failing heart and can't help but wonder if she's partially responsible for weakening it with the added stress she put on her so many years ago. And most of all, Abby thinks about Chloe and Kurt, about how much she's hurt them and about how much she loves them, and about how sorry she is for everything she's done to them. She realizes they may never fully understand why she did what she did, and it's not their fault. Even now, as Abby analyzes the situation from afar, she's not sure what she was thinking either. She should have asked for Kurt's help. Even still, she's hopeful one day they'll give her a second chance—Chloe, as her mom, and Kurt, as his wife—although she may not be deserving of it. Abby's prepared to do whatever it takes to earn their trust back.

The robotic male voice from the GPS leads Abby toward what seems like an abandoned dirt road and toward a trailer park ten or so minutes past the Texaco station. It's the same Texaco she'd driven to a few days prior with the intentions of meeting up with Scott. Driving past it gives her the chills, bringing back the memories of that night—how timid she was, how scared. She remembers the hope she'd felt about seeing Chloe and the disappointment when she'd learned it wasn't going to happen. That was the moment, she realizes, that changed everything. There's no telling what may have happened if the detective didn't follow her that night, or if the reporter didn't follow them both. Things may have turned out very differently.

There's a rusted truck in the driveway of the double-wide as Abby pulls up. The trailer park is deserted, the neighbors hushed, as if they know who Abby is and are afraid to have their children around her. Only a pair of crows occupy the space, but even they fly away when Abby steps out. It hurts, the isolation, but Abby can't blame anyone for feeling that way. Everything she's getting she deserves. The sunshine above her reminds her of the new journey she's about to embark on, and that no matter how many hurdles she might have to clear, there is still hope for her at the other end—that's what she's living for, the hope.

Inside the trailer, there are no lights on and all of the windows are covered with curtains. The detectives had told Abby about the man who'd brought Chloe home—Jordan Huff is his name—and although he supposedly remembers her from their past, she doesn't remember him. Not even the name is familiar. She knocks a couple of times on the screen door, but there's no answer from the other side. The only sound is that of a barking dog from a different trailer somewhere deeper inside the park.

Abby had been hoping to see the man's face, hopeful that seeing him might bring back the memory of how they knew each other. She wants to thank him face to face for saving her daughter, and her own life. He'll never know how much his actions have altered her path. Because of Jordan Huff, the faceless man who enabled her to finally rid herself of the burden she'd been carrying, Abby is on the road to reclamation.

Abby grabs the blank envelope from her purse and slides it in between the door and the frame where it can't be missed. Then she turns and walks back toward the driveway.

***

From behind the sofa, Jordan watches Abby drive away through a slit in the curtain. He saw her approaching and ducked behind it so he didn't have to see her up close. He's not ready for the confrontation. The detective had promised he'd tell Abby that they only knew each other once upon a time, but not from where. Jordan fears retribution if Abby were to find out what he did to her and Scott Baker back then.

While Jordan had been on a high when he'd left the police station, the message on the answering machine when he'd arrived back home quickly ended that. Just as he'd thought might happen, he was terminated from his job at the steel factory for not showing back up after lunch. He'd tried to explain the situation to his boss over the phone the next morning, but no exception would be made—that'd be a bad precedent to set around the others, Jordan's boss had said. The man even congratulated Jordan on his courageousness and thanked him for being a good employee, but the decision was final. The endorsement hasn't made it hurt any less.

Once Abby is out of sight, Jordan heads onto the porch to see what she's left inside the door. A blank envelope falls to the ground when he opens the screen. Just as the crows glide over the trailer and land on their customary spot on the lawn, looking for food, Jordan picks up and tears open the sealed envelope.

Inside is a handwritten note thanking him for finding Chloe. Abby doesn't know how she'll ever be able to repay him, the note reads, but she hopes the enclosed check will be a start. Jordan notices Abby's name is signed at the bottom, but he doesn't read the rest. Underneath the note is a check, made out to Jordan, in the amount of twenty thousand dollars.

The reward money.

Jordan starts to tremble. He'd forgotten all about the money. He only vaguely remembers a mention of it from one of the newspaper articles over the weekend, so it comes as a shock to him. It was the last thing he was expecting. The weakness in his knees forces him to sit on the step, facing the driveway. His breaths are rapid, his heart full of happiness. He wants to scream with joy. Jordan closes his eyes and clutches the check to his chest, hoping it's not a dream. His crow friends sing to him from the lawn as the tears begin to stream down his face.

In an instant, Jordan knows they'll be alright—him and Mindy. Mindy won't have to stress about money and can concentrate on running her business like she's always wanted. This money will give him plenty of time to find another job. This will keep them afloat for a while.

Then something else crosses Jordan's mind. It both excites him and makes him nervous. Even if he spends some of the money, they'll still be okay—there's plenty here. Mindy's not one to care about material objects—hence the modest double-wide—so a little reasonable spending would be acceptable. At the thought of it, Jordan genuinely smiles for the first time in quite a while.

Inside the trailer, Jordan grabs the keys to his truck from the bowl on the counter and rushes back outside. He clutches the check in his hand like it's his lifeline, because it is. The crows fly away when the engine backfires, but they stay perched on a tree limb that hovers over the trailer. It's like they know, like they're looking forward to seeing the end result just as much as Jordan is. He hopes they'll stick around for the show.

Jordan smiles again as he backs down the driveway, his truck clunking, the air conditioner blowing warm air. The ring he's had picked out for Mindy is waiting for him at the jeweler downtown. And now that he has the money, he can finally get it for her. She'll be overjoyed. Tonight he will ask Mindy to marry him, and tomorrow will be the first day of the rest of his life. He has so much to do to ensure the evening goes perfectly.

***

Abby's final stop before heading back home to begin her new life is the hospital in Montgomery. The little town twenty-five miles north of Mifflinburg has become a pretty important place in her life. Not only was that where Chloe was found, but as Abby learned later, that's where she was held too—in a cabin. But more than that, Abby still has some unfinished business she has to tend to before she can leave for good. She holds the recipient dear to her heart.

Abby leaves the envelope with reception. It feels inappropriate to ask to see her, considering the circumstances. The nurse promises to hand deliver it once the patient is well enough, and Abby takes her at her word. The envelope is identical to the one Abby had dropped off at Jordan Huff's place, except the contents are different. Very different. And more meaningful than any dollar amount could ever satisfy.

Abby leaves the hospital. The gas tank is nearly empty, but her heart has never been fuller. Even the growing fetus inside of her seems to be settled now. With a fresh new outlook on how special life can be—especially with such great people around her—Abby heads home with new hope and perspective. She's ready to tackle whatever may come her way, and if that includes paying for what she's done with some jail time, then so be it. She probably deserves it. Regardless of what happens down the line, she now knows where home is. She and Kurt have some work to do to get back to how things once were between them, but that's to be expected—she's just grateful he's willing to try. And she's hopeful Chloe hasn't quite grasped everything that's gone on—hopefully, she'll forget it all someday. But if she does have some pain to rehabilitate, Abby will do her best to help her heal those wounds. Everyone has a lot of healing to do, Abby included. Maybe, if it all works out, they can heal together, as a family. Abby's finally ready to start living.

***

Diane wakes up in the worst pain she's ever felt in her life. Everything hurts. Her muscles ache, her chest pulsates, and it feels like someone has taken a sledge hammer to her temples; her headache is relentless. She's covered in a cold sweat and has lots of bandaging. She just got out of surgery a few hours ago.

Diane had known something different was going on when she felt herself struggling to breathe when the SWAT men raided her cabin. She knew it was different than last time. After all the years of emotional strain, the valve gave way again, just as she knew it eventually would, and she suffered a severe heart attack. To their defense, though, the men from SWAT had no way of knowing her situation was that dire, so Diane doesn't blame them for what happened. She's just happy to be alive, although it is bittersweet in a lot of ways too.

Diane has been in a hospital bed since Monday. She's been begging to go home, but the doctors won't authorize her discharge; she's too sick. On Tuesday evening, yesterday, everything changed. There was suddenly hope. A nurse came and delivered the news.

Scott—who Diane knew had been transferred to a state prison from Mifflinburg—was in the ICU and completely brain dead. Diane was numb—it couldn't be her Scotty. Some of the inmates that had witnessed what happened had said Scott didn't even fight back. The biggest and meanest guy in the place was the one who did the damage. Some of the inmates had speculated it was a setup and that Scott wanted to die, but there'd been no direct evidence of that. Although the note he left behind in his cell said otherwise.

The note had listed out Scott's situation—his blood type, his mother's condition, instructions on what to do with his body, and his last wish. With nothing else to live for, the note read, his last wish was to give his heart to his dying mother as a way to give her a second chance at life. Scott had made such a mess of his own life and had failed to make anything positive out of it, so, in his mind, his mother had been more deserving than he to live on. Diane had to read the letter three times to make sure she saw it right. She recognized his handwriting right away, complete with the trail of ink that always bled from the final letter in his name. Diane was too weak to cry.

The doctors had tried to explain it to her, but Diane barely understood any of it. Her mind was mush, the pain too great. The tricky thing about donating a heart, from what Diane gathered, is that the donated organ has to be alive to do so. That's what made the whole thing remarkable. After the beating, Scott was brain dead but still being kept alive by a ventilator, meaning his heart was still, technically, alive. Diane didn't understand what it all meant.

The best explanation the doctor gave was that, simply put, it was a medical miracle. There was no way, in his eyes, that Scott could have known about the restrictions of donating a heart. Even if he was aware, it would have been impossible to plan it the way he did—his level of unconsciousness, being beaten that close to death without actually passing. The odds of it happening that way are so rare that it's barely even medically plausible. But it did happen, and he was a perfect match.

Diane had a chance at a new heart, and at life.

As soon as the hospital was alerted of the discovery in Scott's cell and his final wishes, the breathing tubes were removed and his heart was extracted and transported north to Montgomery. Diane was sent into emergency surgery and was given the most selfless of gifts possible. Even though the tissue was so similar between the two organs since they had the same basic DNA structure, the transplant was risky. Diane's overall health wasn't good and her chances of survival were low. She didn't care. Part of her wanted to die too, so she could go be with her son. Whatever happens, she'd thought, she was at peace with it. The doctors would try their best.

Five hours later, the surgery was a complete success.

Diane pulled through without a hitch, no worse for the wear. The doctors were even able to use the same scar, not that it mattered to Diane. It's too early to tell for certain if Diane's body will reject Scott's heart or not, but all early indicators are that she won't. She's expected to make a full recovery.

A blonde-haired nurse enters Diane's recovery room to check on the bandages on Diane's chest. She's holding an envelope in one hand, a cup full of pills in the other. "How are you feeling, Mrs. Baker?" she asks.

Diane only nods, in too much pain to speak. Her chest throbs.

The nurse lifts up the blanket from Diane's chest and inspects the gauze for blood. Diane pinches her eyes shut and looks away, bracing for pain. The softness of the cotton balls stick to the crusted blood around her wounds, lightly tugging, as the nurse gently pulls them away.

"Someone left something for you earlier," the nurse says once she lays the sheet back over Diane.

Diane looks at the envelope, strangely, curious what it could possibly be. But she takes it. Her muscles are so weak that even the envelope feels heavy to her. Her fingers struggle to grip it, and she drops it on the sheet on her chest. The corner of the envelope digs into her like a knife, causing her to wince in pain. By the time the pain passes and she looks up, the nurse is gone.

Inside the envelope is a color photo. Diane starts to weep upon looking at it and immediately places the photo to her chest, directly over her son's heart. Her hands tremble, the IV line tugging, as she struggles to steady herself. She thinks back to Scott's final written words, especially the part about him having nothing to live for. He was so wrong. If only he knew.

She pulls the photo away from her wounded chest and looks at it again through blurred vision. Tears dampen her cheeks and trickle down her chin as she rubs the photo with her thumb. She can't help but smile, even though it's painful. She turns the photo over.

On the backside is a small passage, handwritten and signed at the bottom by Abby. With all that they went through together, albeit so many years ago, her heart goes out to Abby. And because she feels that way deep within her heart, she knows Scott must too. She clenches her eyes shuts and prays for forgiveness for what happened with Chloe; she only did what she thought was best at the time. She realizes how wrong she was.

Eventually, Diane opens her eyes, feeling liberated. Her chest aches—both inside and out—but she musters up the courage to read what Abby has written.

For Diane, my second mother. Please accept this photo of Chloe and store it in your memory. Thank you for everything you've ever done for me; I'll never forget it, and I'll never forget you. Maybe one day we can meet again and Chloe can be introduced to you properly, as her grandmother.

The End

About the Author

Dan Lawton is an award-winning literary suspense, mystery, and thriller author from New Hampshire. He is an active member of the International Thriller Writers (ITW) Organization.

His fifth novel, *The Green House*, won the 2021 New Hampshire Writers' Project Literary Award for Fiction, was a Bronze Medalist in Adult Fiction E-Book for the 2020 Independent Publisher Book Awards (IPPY Awards), a Finalist for the 2021 Montaigne Medal (Eric Hoffer Awards) for most thought-provoking book, a Finalist in Fiction for the 2020 Next Generation Indie Book Awards, a Finalist in Mystery for the 2020 Book Excellence Awards, and a Finalist in Literary Fiction for the 2020 American Fiction Awards.

His fourth novel, *Plum Springs*, won the 2019 New Hampshire Writers' Project Readers' Choice Award for Fiction. His first novel, *Deception*, was named one of the best thriller novels of 2017 by the Novel Writing Festival.

Dan resides in New Hampshire.

Website: http://www.danlawtonfiction.com
Email: info@danlawtonfiction.com

Instagram: @danlawtonauthor
Twitter: @danlawtonauthor
Facebook: facebook.com/danlawtonfiction

Author's Note

Dear Reader,

I want to pass along my most sincere appreciation to you for your interest in TAKEN: A MOTHER'S SECRET (formerly AMBER ALERT). My goal is to entertain, excite, and hopefully satisfy you as a reader with a combination of mystery, suspense, and thrills. I hope I did. As an author, I'm most grateful for readers like you and I wholeheartedly want to thank you.

If you enjoyed my work, I encourage you to please write a review to help other readers, like you, discover it. Also, please check out my other novels, which I hope you'll enjoy as well.

If you'd like to stay up to date with future works, I encourage you to visit my website for all the ways in which we can connect.

Best Regards,

Dan Lawton

Printed in Great Britain
by Amazon

60006724R00168